# The Passion of 3

## THE PERFECT NUMBER
### BOOK TWO

**ARIELLA TALIX**

"Nothing is as important as passion.
No matter what you want to do with your life, be
passionate."
-Jon Bon Jovi


"The profession of book writing makes horse racing seem like
a solid, stable business."
-John Steinbeck

One

"What's wrong, Caro?" Zoë asked with a furrowed brow. "You seem a little down today." They were working on Zoë's pet project, the literacy foundation that Zoë had started as First Lady of Kentucky. Caroline Whittaker was her right-hand person and close friend.

"Oh… Jason asked me to marry him last night. Again." She saw Zoë's shocked look and hastened to say, "I didn't accept. But he's an okay guy, and it made me think that maybe I need to… settle."

"Absolutely not! Jason's dull, I'm sorry to say. I never understood the two of you together. To be honest, I always thought of him as a placeholder boyfriend for you." Caro nodded glumly as Zoë kept speaking. "You deserve someone who can make you as deliriously happy as Eli and Tanner make me." Tanner was the governor and Zoë's legal husband, but Eli was married to both of them in all ways that counted.

They had a wonderful triad marriage that they kept secret from the public. Maybe someday they would open up about it, but not yet. At least Tanner had finally given up his ambition to become the president, much to everyone's relief. Their plan was to continue to live quietly in Kentucky when Tanner's final gubernatorial term was over.

"Oh, I know. I'm just feeling my age, and I do want someone in my life."

Zoë chuckled. "Watch it. You're a year younger than I am. Let's not start acting old while we're still in our early thirties!" Zoë absently rubbed her very pregnant belly. This would be baby number four for them, and she was due any day now.

Caro didn't miss the gesture and expected to feel that usual pang stab at her heart. She'd always thought she wanted at least one baby before her eggs dried up. She knew rationally that she still had time, but then again… it wasn't hurting as badly as it used to for some reason. Then she got a wistful look on her face and said—somewhat out of the blue, "I used to be a lot more exciting back when I was a rock 'n' roller touring around and singing with Chaos. Now I feel all buttoned up and proper all the time. Sometimes I don't even recognize myself."

Caroline was a Whittaker from New York, and that meant billions. She'd dropped out of college—much to her parents' horror—when her exciting new boyfriend convinced her that with a glorious, sultry voice like she had, she needed to set the world on fire. It had been the best three years of her life until her parents finally wore her down and persuaded her to come back to the life she was "meant" to lead. Feeling too old and worldly by then to still be in college, she finished her degree as quickly as was humanly possible and went to work for her father.

"I'm going to admit something I've never told anyone before, Zoë." Caro took a deep breath as Zoë's eyes widened with curiosity.

"What is it?"

"I never *really* wanted to leave Nash or the band. I was being a coward. I took the first excuse I could come up with to run away, telling myself I was being smart and protecting my heart. My mom and dad kept laying such a guilt trip on me about the responsibility I had to the family. They made me feel like a naughty child who needed to grow up and face my true destiny. I was supposed to become a New York socialite like my mother, marry a guy they approved of, and then pop out little future billionaires for them to brag about."

"Are you saying you're sorry you ended up with us in Kentucky? It's a far cry from summering in the Hamptons and the excitement of Manhattan," Zoë asked.

"I'm not saying that at all. I love it here, and I couldn't stay in New York once I'd had a taste of the realness of the people I met here. But I do have regrets about not singing anymore, and I've felt terrible about the way I broke up with poor Nash, and… Well, let's just say it wasn't my finest moment. I'm worried that my actions ultimately destroyed the band. Breaking up with Nash Keating was the worst decision of my life. I've never found passion in any relationship I've had since we were together."

"Where is Nash now? He was quite a big deal as I remember. He wrote that beautiful, sad ballad about… Hey! Was it about *you*? They used to play that on the radio all the time. I remember it was number one for quite a while. But I don't remember a female singer with the band."

"That song made them ultrafamous *after* I left. I don't know where he is, and I have always assumed the song was about me, although he refused to name anyone in it—even when he was interviewed about it. But I never got up the courage to ask him or to apologize." Caro looked close to tears. "I used to read about him all the time. Eventually, after their big hit, the band broke up, and he kind of drifted away from the paparazzi's focus. Nothing about him has been made public for a few years now."

"Why don't you try to find him? It's the age of the internet. No one can really hide if you want to find them."

"Because I'm a chicken."

"You are not! You were a rockstar! Rockstars have guts. They go after what they want, Caro." Zoë looked closely at Caro. "Where was he from originally?"

Blushing, Caro looked down and answered quietly, "Kentucky."

"What? Caro, did you move here hoping you'd run into him somewhere? Be honest. I thought working with Eli on Tanner's campaign and then settling here was a little out of character for a city girl, but this is starting to make some sense now."

Caro's eyes looked haunted when she answered. "Zoë, please never think I was using you guys as an excuse. You know I've always been fond of Tanner, and Eli is the best brother in the world. I truly was sick of living in New York and all the pressure my parents put on me to behave just so and marry someone they picked out for me—not that they've ever stopped with the guilt trips. But this was an excellent opportunity for me, and then I became such good friends with you, and life just seemed easier here. I am not at all sorry I made the move." She looked down at her hands. "But maybe, just perhaps, a tiny bit of me hoped I would somehow run into Nash. I didn't expect him to show up for the Honeycomb Fair in Honeybee Hollow." She laughed softly. "But Frankfort is a different story. There is a strong music scene here, and his family lives in Lexington. That's not so far away at all."

"We need to do a bit of sleuthing. What if he's been here right under your nose all along? You did all that wonderful research on Tanner's campaign opponents, so this ought to be easy for you." She eyed Caro again cautiously. "That is if you're actually interested in finding him, and I'm not just butting in when I shouldn't."

"I… uh… don't know." Caro sighed. "It's too late for that. He's undoubtedly moved on. I should just let it drop. I'm sure he's long past over me by now."

Zoë looked at Caro skeptically but kept any other opinions on the subject to herself. "Whatever you say. I just want to see you happy" was all she added.

Later that night, Zoë went into labor, and her conversation with Caro was the last thing she thought about for weeks.

# Two

On a beautiful Saturday the following May, Caro found herself in a private luxury suite—courtesy of Eli—at Churchill Downs with Eli, Tanner, Zoë, their children, and Tanner's parents. Tanner's sister and her family joined them with several other friends. It was quite a crowd. The racetrack was teeming with people, all there to see the famed Kentucky Derby. As governor, it was to be Tanner's job to present the trophy to the winner.

Naturally, all the women at the party wore beautiful Derby Day hats designed by Tanner's sister Madison. Her business continued to employ many workers at her factory in Honeybee Hollow, and her millinery shop in Louisville was second to none. The first Saturday in May was Madison's favorite day of the year.

As the Derby horses were escorted out to the gate and everyone in the stands sang "My Old Kentucky Home," Zoë nudged Caro, exclaiming, "Look at the silks on that last jockey. You don't normally see anything like that." The rider wore only black and white. There was a band around his chest and back that looked like the keyboard of a piano against a black background, and the pattern on his white sleeves was a random design of black musical notes.

"Oh, I love that!" Caro answered with a laugh. "It looks good on that black horse too. You don't see too many of those racing, do you? Most of them are bay or chestnut."

The race was history making, with the two favorites leading the pack for most of the race, battling for the lead back and forth. The announcer barely mentioned any other horse until the home stretch when the black horse, who had been dead last and had come from the outside gate, made a tremendous sprint at the end of the race. In the final moments, and with a breathtaking display of skill, his jockey maneuvered his mount around another horse that was blocking the rail position to overtake the favorites. The odd horse thundered to a win as the stands filled with cries of, *"Who* won? Who's *that? Where did that horse come from?"*

The excitement of having a longshot winner in the Derby was so overwhelming that Tanner announced, "I want the whole family to be in the photo." Addressing Zoë, Eli, and Caro, he said with a laugh, "Everyone, grab a kid!" Tanner picked up their eldest—a daughter named Stella. Eli picked up the next in line—their son Wade. Zoë had her newest baby, Preston, in her arms, and Caro held their younger daughter, Shelby, who favored Eli in her coloring—and thus shared it with Caro as well. All three had black hair and striking hazel eyes—although Caro's were greener than Eli's. Caro was tall and lean like her brother, but her face resembled their mother's while Eli looked like their dad. They'd both been photographed so often with Tanner and Zoë that many people assumed they were a couple.

Off they went, surrounded by security guards, to the winner's circle, laughing and smiling the whole way down to the track.

It turned out that very little was known about the winning horse, whose name was Domino Pip. He was only entered at the very last minute by Best Life Farm as a replacement for a horse that had scratched Saturday morning.

Domino Pip was all black except for an odd cluster of white dots on his forehead where most Thoroughbreds bore a solid white marking called a star or a blaze. When the colt was born, everyone attending the mare laughed and said, "He looks like a domino!"

His breeding was fair, but he didn't have any Derby winners in his lineage, so he'd gone to the yearling sale. The more jaded horse buyers ignored him. The most superstitious potential buyers figured he might even be unlucky, and heaven knows that every racetrack is steeped in plenty of superstition. In the end, Domino Pip fetched a mediocre sum from a young man who was charmed by the colt's unusual look.

Due to his anonymity, Domino Pip had stayed out of the eye of the press in the weeks approaching the Derby. Practically no one had bet on him, and this resulted in eighty-to-one odds. He beat out the favorites by three-quarters of a length with an incredible burst of speed in an already fast race, making it one of the most exciting races Churchill Downs ever hosted.

Neither the jockey nor the trainer had ever been in the Derby prior to this.

The crowd was stupefied.

But quickly, word went around the track from person to person that this was a true Kentucky Bluegrass-born and bred horse, and local pride kicked in for the unusual colt. Furthermore, there were whispers that the owner "used to be somebody famous."

Half the photos taken in the Winner's Circle showed a jubilant young man bursting with pride over his unbelievable win with a horse no one else wanted. A wide grin lit up his handsome face as he shook hands and posed with the governor. The other half of the photos showed the same young man with a dumbfounded and somewhat perplexed look on his face as he stared at a tall, elegant woman who stood next to the governor's wife. Her face was mostly hidden in the photos because of the First Lady's hat.

As the crowd around Domino Pip and his beaming jockey dispersed, the owner of the horse stood his ground, ignoring some of the exuberant well-wishers who kept congratulating him and slapping him on the back. He seemed rooted to the spot, staring at someone. Finally, in a choked voice, he asked, "Caro? What are you doing here?"

Caro knew that voice as well as she knew her own name. She stopped in her tracks and turned to face him. "Nash," she whispered, "what are *you* doing in the winner's circle?"

Nash's eyebrows furrowed as he answered, "Domino Pip is my horse."

The toddler in Caro's arms took that moment to grab at the brim of her hat and yank on it. This made her stumble in her high heels, and Nash instinctively grabbed for her to keep her from tripping. The feel of his arms around her took her back to years ago when it felt like the safest place in the world to her. They stared at each other, and the roaring of the crowd disappeared.

Nash's arms were still strong, his face still chiseled and perfect. His blue eyes penetrated her hazel ones with an undisguised longing tinged with sadness. *Sadness? Why would he be sad?* Caro wondered. *This must be the most exciting day of his life.* She watched spellbound as the spring breeze lifted his bright, wavy blond hair and blew a bit of it across his face. Her fingers itched to smooth that silky tress out of his eyes. She was happy he had kept it long all this time. She always preferred him with longer hair.

Caro forced a smile and said in a cheerful voice, "Well, in that case, congratulations! Does that mean you're Best Life Farm? We've been so caught up in festivities I didn't pay much attention to the *Daily Racing Form*, and I'm not someone who typically bets..." *Stop babbling,* she told herself. "I didn't know, but... well done!"

As if shaking cobwebs from his mind, Nash blinked a few times, stepped back, and answered, "Thank you. You... um... have a beautiful little girl there."

Before Caro could protest that Shelby was not hers, a reporter shoved a microphone between them. In an annoyingly nasal voice, she demanded that Nash tell her "...how it feels to be the second-biggest Derby upset since Donerail, who had ninety-one-to-one odds back in 1913."

As it turned out, Nash would not have another chance to speak to Caro that day. Word got out, however—and was everywhere—that the owner of the mystery horse was none other than former rockstar and lead singer Nash Keating, who had become something of a recluse since his band Chaos broke up and more recently owned and lived at Best Life Farm.

As the cameras swarmed around him, Nash wondered how long it would take before they moved on to something shinier and more exciting than his dull life. This horse entertained him more than anything had since Caro. And Greyson. God, how he missed them. *It seems I'll have to be content with the horse. Maybe we can pull off a Triple Crown. Wouldn't that be something? Today made me nearly $10 million richer between the purse and the large bet I made, so that's definitely something.*

Nash sighed as he smiled for another picture. Truth be told, he just wanted to go home, get out of his suit, put on some music, and relax with his dogs.

Maybe he'd write a song about Domino Pip. Immediately a melody began to percolate in his brain. But all too quickly the zippy, happy tune veered into a melancholy direction as he thought of shining hazel eyes, black waves of hair, and legs that went on for miles. *Too bad she dumped me so decisively. At least I'm rich.* He made a face at himself.

*Big fucking deal. What's the point of money when you're all alone?*

# Three

Nash's phone kept ringing and ringing. He answered a few calls from his agent, but anything he didn't recognize he let go to voicemail. He wasn't interested in rehashing his life story to the public. Maybe buying that goofy horse was a bad idea. Back in the day, Nash had loved the fame his band garnered. But he had done something to earn it — writing an incredible song or performing for a crowd. This time, all he did was pay out a mediocre wad of money for a horse that no one particularly wanted and hire his old man to train the colt.

His dad's career had never made him one of the most sought-after trainers in the field, but the man loved every minute of it and wasn't ready to retire. The fact that he'd been able to give something so important to his father made Nash as happy as the Derby win. *The old man deserves some happiness.*

As he climbed into bed that night, his phone rang once again. It was close to midnight, and he didn't recognize the number, so he let it go to voicemail. But for some uncanny reason, he picked up the phone and listened to this message instead of deleting it.

A tentative and familiar smoky-smooth voice spoke. "Hi, Nash. It's Caro. I don't even know if you have the same number after all these years. Maybe this voicemail is just going into cyberspace somewhere… I don't know. Anyway, I called to tell you congratulations one more time. That was really something today. If you get this message, maybe it would be nice to… um… talk sometime. Uh… well, good-night. I hope you get this. Bye."

Nash frowned at his phone, wondering why she called so late and sounded so unsure of herself. One thing was sure; he wanted like hell to speak to her. But his brain immediately went to a weird place. *Maybe she waited for her husband to go to bed and called me because…* He didn't even know how to finish that thought. So, without delving into whether or not talking to her would be the worst idea he'd ever come up with, he punched the button to call her back.

"Nash! Did I wake you up, or…?" she said by way of answering the phone.

"No, I was heading to bed, but you know me… a night owl." *Lame, you idiot. She doesn't know what kind of schedule you've kept for the past ten years or so.* "Um, it's good to hear from you."

"Is it?" Caro took a fortifying breath and said, "It's been a very long time."

"Caro, I've thought about you every day since you left." *I cannot believe I just said that.*

"You have?" She sounded genuinely shocked.

"Yes, but maybe now's not such a good time to talk about it."

"Oh! I'm sorry if I disturbed you. I hope I didn't disrupt anything… like bug your wife or something."

*She's a fine one to talk.* "No, *I'm* not the one who got married." His voice had an edge to it.

"What are you talking about? Who got married?"

"I assume the little girl you were carrying today has a daddy. Or isn't he in the picture?" *Come to think of it, why were you even in the winner's circle today? You never answered me.*

Caro thought, *Two daddies, actually, who are very much in the picture.* "That wasn't my daughter. She's one of the governor's children. His wife Zoë is one of my best friends, and I was just carrying one of the kids because Tanner—you know, the governor—wanted all their children in the pictures, and they have four of them. Stella, Wade, Shelby—that's the one I was holding—and the baby, Preston. They're all too little to let them wander around on their own in a crowd like that, so my brother Eli and I both grabbed a kid." *It's so frustrating that I can't admit that the little girl is my beloved niece, and my brother is one of her fathers, but that's not my story to tell,* she told herself. "I'm not married, Nash."

Nash released a relieved breath he hadn't been aware he was holding. "Good. I mean, that's good to know." There was a moment of uncomfortable silence before he asked, "Why, after all these years, did you want to talk to me?"

Tears prickled at Caro's eyes when she answered, "I've never stopped thinking about you. And I guess I'm old enough and experienced enough now to forgive and forget and thought maybe we could… you know… talk."

Nash frowned. "Forgive and forget just what exactly? You're the one who ran off and disappeared, and then you blocked me so that I couldn't call you. You broke my heart, Caro!"

"Yeah, I heard the song, but you were the one who cheated! Did you expect me just to say everything was fine and dandy after that?"

"I never cheated!"

"Nash! I saw you. I came into the hotel room that night after having dinner with my family—and listening to them tell me about my bad decision making for the umpteenth time—only to see you in bed with someone and going at it so… enthusiastically… that you didn't even hear me come in!" She scrubbed her hand over her eyes and continued, "So yeah, I blocked you. You were obviously tired of me, and some groupie finally got to you at a convenient time. I went that very night to my parents' place and then got back into school as soon as I could and tried like hell to forget about you. I was crushed!"

In a quiet voice, Nash answered, "You didn't see what you thought you saw at all. It was dark in that room, Caro. I was actually doing exactly what you'd been trying to get me to do for months!"

"I never told you to cheat."

"Of course not. I know you loved me, and I loved you. I

would *not* have cheated. But… remember the more and more we got together with Greyson and started to feel that we'd built a real three-way relationship with him, you encouraged us to get it on? And we wouldn't do any actual… penetration with each other? Well, that night we were watching a movie, and it was boring as shit, so we started to talk about you. Then we broached the topic of trying out more things together. You know we'd at least kissed and touched each other by then with your encouragement. So anyway, that night we went further. Greyson tried some stuff, and I tried some stuff, and we thought you'd be back at any minute, and we'd surprise you, and all of us would have a big ol' orgy or something. It felt like it was going to be great! I have to admit we were a little high, so that might have contributed to our enthusiasm, but the next thing I knew, I was banging his ass. And guess what? He loved it, and so did I!"

"Oh!"

"Yeah, even though we'd never intended for it to go that far. But then we kept wondering where the fuck you were. You scared the *shit* out of us, you know! All of your stuff was still in the hotel room like you were planning to come back, but you never did! I called and called, and just about when I was ready to call the police, I found the number for your dad's office. His assistant wouldn't let me talk to him, but she told us that you were with your family and you were safe. That's all we knew. So don't be telling me that I broke your heart. You broke mine! And Greyson wasn't all that happy either, poor guy." He let out an exasperated sigh and continued, "We should have had this conversation years ago. Unless you decided we weren't good enough for you."

"Good enough? That wasn't it at all. Look, Nash, can we maybe get together over coffee or something? Where do you live now? Are you anywhere near Frankfort?"

"Closer to Lexington, but not far."

"So you did move back here? Are you here permanently?"

Nash shrugged to himself. "For now. I'll see. But yeah. I think face-to-face clearing the air might be a good thing. When and where do you have in mind? Apparently, I have a shitload of interviews I have to put up with for a couple of days, according to my agent, and then I'll be free. I'll warn you the paparazzi followed me home today, and it's a little crazy for me around here. I had to practically barricade myself into the house." He had a security gate around his vast property, so this was a bit of a stretch. The paparazzi couldn't get past the fence legally without his permission.

"You still have an agent?"

"Still writing songs. Just not performing them anymore. Without you and Greyson, it isn't the same. You must be aware that the band broke up."

"Yeah," she whispered sadly. "Where is Grey? Is he okay?"

"I dunno how he is, but he went to live in LA. We tried to keep things going without you, and eventually, he just gave up on me. Said I was a downer, and he needed some joy in his life—whatever that meant. Last I heard, he was freelancing on keyboard and teaching music at some school. I guess he's a regular Jack Black these days." Another pause, and then he added, "I miss him as much as I miss you, Caro. I think we all fucked up pretty badly. I'm sorry."

Caro sighed like the weight of the world had fallen onto her chest. "Can you come to my house on Thursday? I'll have lunch for us."

"You cook now?"

"Pfft. Seriously? That's still not one of my talents." She laughed and then gave him her address and the entry code for her security gate, and he saved it on his phone under her contact information. "When can you be here? Can you come on Thursday?"

Nash sighed. "I think a week from Thursday will actually be better since everything is so crazy right now. If that's okay, then I can't wait."

*Four*

Much like her brother Eli, Caroline Whittaker had a fortune. She had an impressive portfolio, a trusted financial advisor, and a ridiculous amount of money at her disposal. The work she'd done with Eli on Tanner's campaign and with Zoë as her PA and image counselor were just labors of love and things to keep her busy. She also knew her father didn't really need her back in New York working for him. That had just been her family's way of getting her in front of more "suitable" bachelors than a rock 'n' roller. It hadn't worked. Those men bored her. Escaping to Kentucky to help with Tanner's campaign was the only legitimate way to get out of New York that she could think of because her parents adored Tanner and wanted to see him succeed.

Now that Tanner's job as governor was nearing the end, all she had was the literacy foundation she ran with Zoë. She didn't want to let Zoë down and planned to keep working on it with her, but it wasn't enough for Caro. She thought back fondly to the excitement of touring with the guys in the band —both on and off the stage. The rush of performing was incredible, and she was head over heels for Nash. Then when they'd taken Greyson into their relationship… She blushed, remembering how much she'd enjoyed that. *Yes, I'm older now, and maybe I need to be more serious, but that kind of thrill was like nothing else. Also, Eli, Tanner, and Zoë are so great together, and they're all so happy with their family; I'm frankly jealous. What an awful word that is. I just need something… someone… some passion.*

Even with Zoë, Caro hadn't been totally open about how she felt with Nash and Greyson. Out of habit, she kept up the charade that it was only Nash who'd been her boyfriend, and she'd played off their threesome as if it was all just fun and games for some crazy rockers. *Maybe it was for Greyson—I don't really know, but for me, it was real, and it was intense. No one has come close to making me feel the way they did, and that's why it hurt like hell to think Nash had betrayed me. And maybe my parents got to me a little too much that night, talking about my future and responsibilities to the family. They were crushed that Tanner never seemed interested in me. (I wonder why… Hah! He was in love with Eli, not me.) But they would have hitched me to someone stuffy and richer than Bezos if they could have.*

♡♡♡

ON THE DAY OF THEIR DATE, NASH PULLED UP IN A BRAND-NEW pickup truck with mud on its sides and a horse farm logo on the door that bore the name Best Life Farm. The sight pleased Caro, and she was happy he wasn't in some dorky sports car that broadcast "Look at me!" She had considered dressing up for lunch in a killer outfit from her favorite boutique, but this was Nash; it wouldn't have been quite right. She settled on a comfy pair of well-worn jeans, a little bit of fun jewelry—just earrings and some bracelets—and a T-shirt that she knew fit her just so (and made her boobs look great). She was also happy to see that Nash had dressed for relaxation rather than to impress.

Caro opened the door with a huge smile. Her beautiful green-and-gold-flecked eyes seemed to look right into his soul.

The need to wrap his arms around Caro and kiss her stupid made Nash clench his hands and stuff them into his pockets. *Too soon. Let's see how this goes first.* "You look great, Caro." His eyes couldn't help but travel the length of her. Those perfect tits, those million-mile legs that used to wrap around his waist... He stifled a groan. "You're still as beautiful as ever."

Caro blinked at him. The noonday sun was behind his head, making Nash seem to glow with a sparkling aura, and she took in how large and solid he looked. The sleeves of his light blue Henley were shoved up his arms, revealing golden muscles that had been kissed by the sun, and a bit of ink she didn't remember peeked out of his shirt at the open neck. He towered over her five foot nine and a half inches, and his broad shoulders seemed to fill the doorway. She wanted with every fiber of her being to be wrapped in those arms once again. *God, he's gorgeous. How could I have ever walked out on this man?*

"Come in, Nash. Can I get you a drink? Lunch is just about ready, and the day is so perfect. We can have it out by the pool. Beer? Sweet tea?"

"Sweet tea sounds great. You must be turning into a Southerner."

"Maybe. But more likely, it's because my wonderful cook is from Alabama."

Their conversation began superficially—just catching up on her college experience and her move to Kentucky. Nash was pretty evasive about the band's demise—focusing instead on his father and how Domino Pip was turning his dad into a sought-after trainer finally.

"Dad has picked up five new clients in the days since the race, and he's never been so proud of himself." He beamed.

But when the luncheon dishes were cleared away, Caro suggested, "I had Angela, my cook, bake a bourbon chocolate pecan pie. I remember you have a sweet tooth. Coffee? I can lace it with a little something if you like." She thought they could use a bit of loosening up.

"Just plain coffee for me please. Sounds great."

"I'll go take care of that myself then. Be right back." When she stood and turned toward the kitchen, Nash ogled the way she sashayed away. The tight jeans across her cute butt made him get all kinds of dirty ideas. *Down boy,* he told the chubby in his pants. It had been a long time since he'd had a night of sexy fun, and he'd never had anything to rival what he had with Caro… and Greyson. *I'm probably remembering it as more than it was. But… fuck me, it was hot!*

Instead of returning to the outdoor dining table, Caro brought a tray out and carried it to a coffee table in front of a loveseat. Nash thought it boded well that she chose to sit next to him, but she covered it up by saying, "We'll have a better view of the property from here. I especially love to sit and watch the hummingbirds at the feeders." The grounds of her estate were artfully laid out and carefully maintained. It was all awash in brightly colored flowers, and the focal point was the tiled pool with a waterfall at one end.

"Do you swim much?" The thought of Caro in a tiny bikini now invaded his thoughts.

"When it's warm enough, I try to swim every morning. It's great exercise."

"Do you still ride? I remember the stories you used to tell us about your horses."

"I haven't lately, but I must admit I do miss it."

Nash's grin grew. "Great! Besides our broodmares, we have a couple of retired racehorses at the farm and several rescues. Some of them are a lot of fun to ride." He saw her mild surprise and added, "They're fully trained for pleasure riding. I think one of them is right up your alley. We have over six hundred acres for riding, which includes a cross-country course. Or if you'd like to take a spin around the track, we can saddle up one of the retired racehorses and let them take you for a very fast joyride. They still love to run." Nash laughed at her dubious expression. "Okay, I see the track is a no-go. But would you be interested in a pleasure ride?" *Please say yes. Please say yes. I so need to see more of you after today.*

Instead, she asked, "Why do you have rescued horses?"

"Oh, some of them are referred to us when they're in danger of being sold for meat. People buy horses and fall on hard times, or they underestimate the effort and money it takes to care for them." Nash smiled fondly. "One of my favorites just showed up in the pasture one morning a little over a year ago. I think somebody dropped him off in the dead of the night and split. He's big—over seventeen hands—a sweet bay gelding—the perfect size for me to ride. The only way they could have gotten him in was to jump the fence or have someone let him in. So far, no one has fessed up to that, though." He laughed softly. "The only thing I knew about him was from the brass plate on his halter that said ELVIS." Nash laughed with Caro. "He looks like a Warm-blood, and at some point, somebody put a lot of training into him. I asked around for ages, but no one seemed to know anything about him. Anyway, some of them come to us all skinny and sad, and we fix them up and make sure they go to reputable owners. Some of them are oldies, and we just make sure they're kept healthy and can live out the rest of their lives here with other horses around since they're herd animals at heart. But Elvis is one I've grown attached to and I'll keep. Our vet says he's about six years old."

"That's amazing, Nash. Riding with you sounds like fun. And I'm so happy for you that you can ride again. I know you missed it as much as I did when we were touring. You know, I'll probably end up with sore muscles—even if I don't fall off and embarrass myself." She laughed. Caro had a roomful of horse show ribbons and trophies back home at her parents' place, so this was a little *too* self-deprecating.

"You'll be fine. I'm sure of it." Nash took a bite of dessert, and his eyes practically rolled back in his head. "Ohmygod. This is amazing."

"Thanks. I'll pass along your compliments. So, you keep mentioning 'we' at the horse farm. Do you live with your parents there?"

Nash looked down for a moment. "My mom passed on eight years ago…"

Caro gasped. "I'm so sorry! What…?"

"Thanks. She had a massive stroke. No warning whatsoever." He paused for a moment and gathered himself, cleared his throat, and continued. "Dad wasn't handling things very well, and his training was suffering because of it. He lost some clients and couldn't pay his mortgage. So about six years ago, I bought this huge farm from a business that had declared bankruptcy and moved him into the guesthouse on the property. So no, I don't live with him, but I'm near him. Best Life Farm brought him out of his funk at least, and I got him to quit trying to smoke himself into an early grave. Then when I bought Domino Pip to train under the guise of needing a new hobby, he kept telling me the colt had something special. But do you know how many times I've heard that story about horses over the years?" Nash scoffed. "Every new horse he took on he was sure was the next Secretariat." He shook his head slightly and grinned. "Well, finally, he might be right about this one, and it was the best thing in the world for him. Now that he's being acknowledged for his success, I barely recognize the man anymore. He looks ten years younger and hasn't stopped smiling since the Derby."

"That's wonderful!" Caro's grin faded as she gave him a contemplative look. "Nash, not to change the subject, but I have to ask. You said that you and Greyson tried to keep things together after I left. Did you mean the band or the relationship?"

"Going right for the big questions, huh?" Nash sighed. "Grey and I kept the band together, and for a while, things were pretty good. We had that hit song, and everyone wanted to hear it all the time. But the fact was, each time I had to sing it, it ripped a little more and more out of me. I got pretty depressed, even though we loved the attention. But I drank too much and took out my frustrations on Grey. He's the best guy ever, and he took it well for a while, but he didn't deserve it. He was also suffering from losing you, and after a while, he just got so pissed at me for my shitty behavior that he took off. He told me to get some help and get my act together before contacting him again." Nash swallowed some coffee. "He was right. I lashed out at him for nothing just because he was convenient, and he saw that. He knows his worth and that he didn't deserve some drunk idiot picking on him for imagined wrongs. Plus—neither of us exactly saw ourselves as gay men. We loved it when we had you with us but having a relationship with just each other didn't cut it for Greyson and me." He looked deeply into Caro's eyes and could see the compassion there. "If I could do it all over again, I'd be better at it this time. And God knows, I'd love the chance."

Caro started a bit at that news. A small smile softened her look. "Nash, I owe both of you guys a huge apology. I was childish and wrong to leave like that with no explanation. I hope you can forgive me. I would like nothing more than to try again."

Like mirrors of each other, they quickly set down their mugs of coffee and fell into each other's arms. Nash pulled her close and sealed his lips over hers. She tasted sweet like coffee and chocolate and that particular Caroline taste he'd craved for years. Kissing her felt like coming home after an extended exile in a foreign country—one that was a dry desert with no color.

Finally, pulling away, he asked, "Is that too sudden? I'm sorry if it is."

Caro burst out laughing. "Nash! It takes two to make out. You don't hear me kicking and screaming." She grew more serious. "I do think we need to slow down a little and take things carefully. It may turn out that we have nothing in common after all this time…"

Nash interrupted. "Are you attracted to me?"

She nodded and looked away momentarily as she whispered, "Of course."

"Do you still love music, and do you still sing when you drive, shower, or anywhere when a song enters your head and you can't help it?"

She laughed and nodded again.

"Do you crave the kind of excitement we created when we

were together?" He couldn't help rubbing his nose along the side of her neck, delighted to see goosebumps arise on her arms.

She rubbed his biceps and then clasped his hand, answering softly in that smooth-whiskey voice of hers that he'd missed for so long. "You know I do, Nash. No one has ever taken your place in my bed or my heart. But let's be careful. We're not in our twenties anymore. I think maybe we have more to lose now."

They kissed some more, both remembering each other in ways that surpassed words. Their tongues danced, their breathing sped up, and Nash's chubby became a full-blown boner, straining his jeans. He was horribly uncomfortable and completely delighted at the same time. Finally, when he thought he might explode—and didn't want to do that—he pulled away slightly. "Coffee's getting cold." He chuckled.

Caro cleared her throat. "Yeah, right."

After they finished their pie, Caro suggested, "Would you like to cool off in the pool? It's getting pretty hot out here." In fact, it was pretty mild at seventy-one degrees, and the breeze was picking up.

Nash looked at her thoughtfully and then answered, "Not if you want to take things slowly. I'm afraid if I see too much of your body in a swimsuit right now, it might be *too hard* for me."

Caro looked down and realized he was massively turned on. That pleased her more than she could believe, so she couldn't resist answering with a smirk, "Who said anything about swimsuits?"

"There's the naughty girl I've always lo... liked so much." He winked at her as his face turned pink. *Stupid move, man. You'll scare her off. Can't go professing your love so soon after all these years! Although... she did say you're still in her heart...*

"I'm teasing, Nash. Sort of." Changing the subject, she asked, "Do you know how to reach Grey?"

"Yes. I just haven't done it because I was such a jerk, and I thought for a long time that he'd be better off without me. Now that I have my shit together again, if nothing else, I'd sure like to collaborate on some music with him again. He always brought that special edge, you know?"

She smiled. "I do remember. He was always the heartbeat. You're the poet though, and you write wonderful music."

"Caro?"

"Hmm?" She had her head resting on his solid, warm chest and could suddenly barely keep her eyes open; she was so at home and relaxed with his deep voice rumbling straight through her.

"I have a song that I've never shown to anyone."

"Why?"

"It always needed you, and I couldn't bear the idea of someone else singing it."

She pulled away and looked deeply into his eyes. "That might be the most romantic thing anyone has ever said to me."

"More romantic than if someone says I love you?"

"Yep. Anyone can say that, and I would never discount it because it's great, but how many people can actually write a beautiful song and hold on to it for the just-right person to sing it? That's special, Nash, and I'm humbled and… well… blown away."

"You haven't even heard it yet. How do you know it's beautiful?"

"Did you write it from your heart?"

"I did."

"That's how. And now I can't wait to hear it." She snuggled back into his chest, and they didn't speak for a while. They just enjoyed the feel of each other as their heartbeats synchronized.

Finally, Nash broke the silence and sighed. "I have an early flight to Baltimore tomorrow…"

"Oh, that's right. The Preakness is this weekend. Good luck!"

"Thank you. Dad and Pip are already at Pimlico. What I wanted to ask is if you'd like to come to the farm next week for a ride?"

Caro snorted. "On the mare you think I'd like?"

"Who else?"

She pulled back and looked him straight in the eye. "You."

The boner he'd been sporting surged back to life and gave a lurch as he groaned. "You're killing me, woman."

With an arched eyebrow, Caro snickered. "Then I'm doing it right. I can *come* anytime that works for you."

After a tiny growl, he answered, "Tuesday then. I'll text you the address and the gate code. Come around ten. Now you'd better walk me out, or I may never leave."

# Five

After winning the Kentucky Derby, it seemed as if everyone in the country wanted Domino Pip to win the Triple Crown, making him the favorite at two-to-five odds in the Preakness. Nash kept his bet a bit more modest this time, figuring the payoff wouldn't come even close to what he'd won at Churchill Downs at only $2.80 for a two-dollar bet. He also worried that lightning had a poor chance of striking twice in the same place, no matter what his enthusiastic father told everyone. He desperately wanted to be as sure of the horse as his dad was. He just hadn't been born with that same level of optimism.

But given a better post position this time, the colt didn't have to run from the rear of the pack to win. On this fast track, Pip's jockey Jorge rode conservatively and didn't try to lead the pack wire to wire. He stayed in a comfortable position in the middle, nearly giving Nash a heart attack. Nash hated waiting patiently for the jockey to make his move. He worried that Jorge might stay in the pack too long in this shorter race and not have time to surge ahead. But as soon as the horses made it to the home stretch, Jorge gave Domino Pip his head and managed to rocket through and beat the next favorite by two and a half lengths. It was pandemonium once again as spectators knew they were seeing history in the making.

Watching the race at home, Caro screamed so loudly when Domino Pip won she might have been heard all the way in Maryland.

When the cameras focused on Nash in the stands, Caro could see him hugging his dad, who clearly had tears in his eyes. Nash then looked directly into the camera. He flashed the rock 'n' roll hand gesture and then lightly tapped his heart. The rest of the world no doubt thought he meant, "I love rock 'n' roll," but she preferred to think that it was his way of saying hello—or maybe even more than that—to her. He looked ecstatic.

By the time Nash and his dad made it down to the winner's circle, they must have shaken a thousand hands each. Domino Pip seemed to take all the excitement in stride as his beaming jockey alternated between patting the horse's neck and punching the air in victory.

As soon as he had a spare moment, Nash called Caro. "Did you see it?" He laughed joyously into the phone.

"Of course! Congratulations, Nash. This is huge! I'm so happy for you!"

"Will you come with us to the Belmont in three weeks?"

"I… Yes!" *Maybe it's too soon, but I can't miss this.* "When will you be back in Kentucky? I'm not sure I can wait until Tuesday to see you." *So much for going slowly.*

"In that case, I'll come home tonight."

"Nash! Don't you have parties to go to and interviews to give? Everyone must want to congratulate you."

"I suppose. But I'd rather see you, so too bad for them. I'll see if I can get a flight. Hang on, I'll pull it up on my phone." There was a pause while Caro thought about being back with Nash and what that might mean. Immediately she thought that they also needed to contact Greyson. She was lost in thought when Nash returned to the line. "Okay, there's a nonstop flight tonight from Dulles to Louisville, which is good because that's where I left my truck. So by the time I get to your place, it's going to be late, but Caro… I *need* to see you."

He sounded so sincere that Caro smiled to herself. "I'll wait up. If you're sure you don't need to celebrate with your dad."

"He's in his element, bragging his ass off with all of his cronies. Don't worry. I'll just tell him I have important business, and he'll understand."

Caro gave an amused snort. "Yeah, right. Business at one in the morning. Happens all the time."

Nash grinned. Caro was always a sharp one. He'd actually already told his dad all about reconnecting with Caro. His dad had asked why he'd looked so distracted and moony-eyed all of a sudden when he had a major sporting event to consider. Nash hadn't planned to tell Caro about all that yet though; he worried that if she knew how serious he was, it might freak her out.

"I need to go, Caro, but I'll see you in a few hours. I can't wait."

♡♡♡

MUCH LATER THAT NIGHT, CARO WAS NERVOUSLY *NOT* PAYING attention to the book she was reading when a chime told her a car had entered her gate. She dropped her Kindle and rushed to the door, opening it as a truck pulled up to the house and cut its headlights. She tried to look calm as she went out to meet Nash, who climbed out of the driver's seat, still in his suit but looking a bit rumpled and tired. Wordlessly, she walked straight into his arms.

Nash bent his head to kiss the daylights out of the woman he knew he could never be apart from again. Then he said, "This is the most alive I've felt in years, Caro."

"Because of Domino Pip?" she asked with a coy smile as she batted her eyelashes.

"Yeah, that goofy colt with the oddball face really does it for me. No, you crazy women. It's because of you finally! The races are just a bonus and a really, really lucky way for us to get reunited."

"Nash?"

"Hmm?" he murmured while he nuzzled her neck.

"Screw going slow. I've come to my senses. Bring in your suitcase."

"Now we're talking."

"Are you going to need to get back to the farm right away?"

"Nope. We're fully staffed, and the horses are all cared for. Dogs and goats too."

"Dogs and goats?"

"The goats keep the more skittish horses company, and the dogs keep me company."

"Have you been lonely?"

"You have no idea."

"Are you hungry? Did you have time for dinner?"

"Maybe later. I'm more interested in tasting you."

"How about a drink?"

"Stop stalling, Caro." He chuckled. "And for your information, I don't drink much at all anymore. It's not like I checked into rehab or anything, but I took stock of my behavior when Grey left me, and I realized he was right and my liver was going to kill me if I didn't make a huge change. Or I'd go out and have a horrible accident and hurt someone. So now you know. Is this your bedroom? It's nice."

Caro had been leading him by the hand through the house, and they finally made it up the stairs and into a huge bedroom suite with an elegant four-poster, king-sized bed. She'd turned down the lights and pulled back the covers, creating an inviting atmosphere. But now she gave him a shocked look. "I'm so sorry! I had Angela make that pecan pie, and it had a lot of bourbon in it."

"And it was delicious. Don't worry. The pie didn't make me want to go on a bender. I still have the occasional small drink or a beer. I hadn't reached the status of alcoholic yet—I was just a person with a lot of grief and little self-control."

"Was it really that bad?"

"Are you joking? I thought my heart was being ripped out by an angry bear half the time. I was *miserable.* So I started self-medicating with gin." He shuddered. "Now I can't even stand the smell of that shit."

"When Grey left, how did you stop? Did you go to meetings?"

"No. I was convinced that I was too well-known and meetings would be a disaster, but that was probably just my inflated ego talking. The idea of the paparazzi following me to an AA meeting did not sound like a barrel of monkeys. So I went to a shrink for a long time and got some perspective. That's what helped. He was terrific." Nash sat on the edge of the bed. "No one thinks twice about a musician or even a minor celebrity seeing a shrink. We're all such narcissists; we love to have a captive audience listen to us, right?"

Caro laughed with him, knowing full well that there was plenty of pain behind his bravado, but she sobered when he continued.

"He also helped me cope with the sudden loss of my mom, and I got my dad in to see him for some grief counseling as well." He reached for Caro and pulled her close. "That's enough with the heavy stuff. Dad's doing great, and I'm happier at this very moment than I probably have the right to be. Now why don't we lose some clothes and get reacquainted with each other, hmm?" He reached for Caro's shirt and began to push it up and off. As soon as her tummy became bared to him, his mouth started an exploratory expedition across her skin.

Caro shivered with delight as his soft lips painted a pattern of desire across her belly. No one had ever gotten to her the way Nash and Greyson had. She thrilled to his touch, but in the back of her mind, a tiny voice kept asking for the other man as well. *Greyson isn't here. You left him. He left Nash. Be happy with the man you have now.*

In the back of her mind, she knew she wouldn't be able to breathe easy until they fixed things with Greyson. After all, he hadn't been to blame for any of it. *Nash and I were the ones who ruined it for ourselves and for him. We need to make it right.*

"Where did you go just now, Caro?" Nash asked as he pulled away. "One minute you were with me, and then it was as if you checked out. Are you having second thoughts? I can leave if you want me to."

Grasping his biceps, she answered, "I don't want you to leave, I promise. It's just that I suddenly got a flash of what it was like… maybe what it could be like again…"

"With Greyson," they said simultaneously.

Nash smiled at her, and his bluer-than-blue eyes bore into hers. Softly and with great affection, he said, "We'll call him tomorrow. But I need you too much right now. I've never felt like this with any other woman. You need to know that."

"I understand. Yes. We'll call Grey tomorrow." She nuzzled his neck. "Make love to me, Nash. The way only you can do." She pushed his jacket off impatiently and began unbuttoning his shirt.

Nash chuckled softly, saying, "I need to change the lyrics of that song. It's too sad."

"I'm happy to hear that. And I'm anxious to try singing it. I wonder if I can even still sound half-decent."

"Oh please. Of course you can. Do you mind if I pop into your shower for a second? I feel sort of grubby after being at the track all day and then flying."

"Right this way. Want me to scrub your back?"

"I would not turn that down."

The rest of their clothes hit the floor as she led him into her palatial bathroom. He looked around with awe at the spaciousness, featuring marble tiles and modern fixtures. "This is amazing for an older house like this."

Caro laughed. "I sacrificed one of the six bedrooms to make this a bathroom to enjoy, and I've never been sorry."

"It's gorgeous." He eyed her up and down then. "But not as gorgeous as you. You haven't changed a bit, Caro; you look amazing."

Caro snickered. "You don't need to lay it on thick, Nash. I'm a sure bet tonight." She turned on the shower and grabbed some fresh towels. "Ready?"

Their shower was speedy because as soon as they got their hands on each other, they couldn't stop. Their soft caresses over slick, warm skin drove both of them wild, so Nash growled into her ear, "Bed. Now."

As Caro dried off quickly, Nash found his pants and pulled a new box of condoms out of his pocket. He pulled out a single foil square placed on the bedside table. She came up behind him and wrapped a towel around him so he'd stop dripping on the floor. "You paid a visit to the all-night drugstore on the way here, I see. Anxious?" she said with a laugh.

He whipped around and grabbed her into a tight embrace. Bending to kiss her, he stroked her lips with his own and then plunged his tongue into her mouth. She answered with her own tongue and moaned hungrily against him. His arousal was evident as his hardness pressed between them.

"I want to savor your body, but I'm already so turned on I'm afraid the first time might be over a little quickly."

"I understand. It's the same for me. But we have all night." She reached for his cock and stroked him lovingly. "Oh, I missed this," she sighed as she slicked the precum across the head of his massive erection. Her hand made love to him, feeling the steely hardness beneath the silky skin.

"Lie back, Caro." He helped her get into position in the middle of the large bed and knelt between her spread thighs. "So beautiful," he whispered as he briefly took in her toned body, luscious tits, and the glorious, wavy black hair that fanned out across the pillow framing her face. Her expression gave away her eagerness as she looked into his eyes. She was slick and ready for him, just as she'd promised. Scooting down on the bed, he leaned over and kissed her breasts, her belly, and then her thighs as one of his hands began to explore her. "So wet and eager for me."

Finally, when Caro thought he'd taken far too long—although it had probably been only seconds—he kissed her tender parts. One finger slid into her as he licked and flicked her clit with a forceful tongue. "Perfect," he murmured. Then all at once, he sucked her clit into his mouth forcefully as he added a second finger.

It was all Caro could do to keep from screaming. Her orgasm ripped through her like a category-five hurricane. All the years of wanting and pining for Nash and Greyson exploded in a tempest of sensation and relief. "Nash!" she shouted. "Ohmygod!"

Looking terribly satisfied with himself, Nash grabbed the condom and put it on at record speed. Caro was still writhing with spasms when he shoved himself into her. Gasping, she raised her knees up to allow him deeper access and captured him with her long legs around his waist—just the way he'd remembered.

Nash pounded into her because physically, he was unable to slow down. The craving to plunder and pummel took over him, and he watched as her eyes nearly rolled back with bliss. Caro had always been an energetic lover, and he appreciated that, for he too liked things a little fast and rough. He felt his balls smack against her ass as he quickened his pace. Once he was deep inside, his hips made a twisting motion that he knew drove Caro wild. Over and over, he hammered her as he throbbed inside her. All too soon, he couldn't hold back any longer.

Nash ground into her as he declared, "I never stopped loving you, Caro! You're still mine. Now and always!" Then he let out an enormous, primal growl and came so hard that he thought for a moment he might have died of pleasure.

Caro couldn't even count how many orgasms she had before they made a significant dent in Nash's stack of condoms. *This is a night to remember,* she thought. But still, in the back of her mind, she wondered if Greyson could ever be a part of them again. That was her final thought before falling asleep.

Nash too felt more satisfied than he had in over ten years but like Caro, he fell asleep thinking not only of the dark-haired beauty he held in his arms but of a tall, thoughtful, somewhat naïve man he'd loved with his whole heart. *Can we do it all again? Will it be the same? Better? Or is it greedy of me to want more than Caro? Does Greyson still love us too, or does he hate us for screwing up so badly?*

The next morning, Caro awoke to the delicious feel of a warm, hard body curled around her like a big spoon, and she snuggled closer to him. But it was something else that had brought her out of her dream.

The doorbell.

She knew that very few people had the code to her gate, so it didn't trouble her much. With a sigh, she whispered, "I love you too, Nash," and kissed his chest. Then she carefully extricated herself from Nash's heavy arm and found a robe. She padded barefoot through the house, noting that it was after ten already. The doorbell rang again. Expecting to see either Eli or Zoë, she pulled the door open, only to be greeted by an odd bouquet of flowers. The figure holding the flowers held them high enough to block her view of his face. All she could see was a pale masculine hand with black hair on his fingers.

The man in question thrust the flowers toward Caro—who had no choice but to take them—exclaiming, "Good morning! I'm sorry to show up unannounced, but I thought we could finally have that talk you've been putting off. I've given you plenty of time to reconsider my proposal, Carrie. It's time for you to agree so we can get on with it." As he spoke, he shoved his way through the door. "You're not dressed yet? I thought you were an early riser. Are you ill? Whose filthy truck is that? Are you having some gardening done?" He barely took a breath as he peppered her with his inane questions and suppositions. "If you have a worker on the property, you surely ought to have some clothes on."

Caro's hand dropped to her side where she let the flowers dangle as she stared at the man. She briefly pondered how he had managed to select a bouquet with the ugliest assortment of colors she had ever seen. She considered the possibility that he might have picked them up at the grocery store on his way over. *What flower shop would be open on Sunday morning anyway?* she thought. Glancing down at them, she revised her theory. *On second thought, maybe he plucked them up from beside the road.* She sneezed.

Finally, she found her voice. "Jason, I don't appreciate you barging in like this…"

"I'm hardly barging! I'm your fiancé. And I brought flowers."

She tried to hand them back by pushing them into his chest. "No, thank you. You know perfectly well I've never agreed to marry you. And furthermore, I never intend to marry you. Ever."

"What's gotten into you, Carrie?"

A deep laugh rumbled behind Caro, and she saw Jason's eyes narrow as the voice said, "*I've* gotten into her, dumbass. Maybe it's time for you to take your stinkweeds and go."

Jason's narrow eyes went round as he gaped at Caro and then at Nash, who was clothed only in his boxers. His head jerked back and forth between them comically. "What's going on here? Carrie, who is this? Is *he* why you've turned me down?"

Ignoring Jason's whiny outburst, Nash wrapped his arms affectionately around Caro and kissed the top of her head. Addressing her, he murmured, "I heard what you told me. Best way to wake up ever." Then he looked Jason in the eye. "Like I said, whoever you are, it's time to go. Caro and I have unfinished business this morning." He couldn't resist a lewd little grind against her bottom from behind.

She stifled a giggle and leaned backward into Nash's embrace. She also noted how his naked biceps bulged and flexed as he held her in his protective embrace.

"Nash, this is Jason, whose proposals I've rejected several times. Jason, this is Nash…"

"Nash Keating!" Jason's face took on a look of wonder. "May I have your autograph?"

"Now isn't the time," Caro intoned as Nash snorted behind her.

"Nice to know he at least has good taste in women and mus—" Nash tried to say.

Jason interrupted, "You own that amazing horse!"

"...and horses," Nash deadpanned. "So much for *my* talents."

"Congratulations!"

"On what? Winning the Derby and Preakness or wooing Caro back into my good graces where she belongs finally?"

Jason frowned. "You knew Carrie before?"

Caro sighed. "Look, you guys, I'm dying for some coffee. Would it be okay to take this discussion into the kitchen?"

"You two don't want to put on some clothes?" Jason asked, wrinkling his nose.

Nash gave a belly laugh and answered, "Why? She'll just rip them off of me again as soon as you leave—which I hope will be right away."

"Nash, don't be rude," she said, stifling a chuckle.

He bent and bit her ear gently. "Not rude. You know it's true," he growled at her.

Once they made it to the kitchen, Caro dumped the flowers onto the counter. Then she headed to the coffee maker, poured three mugs, and handed one to each man. Nash thanked her politely and took a sip, but Jason looked at his cup mournfully.

"You know I don't drink black coffee," he bellyached.

Caro gave an I-don't-give-a-fuck shrug and answered, "I actually didn't know." Then she took a sip of her own and let out a contented sigh. "You can find the refrigerator, and the sugar bowl is over there." She smacked a spoon onto the counter by the sugar bowl as Nash sat down at the kitchen table. When Caro moved to sit beside him, he grabbed her and pulled her onto his lap. "Possessive much?" she whispered to him as they watched

Jason pour a quarter of his coffee into the sink. Apparently, he needed to make room for all the milk and sugar he added.

Nash stifled a gag when he saw Jason take a tentative sip and then add another heaping spoonful of sugar to the travesty in a cup. Then he broke the silence as Jason sat across from them. "You need to know, Jimmy, that Caro's mine. She always has been and always will be."

Jason frowned, "It's Jason." Looking at Caro, he asked, "Were you cheating on him with me?"

Nash snorted, and Caro bristled, answering, "No. Nash and I weren't together for several years, and now we're back where we belong. Besides, I don't recall doing anything with you that would have been considered 'cheating' on anyone."

"That's a relief," Nash muttered into her ear. "I'd have hoped you had better taste…"

"Shh!" She pinched him. "Be nice." Addressing Jason again, she explained, "Nash and I were together a long time ago and broke up due to some unfortunate misunderstandings. The feelings I have for him now are the same as they were back then. And while I'm glad to have spent time with you, Jason, it ends now." She looked at his hangdog face. "Actually, it ended months ago when I told you no the first time. In the future, when a woman says no, remember that it means no. Have some self-respect. You'll find someone wonderful, I'm sure. It's just never going to be me."

"But, Carrie…!"

"And please stop calling me that! My name is Caroline or Caro, and you know it."

"It's just my special pet name for you, Carrie…o."

Nash rolled his eyes, and Caro shook her head. "Thanks for stopping by and for the… uh… flowers. Nash and I have to go and get ready for an appointment." She stood and grabbed Jason by the elbow. "I'll see you out."

"I didn't get my autograph!"

"Some other time." *Like never.* "You've caught us at a bad time, Jason. Really." She almost shoved him through the door and locked it behind him. Then she waited a moment to be sure she heard him drive away. When he did leave, she breathed a sigh of relief.

When Caro made it back to the kitchen, she found Nash pulling things out of the refrigerator. There were eggs sitting on the counter as well as bacon and a few things that might taste great in an omelet.

Hearing her footsteps, he turned around and grinned. "I never got to eat any dinner last night, and I'm sorry to say that I'm about to chew my own arm off if I don't get some real food in me. What do you usually have for breakfast?"

Caro sheepishly answered, "Angela makes delicious breakfasts all week long, but she has Sundays off, so I usually just have cold cereal or a bagel then. Or sometimes, I go over to Eli's house for family brunch. If you can cook though, have at it. I'll enjoy the view and eat anything you offer. I've never been fed by a half-naked man."

"Then relax and drink your coffee while I make us a masterpiece. We need our strength." He winked at her then sobered. "We also need to call Grey—although it's still early in LA. In some ways, calling him scares the shit out of me, and in other ways, I can't wait to talk to him."

A few minutes later—after Caro deposited the ugly, sneeze-provoking flowers into the trash—they sat down to a scrumptious meal, and Nash asked with raised eyebrows, "So you and the tool, eh? What was that about?"

Caro let out a long sigh. "Nash, it was not easy to find a great guy who could take the place of you and Greyson. So I went out with a series of reasonably attractive and utterly unremarkable men over the past ten years or so. Sometimes I needed an escort for events, and frankly, sometimes, I got horny. If that makes me a bad person, well… then I'm bad. I make no excuses.

"When I first met Jason, things were fine for a while. He was good enough company. But then he started to get really clingy and made lots of noise about forever. I'd never thought we had a serious relationship at all and assumed we were just friends because of the lack of anything physical. We hadn't ever even shared a night together when he proposed. Then he asked at least four more times after that. Each time I turned him down. Finally, a couple of months ago, I told him to just leave me alone, and I didn't hear from him until this morning. He seemed to think I was taking time to consider his offer. I could kick myself for being so naïve and not changing the security code on the front gate back then. I'm changing it today, by the way. At least he doesn't have a key to the house."

"Alright. I get it. And I won't bring him up again. Now, let's talk about what we're going to say to Greyson."

It was then that something dawned on Caro, and she got a chill. "Nash, wait."

He looked at her nervous expression and said, "We don't *have* to call him right now…"

"No," she interrupted. "It's not that. Did you hear the gate chime after Jason left? I don't remember hearing it. He might still be on the property."

"I'll go check if you want me to."

"Yes please, if you don't mind. But at least put on shoes and a pair of pants. It's no fun walking on the gravel drive barefoot. Should I call the police?"

"Not yet. Let's see what we're dealing with first."

Caro couldn't help but think that Nash looked ridiculously sexy in nothing but his suit pants and dress shoes as he marched out the front door.

Nash looked down the long, tree-lined drive toward the street, and sure enough, Jason's car was still inside the gate, about two-thirds the way down the drive. "Little dirtbag," he muttered. "Couldn't take no for an answer."

Striding purposefully toward the car, Nash saw the silhouette of Jason's head whip around and stare for a moment. Then the car started up and swerved backward up the driveway toward Nash, nearly taking out a few shrubs along the way. Nash had to jump behind a large bush to avoid getting hit by the jerk. When Jason pulled to a stop, Nash glared at him.

"Did you remember my request for an autograph finally?" Jason asked in a plaintively hopeful voice.

"No, asshole. I came out here to tell you that if you're not gone in fifteen seconds, we're calling the police. Caro asked you nicely to leave, but I'm not feeling quite as polite now, seeing as how you almost flattened me with your car!" Nash cracked his knuckles and flexed his muscles—giving his best impersonation of a barbarian.

Jason sniffed and muttered, "You're just lucky you're agile. It would have been fun to run you over." Suddenly, he gunned his engine and was off in a flash of spraying gravel and exhaust. Lucky for Jason, the electric eye triggered the gate to open for an exiting vehicle, or he'd have collided with it.

Back inside, Nash found Caro clearing the table. "He's gone now. You need to go program a new gate number immediately. The little fuckwit tried to run over me going backward."

Caro gasped. "*Now* do you want to report him to the police?"

"Nah, I'm fine. Let's just forget about it."

Caro immediately took care of the gate security and made a mental note to give her new code to all the appropriate people. It was a relief to know that they wouldn't have any more unwanted company this morning.

After loading the dishwasher with their breakfast things, they headed back to the bedroom. Nash watched as Caro's sexy hips swayed in front of him all the way up the stairs. He couldn't take it. With a growl, as soon as they reached the second floor, he swept her up into his arms and whooshed her into the bedroom again. She giggled as he tossed her onto the bed and tore off his pants and shoes. Nash was fully erect and looking fine.

"Ravage me," she pleaded with him in a breathy voice. "I need it hard, Nash." The twinkle in her eye and her tiny snort told him she knew she was being corny and didn't care. He bent over her and whipped off the sash of her robe, then flung it open.

"You just get more beautiful each day." He nearly fell onto her, kissing her hungrily and stroking her body. He caressed her breasts and toyed with her nipples with his fingers and his lips until she writhed beneath him.

"Fuck the foreplay, Nash! Get inside me. I need to feel you in me!"

With a mouth full of boob, he laughed and muttered, "So bossy and demanding!" When she moaned at him for more action, he asked, "Condom?"

"Not necessary. If you're okay, then I'm okay. Here, sit up for a second."

Nash retreated with a questioning look until Caro flipped over and got up onto her knees, then laid her upper body back down onto the bed. "Fuck me doggy-style. I miss that. You get so deep that way." She reached between her legs and grabbed his dick, pulling him toward her body. She guided him into her slick pussy and sighed as he filled her. "Yes! Now beat me with that stick!"

"I like to think of it more like a pole myself." He snorted as he pulled back and pounded in again with an enormous thrust. His hands gripped her hips as he plundered her.

Caro cried out, "Pole, stick, whatever. We both know you're huge. Now let me have it with that monster! Yes, like that!" Caro started rubbing her clit with a vengeance, keeping time with Nash's plunging rhythm.

Once they established a cadence that seemed to propel them both equally toward the ultimate goal, Nash released one hand and stuck his thumb into his mouth. He quickly rubbed his saliva around her rear door and slid his thumb inside her.

Caro's surprised intake of breath was so sexy, it almost

made him spill everything he had into her right then. He had to force himself to hold off until he knew she was completely ready. He slid his thumb deeper into her body and then proceeded to alternate his prods. As his dick retreated, his thumb shoved in, and as his thumb pulled back, he pushed back in with his cock. Within moments, Caro started moaning, "I'm coming, ohhh, now, Nash! Fill me up, honey."

And that was it for Nash. He could feel the fabulous contractions of Caro's muscles around him as she rode wave after wave of orgasmic sensations, and he exploded inside her. It was messier than with a condom, but the thought of filling her with his seed made him come even harder than he had the night before. He was home. He was inside his woman. Bare.

He delighted in watching his cum dribble down her thigh after he pulled out. It made him want to pound his chest and holler, "Mine!"

Now he just needed his man too.

After a quick shower, they dressed and got comfortable in Caro's living room. The phone was on the coffee table in front of them.

"Ready?" Nash asked.

"As I'll ever be."

Nash hit a button, and as the phone rang, he switched to speaker mode. "I hope he answers," he muttered as it rang a third time.

Finally, after five interminable rings, a familiar voice answered, "Well, it's about damn time, asshole."

Caro gave Nash a questioning look, and he flinched. "Um… sorry? What has you in such a fine mood today?"

With obvious pain in his voice, Greyson asked, "I sent him months and *months* ago, and you're just *now* calling to acknowledge it?"

"Whoa, wait. Back up, Grey. What are you talking about, and who is he?"

"The big horse, you jerk. Elvis!"

"*You* sent Elvis? Why? I mean, thank you. He's fantastic, but I don't understand! How and why did you happen to send him, and why didn't I know about it?"

"Yeah, right. I wrote a long letter to you about him and duct-taped it to his jacket-thingy he was wearing in the big transportation van that took him to you. I thought he would be a special gift that you'd *appreciate*."

"Well, that explains a little of the story, but not all of it. Elvis just showed up in the pasture one morning when I went out to check on the horses, and all he had on was his halter. He wasn't wearing a blanket."

"Are you shitting me?"

"No, Grey! I had no fucking idea how that horse got here or why, and no one would tell me anything about how he got into the farm. I thought someone might have jumped the fence with him and dropped him off."

"*Dropped off* a $50,000 horse?! Are you out of your mind?"

"Hey, it happens. People do weird things all the time. We have another great horse that... Oh, never mind. But let's back up a little. How did he get in? Who helped you?"

"Your dad."

"What? How?"

Greyson gave a big sigh. "Look, Nash, I've been worried about you, okay? Even though I was too hurt to call you myself, I've checked in with your dad every once in a while over the years. I'm sorry as fuck about your mom, by the way."

Nash mumbled his thanks.

"Anyway, I know about the counseling you got, and I know about your ups and downs."

At this bit of news, Caro narrowed her eyes at Nash and cocked her head questioningly.

"Then, when I heard that you'd gotten a great deal on some big-ass farm and got your dad straightened out, I decided to send you a congratulatory gift. I talked to some people who knew some people, and they all agreed that Elvis would be the perfect horse for you. You know—kind of a barn-warming gift." He chuckled at his own joke. "His name was Pete back then, but I thought Elvis sounded like more fun, so I insisted that they change it. He has some fancy registered name too. I'll send you those papers now that I know you've kept him at least. Anyway, I hired a trainer to do all the right shit with the horse, and when he decided the big guy was ready to go, we shipped him to you. I made your dad promise to keep his mouth shut and told him I'd explain it all to you. I had no idea the guys with the truck would take the jacket thing off the horse. I thought it came with him or something."

"He probably got too hot, and they took it off and then didn't remember to leave it here," Nash mused out loud. "Anyway, that's amazing, Grey. Thank you from the bottom of my heart. He is a terrific horse, and I have a lot of fun with him. I just can't believe you went to all that trouble and didn't tell me sooner. Why didn't you?"

"I thought maybe you were pissed at me for saddling you with another responsibility or some shit. I didn't know what to think, actually. Maybe you didn't like the horse, maybe your dad was lying about your success, maybe this, maybe that. It hurt like hell though that you just *ignored* me. Again."

Nash's voice softened, "I never would have ignored you if I'd known. And I didn't call sooner about anything else because I was afraid you wouldn't want to hear from me."

Greyson scoffed. "Right."

"No, really. I know how badly I hurt you, and my behavior was horrible. I never want to hurt you ever again, Grey. And I have something to tell you…"

Greyson interrupted, "Hang on, Nash." It was obvious that he'd turned his face away from the phone when he asked someone, "What is it, babe?" Then there was some muffled conversation they couldn't make out. Finally, Grey came back and said, "Look, Nash, I'm glad we cleared the air, but I have to go. I'm… uh… getting married in a few days, and apparently, I need to go over some of the plans with my fiancée now."

Nash's face lost all its color, and Caro's tummy gave an uncomfortable flip.

"Hey, you should come to the wedding! Will you be my best man?" Greyson asked with obvious hope in his voice.

In the background, they could hear a female shout, "Greyson! What about my cousin? He's expecting to be your best man."

Greyson answered her, "Look, this is my *friend* on the phone, and I've never even met your cousin. I doubt he'd even give a damn if we gave that honor to someone else." There was more muffled conversation, and Greyson came back to the phone. "Can you make it? It's this weekend. Saturday night. Please? You have a tux, right?"

Nash closed his eyes against the pain and blurted out, "I hope you know what you're doing, Grey. I'd be honored to be your best man, and I have a tux. We'll be there."

"Who's we? Do you have a girlfriend? If so, I'd love to meet her."

"As a matter of fact, you already know her. Quite well, actually. Caro and I are back together, and we were calling you to tell you how much we'd love to get back with you too."

Caro tried to muster up a cheerful tone in her voice when she said, "Hi, Grey. Um... congratulations." Her voice cracked in pain. "We miss you!"

When there was no reply other than a huge gasp and then dead silence that went on and on, Nash disconnected the call. "Well. That wasn't anything like what I'd expected," he said in a flat voice to Caro.

A tear streaked down Caro's cheek before she angrily swiped it away. "This situation sucks. I'm not even sure Grey sounded all that excited about getting married. What can we do?"

"I think we should take a trip to see him. There is still time before the wedding, but if we can't fix things with Grey immediately, we're all screwed."

Caro looked thoughtful for a moment and then sighed.

"But what if he *is* truly happy? I don't want to ruin it for him. And his fiancée… I don't want to blow up her life by showing up and luring him away or anything."

"If we can lure him away, isn't it better for her to know now? Isn't it better for all of us if we clear the air before he goes and makes some lifelong commitment?" Nash shook his head. "I need to go home and grab some clean clothes to pack... and my damn tux. I only have dirty stuff in my suitcase, and it was just enough for a couple of days anyway. I'll be back as soon as possible. Maybe two hours tops. Then if we can't take your plane, we'll have to drive to Louisville to get a late flight to LA…"

Caro put her hand on Nash's chest. "Wait a minute. Let's slow down. I want him to want us too—I really do. But why don't we give this some more thought, Nash, before we barrel in there with guns blazing and mess up his life?"

"Because we'd be fixing it, not ruining it!" he nearly yelled at her. "He *can't* have the same thing with someone else that he's had with us."

Soothingly, she said, "We don't really know that. It's been years, and we've all grown and changed."

"Did he really sound happy to you?"

Tears sparkled in Caro's eyes. "Well, not exactly, but maybe it's just last-minute jitters, and she's a great match for him."

"Look, Caro, if you don't want to come with me, that's fine, but I'm not letting Greyson get married to some stranger without a fight."

She smiled fondly at him. "Nash, I know this is upsetting, but let's give it a little time. If he's unhappy, it's up to Grey to decide. It's not our place."

"It *is* our place. He belongs with us!"

"Alright, let's compromise. I'll pack a bag and come back to your place with you. We ought to give him at least twenty-four hours to think about what we told him anyway. I'm sure it came out of left field and was a pretty big shock to Grey. We can text him and ask him to contact us later tonight or tomorrow, and we can also let him know we plan to make a trip out to California to see him—no matter what he decides—in the next couple of days. He'll either be adamant about not being with us and going through with the marriage because he's madly in love with Whatshername, or the seeds of doubt will grow because of what we've offered him, and he'll make the right decision. Can you do that?"

"As long as you're with me, I can." Nash kissed her. "And I need to have a chat with my dad too about playing games and acting like he knew nothing about Elvis. I wish he were at home, but they've taken Pip up to New York to get him settled in there. I won't bother my dad about this until after the race." He put his face in his hands. "Everything's happening all at once."

"Most of it is good, at least," she said while rubbing his back. "Just a little overwhelming, I suppose. Anyway, come and keep me company while I pack for… whatever we're going to be doing for the next couple of weeks. And you can think about what you want to text him."

Nash harrumphed and followed her up the stairs. Settling into a comfy chair, he took out his phone and stared at it while Caro went to fill a bag with her essentials.

*Definitely some riding clothes and a bathing suit or two and some killer outfits… Hmm…*

# Nine

One thing that can always be said about Kentucky is that it's beautiful, especially when you get into the horse country parts. Caro gasped with pleasure as they pulled through the gate of Best Life Farm. Rolling pastures, a small lake, several barns and assorted outbuildings, a practice racetrack, and a guesthouse were evident immediately, but as they wound through the tree-lined drive, the actual house came into view. It was breathtaking. Surrounded by tall, majestic trees and colorful flowering bushes, the enormous house looked like a country club. It seemed to sprawl in every direction, all on one level.

"This place is huge! And it's gorgeous, Nash. Do you really live here by yourself?" Caro was no stranger to large houses since she'd grown up summering in the Hamptons and wintering in her parents' colossal, three-story penthouse in Manhattan, but this still floored her.

"You'll meet my roommates soon enough," he answered with a smile. He pulled his truck into a garage and grabbed their luggage as she noticed he had a few other cars. There was a golf cart, a Tesla, a vintage Bentley, and something else that was covered with a tarp that she guessed might be a motorcycle. "Come on in." He led her in through a mudroom and into a modern kitchen that would rival that of a fine restaurant anywhere. Walking through the house, Caro took in the masculine charm of the place. Everything seemed cozy despite the towering ceilings and massively proportioned rooms. Splashes of color made it feel warm and inviting.

Eventually, Nash dropped their bags in the master bedroom and led Caro back out again before she could even look around. "We need to find the crew," he explained.

"Did you get lost in here much when you first moved in?"

"Nah, I have an excellent sense of direction." They passed by a home theater and what appeared to be a fully equipped recording studio as he led her to the back of the house. Finally, he slid open a patio door and stepped outside onto the brick expanse that was partially covered and led out to a magnificent pool. He let out a sharp whistle and looked at Caro. "Brace yourself for the onslaught. They might be muddy, and if so, I apologize. We're heathens around here apparently."

Caro could hear the sounds of deep barks as a trio of large, shiny black-and-tan dogs galloped out of the trees toward them. The dogs' tongues lolled out of their happy faces.

"Rottweilers!" Caro exclaimed happily. "They're magnificent!"

"Sit!" Nash commanded them as they approached at top speed. Simultaneously, three doggie butts hit the ground, and they all whined and squirmed for attention. Nash knelt in front of them and gave them all cuddles and pets until they turned their attention on Caro with curiosity. "Come and meet my buddies," he invited her. "This one is Jimi Hendrix, this is Sid Vicious, and this little beauty is Janis Joplin. They're friendly, I promise."

Caro extended her open palm toward the dogs, and all three crowded around her, alternately headbutting and licking whatever they could reach without jumping. The nubs of their tails batted back and forth eagerly. Caro laughed and doled out plenty of ear scritches and hugs. "They're wonderful," she exclaimed. "I can imagine though that their appearance makes them fearsome guard dogs."

"Well, unfortunately, Sid Vicious would probably turn tail and run away from someone who looked threatening, but Janis and Jimi might be pretty intimidating. I'm just glad they like the horses and goats and don't get in the way."

"Are they house dogs?"

"Oh sure. They're excellent roomies." He laughed. "They aren't picky about the menu, and they don't hog the blankets." Nash rose to his feet and dusted off his jeans. "Care to go meet Elvis?"

"Definitely!"

"We could go for a ride unless you're too tired… or sore." He winked at her.

"I'd love that, actually. Just give me a minute to get out of my shorts and into some breeches."

"Yeah, me too."

Somehow this surprised Caro. She expected Nash to wear jeans and cowboy boots, even though he'd described his horse as a Warmblood. That could mean the horse had been trained to do several things, however, so she kept an open mind.

Nash pulled out his phone and called someone. "Hey, Benny, everything good? Yeah? Great. Do you think you could saddle up Elvis and Lady G for us? Yes, English tack for both horses. Thanks, we'll be down to the barn in about twenty minutes."

"Lady G? You named her after Lady Gaga? Is she a blonde?" Caro laughed, picturing a palomino with a white mane.

"She is not a blonde, but she has a *lot* of attitude. I thought you'd appreciate her spirit."

"Ah, figures. That's perfect."

A few minutes later, Caro had the distinct pleasure of seeing her tall, built boyfriend clad in a polo shirt, a pair of tight riding breeches, and well-worn field boots. *Masculine perfection*, she decided.

Likewise, Nash enjoyed the sight of Caro's long, lean legs and perky bottom dressed the same way.

"It's a long walk down to the barn, so we can take the cart."

Leaving the dogs to relax in the shade of a beautiful tree outside, Nash led them back through the kitchen—where he picked up a baggie full of chopped-up carrots—and out into the garage.

At one point, Nash veered off the tree-lined drive toward a gate. On it was a placard that read THE MÖTLEY CRÜE.

"These guys are the rescues," he explained. He picked up the carrots and opened the gate so they could step inside. Immediately they were surrounded by an assortment of horses—all colors and sizes—all nosing at them impatiently for a treat. Nash introduced each one by name and told Caro what he knew of their background. Quickly they handed out pieces of carrot to the grateful recipients. "Mostly, they all needed some love and some friends to hang with. A couple of these guys are too old to leave, but they'll always be welcome here."

"Nash, you're amazing. This just makes me love you even more." She patted a tall white gelding with a brand on its flank. Nash called him Pearl Jam. Then a little roan mare headbutted her in the back. Caro laughed and scolded gently, "Hey, I'm getting to you!" She fed the mare half a carrot too. Finally, everyone had a treat, and they headed back to the cart.

"Where are the goats?"

"Mostly, we keep them in with the racehorses. Those guys tend to be a lot more high-strung and need companionship. For a while, we had a donkey, but we sold his horse, and the donkey went with him." He shook his head at the memory. "Frankly, I like the goats a lot more. That little shit was always crabby about something and liked to bite me in the ass whenever he could."

Caro laughed at that mental picture. "Does Domino Pip have a goat buddy?"

"No. He's remarkably chill on his own, so not much bothers him. Okay, here we are." He parked the cart off to the side of a large barn door.

Caro noted that the entire stable smelled of fresh wood shavings and was spotlessly clean. Someone had done a magnificent job keeping up on barn chores. Then she saw two horses in cross ties that were obviously Elvis and Lady G. Elvis was huge and terribly handsome, with a lustrous mahogany coat and shiny black mane and tail. He was a flashy guy with four white socks and a wide blaze running down his face.

Elvis gave a friendly nicker as soon as Nash approached him. The look on Nash's face was so affectionate that it was clear that the mutual admiration ran deep. Nash patted the big guy's neck and introduced him to Caro. "He's pretty great, isn't he? I can't believe Greyson found him for me and sent him like that." He sighed. "Maybe there's hope for us yet with him."

Lady G turned out to be a lovely, leggy Thoroughbred with a dappled gray coat. Her eyes were so dark they were nearly black, with a definite sparkle of mischief in them. She pawed the floor impatiently as if to say, "Let's get a move-on!" Caro chuckled as she approached the mare and fed her the last small piece of carrot she'd saved in her pocket.

"Trying to butter her up, are you?" Nash laughed. "Just be careful when you mount. She's well-behaved, *except* that when someone climbs on board, she tends to want to kick up her heels a little and assert herself. It won't last, but I landed on my ass the first time she pulled that stunt with me because it caught me so off-guard. So far, nothing we've done helps, so just get on quickly and stay loose. I'll hold her head for you at least while you're getting on." Nash grabbed a couple of helmets for them to strap on. "Does that fit comfortably?"

She nodded.

Caro adjusted her stirrups by measuring the leathers to the length of her arm, and then she undid the cross ties that tethered Lady G in place. Nash led the horse over to a mounting block, and Caro climbed up. As soon as Caro's left foot wedged into the stirrup, she swung her right leg over the horse and barely had a chance to settle in. Sure enough, Lady G's front feet left the ground instantly, and her back feet kicked out in protest—or maybe it was in celebration that she was going to be ridden—and she let out a loud squeal. Caro laughed and adjusted her reins. "Ooh! Thanks for the warning, Nash. Lady G, you're a troublemaker!"

Nash answered in a flat voice, "I think she was born this way." Then they both cracked up. He quickly mounted Elvis —who stood still like a gentleman—and led the ladies out of the barn. "The reason we have Lady G is because of that behavior, actually. Some rich guy with no sense or riding ability bought her—back when she was called Misty. The first time he tried to ride her, she did her little trick, and the guy fell off and broke his arm. That was the end of their short relationship. He told the trainer that she was a dangerous killer who ought to be destroyed, so the trainer called my dad immediately, and we went to pick her up. The owner probably thought we were taking her off to… you know…"

Caro's horse behaved perfectly for the rest of the ride. They started out warming up in a small ring so she could get the feel of Lady G, and when it was obvious things were going great for them, Nash said, "Let's go explore the farm. I can check on things, you can see the place, and we have a bunch of cross-country jumps set up here and there that we can take or not, depending on how comfortable you're feeling."

The farm was enormous and as picturesque as anything Caro had ever seen. Her favorite part was when they went by the pasture containing the broodmares and their foals—at least a dozen of each, and the sight took her breath away. Nash urged Elvis into a gallop alongside the fence, and the little foals all took that as a cue to follow with their dams keeping pace beside them. There was nothing more beautiful, Caro decided, than galloping Thoroughbreds running free and with joy through the famed bluegrass of Kentucky. Caro also took off behind Nash and loved watching him sail over a low stone jump ahead of her. Something caught her eye when the horse was in midflight. Elvis was wearing… blue shoes!

Laughing, she pointed Lady G toward the jump as well, thinking, *Here goes!* Up and over they sailed—bringing a huge smile to Caro's face. "God, I've missed this!" she shouted.

Ahead of her, Nash slowed Elvis down and turned to look at her. Her eyes were alive with excitement, and her face was flushed. He was sure that she was the most beautiful sight in the world. She slowed her pace and rode up alongside them, laughing as he asked, "Care for some more jumps?"

When she cried, "Hell, yes!" he turned and pointed away from the broodmares.

"We'll go through that path there, and on the other side of that grove of trees, we can have some fun. Ladies first." He really wanted to watch her from behind, and since there was only one path, she couldn't get lost. Happily, Caro took off at a trot.

Caro appeared to be completely comfortable on Lady G, and she had a lovely economy of motion when she rode. He knew Lady G's gaits were smooth, but Caro blended with the mare perfectly. It felt as if the horse had been fated to come to him to entertain Caro and vice versa. He couldn't stop smiling. As they exited the forested path and reached sunlight once again, he could see Caro sizing up the jumps laid out ahead of them.

Without a backward glance, she took off at a canter and picked up speed as she approached the first obstacle: a wooden jump filled with greenery. Effortlessly, Lady G flew over the fence. She truly loved to jump. And then there was an in-and-out that Caro urged her through perfectly—no extra stride in the middle, he noted. He stopped gawking then and let Elvis have his turn at the jumps. It was exhilarating.

After both of them had taken all obstacles in the large field, they pulled up alongside each other once again.

"We better let them walk a while," Caro announced.

"Are you saying you're tired?"

"Not me, but Lady G here says she wants to stay firmly on the edge of glory and doesn't want to get too worn out. And we don't want Elvis to get all shook up, do we?"

Nash rolled his eyes. "Funny girl."

"Do you have a Barbra around here too, somewhere?"

Nash laughed and answered, "Not yet, we don't."

For the next fifteen minutes or so, they walked the horses back in the general direction of the barn where they'd started. They weren't overly taxed or lathered, but the day was warm. Nash finally pointed and said, "There's a small stream over that way. We can let the horses have a little drink and rest in the shade." He gave Caro a pointed look and added, "No one else ever comes out this way."

They dismounted and led the horses over to a bubbling brook that ran through the lower part of the pasture. "This is truly like heaven on earth, Nash. I don't know how you could ever think of leaving this."

"With the right incentive, I'd stay forever. That's for sure. It's just been a little lonely until today." He took her hand and brought it to his lips.

After the horses had their drink, he looped their reins over a low tree branch. The horses were obviously content with each other. Their eyelids drooped, and they seemed to be settling in for a nap.

"Come relax and get comfortable with me," Nash said as he sat on some long grass.

Caro didn't waste any time snuggling into him. The grass was cool and soft, and Nash was hard and warm. He smelled like sunshine and lust as he pulled off their helmets, wrapped her in his arms, and kissed her. Then he eased her back onto the grass and pushed up her shirt. He rubbed his face on her warm belly and finally laid his head on her chest, nestling between her breasts.

Caro expected things to heat up quickly, especially after Nash had mentioned that the area was private, but she could tell he actually just wanted to hold her and not much else. So she luxuriated in his embrace for a while, and they listened to the birdsong around them. This felt intimate too.

Breaking the relative silence, she finally asked, "I can't believe I never asked you this before, but when did you start riding?"

He laughed softly and sat up. "Probably before I could walk. I don't honestly remember. I was just always on a horse. Dad had me exercising them all the time. It was obvious I was never going to be a jockey, but I did spend a lot of time at the track with Dad. I rode some of the lead horses that pony the racehorses out to the starting gate. That was always fun. The jockeys are incredibly superstitious, so if you ponied one out and he won, chances were good that he'd ask for you again. I did that whenever I wasn't too busy with school. But then I got much more interested in my music and knew I had to work really hard on that if I wanted to get into Berklee College of Music. So as an older teen, I didn't ride as often. It was important for me to get a scholarship, so I had to stand out and be something special."

"Even though we were more concerned with other things at the time, I seem to remember you mentioning something about it way back when. You did get it, didn't you?"

Nash smiled, "I was awarded the Presidential Scholarship."

"Sounds impressive."

He nodded. "I guess. Greyson was also there on scholarship. Something else we had in common." He kissed her again softly and said, "Let's get the horses back and try getting hold of him again."

Nash gave Caro a quick leg up into the saddle, and Lady G let out a half-hearted squeak and again kicked out her back feet. At least this time, she didn't go airborne. Caro just laughed at her antics. "Naughty girl," she scolded good-naturedly.

"We'll go back by the clinic area this time. It's interesting." Nash led her through some buildings that he explained held a water therapy facility and a surgical center. They had a full-time vet on the premises as well as a physical therapist. There was a dormitory for the grooms, the groundskeepers, and a general handyman, but the rest of the staff lived nearby. The farrier made weekly calls.

"Speaking of the farrier, I noticed some fancy blue suede shoes on Elvis. What's that about?"

"They are a synthetic material that is supposed to be better for the horses' feet and legs. We're trying them out on Elvis. I couldn't resist the blue ones for him."

After seeing to the horses' baths and cooldowns, Nash led Caro back to the cart, and they drove back to the house. The three dogs were all sleeping in the shade of a tree in front of the house, but they roused themselves when they realized Nash was home again. They trailed in after them, and Nash made sure everyone—dogs and people—had some fresh, cold water to drink.

"Do you think we ought to call him again, or are you planning to text him?" Caro asked. "It's been hours now since we spoke with him."

"Let's send him a text and see if he responds."

Nash: Caro and I are coming to LA.
Call us ASAP.

"How does that sound?"

She smiled at him and answered, "It's very direct and to the point. Do you think he'll call?"

"I sure hope so." Nash hit the arrow button to send his message. "Now we wait. If he doesn't call back right away, we can go shower, and I'll figure out some dinner for us."

But no sooner had Nash said that when his phone rang, and the caller ID announced that it was Greyson Foster.

"That was quick," Caro observed as Nash answered and put Grey on speaker.

"Look, you guys, I'm anxious to see you and have you meet Britney, but don't go trying to mess things up with us, okay? I heard what you said about getting back together with you, and that's not happening."

"Are you telling us that she's definitely the one for you, Grey? And how long have you known her?" Caro asked.

"Um. Maybe. We started dating maybe five or six months ago."

"A ringing endorsement if I ever heard one. Do you know what the hell you're doing? This is a big step!" Caro tried to keep her voice calm, but it wasn't working too well.

"Come on, you know what I mean."

"No, we don't, Grey. It sounds like you barely know her. Does she make your life better just by being with her? Does she understand all of your faults and love you in spite of them? Does she even know that you're *bisexual*? Does she—?"

"Okay, I get the picture. You might not approve, but I'm getting married, and that's it."

"Why?" Caro and Nash asked simultaneously.

"Maybe because I want to! Did you ever think of that? Did you ever consider how hard it's been for me the past several years? I missed the two of you so badly that some days I could barely get out of bed!" *Fuck. Why did I admit that?* Greyson thought to himself. "So now I finally have someone who wants to be with *me*, and maybe I want to be a husband and not some cast-off *toy* you got tired of playing with!"

"Oh, Grey, we had no idea you felt that way," Caro said softly. A tear rolled down her cheek as she continued, "Never, *ever* think that. I left because of a terrible misunderstanding, and Nash has forgiven me. I was completely wrong about... so many things. It was a mess the way we ended our relationship, and I'm so sorry if my anger toward Nash affected you so badly. I never want to hurt either of you."

Nash interjected, "Don't forget that *you* were the one finally who took off, man."

"Because I couldn't stick around and watch you self-destruct and take advantage of me in the process. I lo… *cared* too much, Nash, to let you drag me down while you ruined your life. You wouldn't let me help you, so I removed myself. I didn't know what else to do to make you understand that I meant business."

"Grey, we're coming out to LA. We can fly out right away, and we're going to prove to you that we're still here for you. Whatshername can join us or not. It's up to you."

"Her name is Britney, and I insist that you two treat her well because I love her."

"If you say so. I'll be on my best behavior. Look, Caro has access to a private plane, and we'll be on it as soon as they can fuel up and get clearance. Don't do anything stupid in the meantime like run off to Vegas and get hitched."

Greyson snorted. "As if. Britney and her parents think this wedding has to be the Beverly Hills social event of the year. She'd never elope." In a nasal, feminine falsetto, he added, "'It just wouldn't be right'—according to her mother."

Caro was busily doing something on her phone and looked up. "I just booked us a suite at the Beverly Wilshire, and a driver is coming to get us in two hours to get us to one of the family jets. When I told Eli that it was important, he didn't even ask questions; he just leaped into action. He's the best brother ever."

Smiling at her, Nash said, "Sounds good to me. It'll give us plenty of time to shower—since we smell like horses—and get ready to go. I need to let a few people here know I'll be gone a while too." Looking back at the phone, he addressed

Greyson again. "Come see us in the morning at the hotel, Grey. If you don't show up by eleven, we'll track you down."

"I have a tux fitting at nine."

"Perfect. Bridezilla won't accompany you to that, will she?"

"Don't call her that, but no."

"Then come over as soon as you're done. I mean it, Grey." Nash added, "Please. If nothing else, come and let us say goodbye to you for once and for all before you get married." He looked at Caro with the saddest expression and added, "We promise not to pressure you if your mind's made up. We owe you that."

"Alright," Greyson answered softly. His blood stirred at the thought of seeing them again. *I could never resist them. What am I going to tell Britney?*

Their driver showed up as scheduled by Eli, and off they went to the closest charter airport outside Louis- ville. "Eli said we'd need to take the Challenger 300 because of the flight distance. It's equipped with a JetBed, but not a private bedroom, in case you're curious," Caro explained with a twinkle in her eye. "The flight attendant knows to leave passengers alone if they ask, but I don't think any in- flight hanky-panky is a great idea."

Nash shrugged good-naturedly. "It's fine. We have all night." He kissed her neck, and she snuggled close to him in the back of the limo. In her heart, Caro knew there was a lot on Nash's mind and that had something to do with why he wasn't jumping her bones at any possible moment. He was affectionate, but he was also somewhat distant.

So they enjoyed the exquisite meal served on board, chatted a lot, and read a bit. A little over five hours later, they checked into the Beverly Wilshire Hotel. "That's really the way to travel, isn't it?" Nash asked with a chuckle. "It's a far cry from the old days, when I used to stick my thumb out or ride my ratty old second-hand bicycle along Kentucky dirt roads."

"You've come a long way, Nash."

"Yeah, thanks to you."

"Me?"

"You left me heartbroken, and my sorry state of mind prompted me to write a song that became a major hit in several countries. The fans suddenly couldn't get enough of us, and Grey and I ended up filthy rich. We were miserable but rich."

"Well, thank heaven for small favors, I guess," she mused. "But surely it wasn't just that one song."

"Not entirely. We had other hits and sold a couple of very popular albums before everything went south. Greyson was right to leave. I had to have been miserable to work with, and I turned into a horrible person for a while."

"That's so hard to believe."

Nash hung his head and looked at his hands that were folded in his lap. "Believe it. I blamed everything that went wrong on Greyson, even when I knew it wasn't his fault. He understood, naturally—because that's the kind of guy he is— that I was in pain and it actually had nothing to do with anything he'd done. A fact that he pointed out to me on more than one occasion. I think he's such a kindhearted soul; it was too easy to dump on him. Now, after counseling, I'm embar- rassed by my actions, and there is no excuse for me taking so long to apologize to him. It's no wonder he left. He stayed as long as he could stand it out of loyalty to Chaos, but once our touring schedule was over, that was it for him."

"What happened to the other guys?"

"They were all such great musicians; they immediately joined other bands. I've lost touch with them personally, but I know they're all working. I read about them here and there. And believe me, they all still get their share of the royalties."

Caro nodded. None of this had happened for them while she was touring with them, so she'd never expected a share. It surprised her when he said, "Your shares of the royalties have all gone into a special fund for equine disease research. I know technically you didn't sing on the albums, but you were there when we were young and new. It just seemed right. I also knew you didn't particularly need the money. So a donation is done annually in your name."

Caro blinked at him. "Well, that explains some of the mail I've gotten over the years. I get annual reports and whatnot, and I've always wondered why."

"Did you ever look in the back of one of those reports and see your name as a contributor? It's under the listing 'Anonymous.'" She laughed and rolled her eyes at him when he added, "Your accountant knew about it, just in case you're worried about anything."

"Thank you. That's extremely generous of you to do. How did you find my accountant?"

"I asked your dad."

Caro sat back and stared at him. "You contacted my dad?"

"He never spoke to me directly, but I explained the situation to his assistant and got the information I needed that way."

Sighing, Caro murmured, "So many secrets. He could have told me."

"Maybe he thought you knew? I don't have an answer for that other than he was undoubtedly glad you were through with Chaos."

"Nash?"

"Hmm?"

"Let's forget the past for now. Come to bed with me. I need to show you how much I love you."

With a broad smile, Nash took her hand, and they headed for the bedroom in their suite. Eyeing the lovely bed with crisp white linens, he pulled his shirt off quickly and stepped out of his shoes. Caro stroked his bare skin and walked around him, admiring his fine form. "You've definitely been hitting the gym; you're even more exquisite than I remember." She traced her fingers over the tattoo that covered his left pec. It was an intricate, stylized design that had a broken heart in the center. The sight of it made her sad for Nash. "When did you get the ink?"

"A couple of years after Greyson left, when I was starting to see some improvement with therapy. I wanted to remind myself never to be such an ass to someone I loved again. It wasn't any hardship because the only two people I was in love with were gone."

"Well, maybe we can repair this," she said softly as she kissed his chest. Then Caro dropped to her knees and undid his pants. Quickly she pulled them down his long, strong legs, and Nash accommodated her by stepping out and kicking them away. Caro rubbed her face into his abdomen and nuzzled his groin, breathing in his manly scent. One hand cupped his ass cheek, and the other grasped his hardening cock. Before he was all the way erect, she sucked him into her mouth.

Nash gasped in pleasure. "Yes. That's the way. You always know how to do that just right." He clenched his butt and locked his legs as Caro sucked him down.

She began a rhythmic stroke with her hand around the base as her head bobbed, sucking and pulling at him. Her tongue created a busy pattern on him as she flicked and laved his head. Looking up, she saw love shining in Nash's blue eyes. With his golden waves around his face and the defined muscles of his arms and chest, he looked like a conquering Nordic warrior, but his expression was so soft and loving her heart melted for him.

He couldn't take his eyes off her as she sucked and retreated over and over. Her big hazel eyes sparkled with specks of gold as she stared up at him. *Such trust and love in that gaze,* he thought. *Do I really deserve her? The only thing that could make this moment better would be if Greyson were here right now—naked and expressing his love as well.* "Caro, I have never told you often enough that I love you. Whatever happens with Grey, I'm here with you as long as you'll have me. You know that, right?"

She smiled sweetly around her mouthful of dick and nodded. Then she upped her speed and suction. Over and over, she played him like a slide trombone until he hollered and came down her throat. Sitting back on her heels with a cocky grin, she wiped her mouth with the back of her hand and said, "I love you too. So much."

"Lose the clothes. It's my turn." Nash reached for Caro's top and pulled it up and over her head, tossing it onto the pile of his own discarded clothing. She stood and unzipped her pants, and he divested her of those as well. "Lie back; I'm going to see how many times I can make you scream," he announced with a gleam in his eye.

She gave him a saucy look and said, "We ought to be respectful of our neighbors. This is a hotel, you know. But when I scream, do you want me hollering your first *and* last names or just Nash?"

He burst out laughing and answered, "Just whatever comes naturally. I don't really need the advertising though, now that you mention it. Especially since we saw the paparazzi giving us the eye when we got out of the limo."

"They were eyeing you, not me. I could be anyone as far as they know. You're the one with the fancy, world-famous horse and the interesting background."

"Don't be so sure. They might have you all figured out too. You know how nosy and persistent those weasels are." He picked her up and laid her carefully on the bed. "Now... forget about everything else and go with the flow here, sweetheart."

Caro wound her fingers into Nash's golden waves as he bent over her. He worshipped her body with his tongue and his lips, kissing and plucking at her breasts, sucking her nipples into his mouth—driving her crazy with want. He kissed a path down her tummy and spread her legs, raising her knees so he could get a good look at her most feminine parts. She glistened with arousal, and he licked his lips. Tracing a pattern around and around softly, he watched her facial expression morph from interest to mild exasperation.

"Stop teasing me!"

"I know you love it. And what's the rush?"

"I need you!"

Nash chuckled and bent over her, giving her pussy a firm lick. "Mmm," he moaned as she squirmed.

"More, Nash, *please*."

Nash circled her opening with the broad end of his index finger and licked more directly onto her clit.

She groaned, so he slowly shoved his finger inside her and licked harder. Caro's back arched, and she breathed out, "Yes, like that. Oh yes."

He pumped in and out and firmed up his tongue, lashing her now with it. Then he added a second finger and alternated sucking her clit into his mouth and flicking it with the end of his tongue. Each time she thought she'd fall over the edge into orgasmic oblivion, he would slow down or back up a little. So she began to beg. "I need it, Nash. Give it to me *please*." Then, "Yes, that's it. Right there. Oh yes." Her legs went rigid as she clamped down on his fingers with her muscles, and once again, he stopped for a moment. Caro was on the verge of screaming in frustration when she saw him put his other index finger into his mouth. She knew what was coming, so she kept her complaints to herself. She loved being penetrated everywhere, so she let out a satisfied moan when he slid the wet finger into her butt and went back to sucking her clit into his mouth. His eyes were on her face the entire time—something she found ridiculously sexy.

With both hands manipulating her and his lips and tongue driving her wild, Caro succumbed to pleasure so deep and profound she thought she might never come down from the high. Spasm after spasm coursed through her body, warming her and tingling her from brain to toes. "Whew," she finally breathed out. "Talk about a full-body orgasm." Nash took that moment to position himself atop her and enter her, eliciting more groans, more spasms, and more declarations of love until they both lay spent in each other's embrace, trying to catch their breath.

The next morning, they woke refreshed and starving. "Want to go for a swim or eat?" Nash asked.

"I'd love to hit the pool before it gets crowded."

So off they went and swam laps until they wore themselves out again. They then donned robes and ordered coffee and bagels poolside. It was still only nine o'clock by the time they were done. Nash couldn't stop himself from checking his phone every few moments to see if he'd missed a call or a text from Greyson.

"He'll be here. Did you text him our room number?" Caro asked in a soothing voice.

Nash typed something quickly and looked up. "Good thinking. I guess I kind of forgot. Let's go shower and get ready to see our man."

At ten o'clock, all they'd had from Greyson was radio

silence. Nash was getting fidgety, and Caro finally began to look worried.

At eleven o'clock, Nash was pacing and eyeballing the contents of the minibar, even though he knew better. Still nothing from Greyson.

At noon, Caro optimistically ordered lunch for three to be sent to their suite. She tried to remember what Greyson liked and thought a positive outlook might help Nash's attitude. He looked like a nervous wreck at this point, though he had not yet raided the minibar.

At a quarter past noon, someone knocked on the door, and Caro opened it, expecting a waiter. She turned toward the room, holding the door handle, without paying attention. "You can serve it in the living room," she said and walked away.

"Serve what?" asked a deep voice as dear to her as Nash's. She whipped around and flew at Greyson, crying, "Grey! You're here!" She flung her arms around him, feeling his muscles stiffen at her touch. His arms did not embrace her back, so she stepped away and noticed the firm set of his jaw and the steely look in his eyes. "Sorry. I didn't mean to tackle you; I'm just so excited and happy to see you."

Nash also stopped his pacing and rushed to greet Greyson. He tried a one-armed bro hug, exclaiming, "You made it!"

Greyson didn't say anything when someone proclaimed, "Your lunch is here," through the still-open doorway. This time it was the server, so Caro ushered Greyson in, and they all quietly arranged themselves in the living room around a table.

"Want a beer?" asked Nash.

Greyson narrowed his eyes and asked, "Are *you* having one?"

Nash shook his head, and Caro piped up with, "I'll have one with you." She opened two of the chilled bottles that she'd ordered with the meal, remembering Grey's favorite brand—she hoped—and opened a chilled water for Nash.

When she set the water down in front of Nash, Grey couldn't miss the affectionate gesture and look she gave Nash when she stroked his hand and smiled. His shoulders seemed to relax just a bit.

Clearing his throat, Greyson began, "The two of you together still make the most striking and attractive sight I can recall. I've always thought of you as the black and white keys on the piano. They make beauty together, although they are as different in appearance as night and day. Nash is all large, fair, and bright, and Caro is smaller, dark, and sultry." His face colored with a blush as he realized how telling that sounded, and he took a gulp from his beer. He clammed up and looked down.

"Thank you. That's a lovely compliment. We're so happy you decided to join us, Grey." Caro tried again. *Way to sound like your grandmother, Caro.* She sighed inwardly.

Greyson wiped his hand over his face and admitted, "I've been here for a while, actually. I drove to the hotel after my appointment and just sat outside in my car until I could muster up the courage to come in." He sighed heavily. "I wanted to see you both so badly, but after what you said, I thought maybe it was a terrible idea. Maybe it was sheer curiosity or... I don't know what, but suddenly my feet started moving, and here I am."

Nash remained silent while Caro prompted Greyson, "So tell us about your fiancée—Britney, is it? How did you meet her?"

Nash's eyes blazed icily when Greyson answered, "We met at a party in Malibu about six months ago. She's a dancer who's been in a few music videos. Her father actually introduced her to me."

"Six months," Nash muttered. "How long was it before you proposed?" he demanded. His irritation and incredulity poured off him like steam. Caro gave him a warning look and stroked his arm.

"Oh, um... a couple of months," Greyson muttered.

"And this is true love, I'm to assume? Give me a break, Grey! Is she a gold digger or...?" Nash fumed.

"Stop trying to act like you're my father. You don't know anything about Brit. And what happened to you showing up to visit and not pressuring me? Isn't my best man supposed to be here for support?" Greyson all but shouted in Nash's face. He stood as if to leave. "Obviously, I was wrong to get out of the car after all."

Caro and Nash also flew from their seats, and the heated looks that went from face to face could have started a forest fire. Suddenly Nash threw his arms around Greyson and buried his face in his neck. "I'm so sorry. If you're in love, great. I'm happy for you." Then he added, "Even if it is hard to believe." Nash kissed Greyson's skin behind his ear as if he couldn't stop himself. "*Please* think about this extra hard, Grey." Nash realized that Greyson's arms had wound around him as naturally as breathing. They slid away as Nash stepped back. "Let's start over. I'm sorry for acting like a dick, but you have to agree that this is a bit of a shock, and it sounds pretty fast." Nash made an exasperated face. "Sorry again. Let's eat our lunch and talk about something else. How long can you stay?"

"I have a couple of hours. Britney is tasting cakes or hors d'oeuvres or... I don't know... *something* with her mom today."

"Didn't she want to know your opinion too?" Caro blurted out and then wanted to bite her tongue.

With a mirthless laugh, Greyson answered, "She didn't think I'd have the 'proper palette' to approve of the right thing. We all know I grew up under a bridge eating canned beans and stale Twinkies."

Nash and Caro shared a quick look. Greyson had come from a modest background, but it was far from what he described.

Caro frowned and asked, "Is Britney's family somehow prominent? Why the emphasis on what you called the social event of the year?"

"Not particularly—except in her parents' eyes. They think that now she's such a sought-after dancer, she's an important somebody. The truth of it is, she appeared on *So You Think You Can Dance* and made the first cut before she got dumped, and that made her mom think she's something extra special. I mean, she's been in a couple of music videos, but…" He gave a small shrug. "I think they might look at this wedding as an opportunity to make connections somehow. She's never been a featured dancer or anything. I always hoped I could help with my music contacts. She's beautiful, she works hard, and she just needs a break."

"What about her dad?" Nash asked.

Greyson made a face and took a drink, then answered, "Her dad is a piece of work. He calls himself an agent, but he just seems to make a lot of phone calls and bug people about what he can do for them. He has a few B-list clients he's always going on about." Greyson rolled his eyes. "He's assured me several times that he could manage my career, but he doesn't know the first thing about music. He's always trying to make a deal, and he's as pushy as hell. It's pretty annoying, actually. Believe me, I'm not marrying her for her parents. She loves me and treats me like I'm the most important person in the world." Greyson's forced words seemed at odds with his expression. He didn't look at all sure of his conviction.

*Why didn't he say how much he loved Britney?* Caro wondered and started to think she might understand some of the attraction Greyson had for Britney. But she still had major doubts about the health of the relationship. Caro asked, "How much does she know about your background, Grey?"

"I told her I used to be in a band, but I've kept things pretty simple in my life for the past few years. My house is fairly basic, and it's rented, and I haven't ever been a big spender—except for a certain gift horse"—he smiled ruefully

—"because I never knew when I might have another break like what we had before disbanding. Quite honestly, the teaching gig is just so I have somewhere to go regularly, and it forces me out of the house on a daily basis. She might think it's my source of income." He snorted. "Pfft. A part-time music teacher's salary. As if. I couldn't even pay the rent on that."

"She's aware that you have plenty of money though, right? She might not be as naïve as all that." Caro prompted. She always had her antennae tuned for people who wanted her for a meal ticket, and the feeling was a terribly uncomfortable one. She could spot them miles away at this point, and Britney and her family certainly seemed to fit the profile. "As much as I hate to mention it, this doesn't sound too good in that regard. They could have easily found out about you and targeted you from the get-go." She saw the anger in Greyson's eyes and hastened to say, "I am not trying to say she's definitely a bad person, but you need to be cautious. If my dad taught Eli and me anything at all, it was to look out for opportunists who wanted to take advantage of our wealth."

Greyson gave her a puzzled frown. "You're wealthy?"

Nash burst out laughing. "She's a fucking billionaire, dumbass!"

"Oh." Greyson blinked at her. *Now the mention of the planes makes sense.* He'd never thought about her financial status years ago when they were more concerned with Chaos.

"Well, not really. I mean, I will be someday, but let's just say that for now, I'm more of a prebillionaire with plenty of trust money at my disposal. But my point is, you need to be careful. And I'm assuming that they expect you to be paying for every last expensive thing associated with this wedding?"

Greyson's cheeks flamed, and he looked down. "Um, yeah. But she deserves the best!"

"If you say she does, and you love her, then that's fine. We just want to hear that you're happy." Caro gave Nash a tiny poke with her toe under the table when he opened his mouth to say something. The look on his face said it was not going to be complimentary. He closed his mouth.

"How about if we get together with you and Britney this evening? We can go out and celebrate and get to know each other." Caro looked hopefully back and forth between the men and waited for Greyson to answer.

Nash looked hopeful and interjected, "If you like, this could be in lieu of the bachelor party I'm supposed to throw for you as your best man. Britney can meet us both this way."

"Okay. Brit and I didn't have any special plans, and her cousins were too cheap to spring for a party, so let's do it. I'm sure you'll both love her as much as I do."

They had their doubts.

They decided to meet at a local hotspot that served dinner and had live music for dancing. Nash and Caro got there first and were waiting at their table for a good twenty minutes before the others showed up. "Something tells me that Greyson's fiancée might be a little high maintenance or they'd be here by now," Caro remarked.

Greyson and Britney managed to make an entrance that had people staring. He was tall and slender, looking like a male model in an expertly tailored navy suit. He'd always had a smooth grace about his movements. His expressive brown eyes and heavy brows gave him a Colin Farrell-ish look, and his dark, wavy hair had been tamed and styled in a way that he never would have attempted when he was in Chaos. Although he looked amazing, it was completely out of character for the Grey they knew and loved.

On his arm was a diminutive blonde with a tight little dancer's body. She had a similar look to Julianne Hough—something she liked to capitalize upon—only several sizes boobier. Dressed in a low-cut micromini dress, she strutted and sparkled her way through the restaurant in glittering gold, glancing around as if to assess her successful appearance. When her eyes lit on Nash, however, she suddenly looked like a heat-seeking missile. She tapped Greyson on the arm and whispered a question to him, and he grinned at her, nodding.

Britney seemed momentarily at a loss for words though when Greyson led her straight up to Nash, who'd politely stood to make her acquaintance. "Guys, this is Britney Hunt. Britney, this is Nash Keating and Caro Whittaker."

She blinked at Greyson before gushing and sticking out her hand to Nash, completely ignoring Caro. "I'm so honored to make your acquaintance, Mr. Keating," she said in a breathy voice. "Congratulations on winning those races with your horse! I wish we could stay and chat, but we're meeting some old friends of Greyson's." It was then she realized that Greyson was holding out her chair for her.

"Sit down, babe."

"Nash *Keating* is your old friend?" Britney whispered with a scarlet face. She plunked down into the chair, looking like she wanted to hide.

"Who did you think I meant? We've been friends since college."

Britney's mouth opened and closed like a baby bird until

Caro saved her. "It's nice to meet you, Britney. That's quite a dress."

Blinking at Caro as if she'd appeared out of nowhere, Britney tried to perk up. "Thank you! Greysie bought it for me. He loves sparkly things." She waved her left hand around in the air, demonstrating that fact and showing off the impressive diamond ring she wore. Looking fondly at the ring, she declared, "He's just the best. What was your name again?"

"It's Caro, and he certainly is," she agreed, staring pointedly into Greyson's eyes. "The best." *Did you buy her the boobs too, Grey?* she wondered with a cocked brow.

Britney frowned slightly in obvious confusion, and then she turned her attention back to Nash. "So Mr. Keating, I just adore horses, and the racetrack is such an exciting place. My dad loves it, and he taught me all about betting odds and how to read the Racing Form. How do you like your chances in the Belmont?"

Thinking she sounded like a reporter, he ignored her question about his horse. "It's Nash, please. You make me feel old calling me Mister."

"Sorry, I was brought up to respect my elders, but…" She gave a horrified gasp and covered her mouth. "Ohmygosh! That was worse, wasn't it? I'm so, so sorry!"

Caro stabbed her with a pointed stare and asked, "Do you call *Greyson* Mr. Foster very often? They're exactly the same age, you know."

"Oh, I uh… Greyson is *that* old?"

Greyson covered his eyes and shook his head. Dropping

his hand finally, he said, "We're both thirty-six, Brit. I told you that when we met, remember?"

"Um. No. I mean…"

"Just out of curiosity, how old are you, Britney?" Caro asked.

"Twenty-one."

Nash ground his teeth and muttered, "Fifteen fucking years, Grey? Seriously? At least she's legal drinking age." Then louder, he said, "Let's order some champagne to celebrate."

"Are you sure?" Caro asked with a nervous look in her eyes. This evening was getting off to an uncomfortable start, to say the least.

"Absolutely! How often does my *best friend in the world* get married to the love of his life? It's a one-time deal."

So they ordered a bottle of fine bubbly—which ended up being a few bottles of bubbly—and a lovely dinner that Britney seemed to poke at and shove around her plate. She only took a few tiny bites while everyone else ate with gusto. She did put away several glasses of champagne, however, and the more she drank, the more goo-goo eyes she made at Nash. Somehow, as if by magic—or the combined efforts of both the waiter and Nash—Britney's glass never seemed to empty.

Greyson tried to explain to Britney that he and Nash had been best friends at the Berklee College of Music, but she kept getting confused. "Did you like living in the Bay Area?" she asked at one point.

Greyson's eyes scrunched up, and he asked, "You mean Boston Harbor, or…?"

"No, silly. Berkeley. In the Bay Area. Where they used to have hippies and demonstrations and all that stuff. I've heard about it."

Nash squelched a snort, and Caro put her napkin over her mouth.

"Babe. We went to Berklee, B-E-R-K-L-E-E, College of Music in Boston. Not the University of California. Surely if you're a dancer, you know people who've gone there. It's a famous school for music and performing arts."

"Oooh. Um. Maybe. I guess I thought… Never mind."

Nash spoke up then and asked, "Have you ever heard of a band called Chaos, Britney?"

She got a thoughtful look and answered, "I think they might play it sometimes on the oldies station. Why?"

Caro wheezed and coughed. Waving her hand in front of her face, she apologized, "Champagne went down the wrong way." Her eyes were alight with humor.

"Did you know that Greyson used to be in that band?" Nash asked.

"Really?" She looked at Greyson questioningly. "Did you tell me that? I don't remember." She giggled. "I thought you were just a piano teacher who inherited a bunch of mon…" She clapped her hand over her mouth then and hiccupped.

"Ah, you do know all of Grey's secrets then," Nash intoned. "How he's secretly a multimillionaire and a musical genius."

Greyson glared at Nash, whose tongue had been seemingly loosened by the champagne. The truth was, he'd only had one glass, but Caro was the only one who'd noticed that fact.

"Really? *Lots* of millions?" Dollar signs seemed to sparkle in her eyes when she looked at Greyson.

"Oh yes. He's a former rockstar and frankly ought to still be one, and he's co-written many of the hits you hear all the time. It's nice to know how interested you are in his life, Britney. You're obviously so well-informed."

"Nash." Caro looked at him with a censoring look. "Careful."

With an angelic expression, Nash asked Britney, "What's Greyson's favorite food?"

She blinked a couple of times and answered, "Uh… popcorn?"

Nash smirked and asked, "He's allergic to corn. When is his birthday?"

"Um. Why? Don't you know?"

"What rather unusual thing does he love to do before going to sleep at night?"

"I know this one! He likes to have doggy-style sex!" Britney looked smug.

"Duh. I meant after that." *Although I wonder why he wants to do it doggy-style all the time now. He never used to. It was always more my thing than his. Does he not want to look at her?* "He likes to sing. Says it puts him in a good headspace for pleasant dreams."

Britney's head swiveled toward Greyson and asked, "You do? How come you never sing to me then? We just have sex, and then you go to sleep."

Greyson glared at Nash, who continued his barrage. "Have you ever been in a threesome?"

Britney's eyes popped so wide that she looked like a scared cat. She gasped, "No! What's the matter with you? And that's a pretty personal question, Mr. Nosypants!"

"How do you feel about bisexuality?"

"Ew!" She made a face like she smelled something gross. "Greysie baby, make him stop asking me such nasty questions. I was raised better than that!"

Nash raised both hands in surrender. "I'll stop. My work here is done. We'll grab the check. Caro and I would like to go dance for a while."

Greyson stood and grabbed Britney by the elbow. "We're leaving. I'll speak to you later, Nash. Good night, Caro."

"Night, um, Carol," Britney said, blinking at Caro as if she still wondered what she was doing there. "Night, Mr. Nosypants." Then she giggled and stumbled her way back out with Greyson holding her tightly by the arm. She stage-whispered to Greyson on the way out, "Carol's really pretty for an older woman. Does Nash like her? He's hot, but he sure is weird asking those creepy questions."

"I cannot believe you, Nash," Caro said as she glared at his innocent expression. But she couldn't keep it going and suddenly burst out laughing. Finally sobering, she added, "Poor Grey. He's going to have a tough night ahead of him."

Nash took her hand and kissed it. "Thank you for being so

wonderful, Caro. You're the most real woman I've ever known. Come dance with me so I can hold you and grind on your beautiful body in public. I'm obviously a dirty old man."

Shaking her head and laughing, she answered, "Let's go, Mr. Nosypants."

# Thirteen

It was somewhere south of three thirty in the morning when Nash heard pounding on the door of the hotel suite. Caro was still asleep, and he could barely blame her. They'd danced like fools until their feet gave out and then came back to the suite, where they had extremely energetic sex. Caro had been in one of her goofier moods and ended up wanting to ride him after they'd fucked on several different pieces of furniture around the suite. She'd boisterously boinked him as he lay on the bed, then decided to turn around and go at it reverse-cowgirl-style, giving him a prime view of her cute butt as she bounced up and down on him. After countless orgasms and lots of noise, she'd finally fallen off him and apparently into a sex coma.

Nash had a sneaking suspicion as to who might be pounding on their door, so he didn't even bother grabbing pants. He just went to the door, peered through the peephole, and opened up to a very agitated Greyson Foster. At least this time he was properly attired in jeans and a T-shirt, and his hair was its usual mess, falling over his forehead and nearly into his eyes.

Eyeing Nash's lack of clothing, Greyson's eyes flashed as he barged in. "Nice outfit, asshole. Do you always answer the door like this?"

"Only when I want to make a good impression. Come right in, Grey." Nash opened his arms in a welcoming gesture and smiled beatifically. "I take it you have something to say?"

Greyson glared at Nash for a few seconds before his shoulders drooped, and he admitted, "I almost broke off the engagement tonight, but I was afraid she was too drunk to remember it when she wakes up. I'll have to deal with that tomorrow, I guess." Grey plopped down on the couch and ran his fingers through his hair a few times. "I honestly don't know whether to thank you or punch you in the nose."

"Grey..." Nash sat down next to him. "Marrying that girl would be a short-lived disaster. You know what she did when you went to the bathroom?"

"What?"

"She leaned over and whispered in my ear that she'd love to give me a blowjob. And she suggested I meet her behind the restaurant in the alley before you returned to the table."

"Holy motherfucking shit." Greyson stared at him. "Are you telling me the truth?"

"I swear on Elvis. She did. You'd be lucky to be rid of her."

"Real classy move, Britney." Greyson moaned, "Fuck me."

"I'd love to."

"So would I," came a sultry voice from the bedroom door. "But I'm afraid my hoo-ha might be broken after what Nash and I've been up to." Caro stepped into the room, and she too hadn't bothered with clothes. "It's way too late for any serious discussions, you guys. Come to bed, and let's get some sleep please. I'm beat." She yawned and held out her hands, taking theirs as they approached her as if drawn magnetically. "Grey, you have on way too many clothes."

He started to protest, but he was bone-tired and weighed down with emotional baggage, so he allowed them to strip him bare. Caro got on one side of him and Nash on the other, and they pulled the bedclothes over themselves. Greyson's final thought before oblivion took over was, *I'm home.* "I miss us," he whispered *almost* inaudibly and felt hands squeeze him on either side. They were all asleep within moments.

When they awoke the next morning, however, Greyson was gone.

# Fourteen

Except for a hand-delivered wedding invitation that arrived by courier, there was no other communication from Greyson over the next day. He'd included a note saying that he still expected Nash to be his best man and that was it. Attempts to call him ended up going to voicemail.

Apparently, the wedding was still on.

Nash swore so much he had to make up a few new colorful words to express himself properly.

"Do you think he's doing this out of his deep sense of duty?" Caro asked. "He can't possibly love that girl the way he professes to. We know him better than that."

"Maybe he's afraid of something—or of us. We broke his heart once before. There's no telling." Nash sighed like the weight of the world had landed on his chest. "We tried our best, so I guess we have to accept this for what it is. Grey's making his own mistake, and we can't fix it. And... I don't want him to hate us. This marriage will end sooner or later, and maybe we can pick up the pieces if he'll let us then."

"I guess." She sighed too. "We probably need to get over Grey and concentrate on what we have together with the two of us. Maybe we should accept that what we did was fun, but now we're older and more mature and just need to chalk it up to a fun experience we once had."

Nash snorted quietly. "You don't really believe that do you?"

Eyeing him with a flat look, she answered, "I'm trying to." Then she perked up. "Anyway, I can't wait to see how handsome you look in your tux. I can gloat and tell myself over and over that you're all mine." She pulled Nash close and kissed him deeply. It was impossible for either of them to miss the tinge of sadness that hung over them like a pall, however, shading their kiss with melancholy.

♡♡♡

Late on Saturday afternoon, they dressed to kill and took off for the wedding venue. "Remember our agreement: we're both going to be on our best behavior," Caro said.

"Yep." Nash was becoming less and less talkative as they neared the church.

The sanctuary of the ultra-modern building was bustling with florist's assistants who were fussing with their displays, workers who were installing a white carpet runner, and a sweaty-faced, officious wedding planner barked out unnecessary orders like a wannabe drill sergeant. There was no feeling of excitement in the air—just nerves and bossiness. There were no guests in evidence this early, but the parents of the bride stood in the back corner watching everything like a couple of hawks.

Always mindful of her manners, Caro took Nash by the arm and led him up to the couple. "Hello. I assume you're Britney's parents. I'm Caroline Whittaker and this is my boyfriend, Nash Keating. We're old friends of Greyson's." When they didn't answer right away, she continued. "I'm sure this must be such a happy day for you."

Finally, the father-of-the-bride extended his hand with a narrow-eyed, calculating look. "Nash Keating, you say? The man with the horse?"

"Yes sir." Nash sighed inwardly. As excited as he was about Domino Pip, he'd love for people to forget about his connection to the colt. "I'm Greyson's best man."

"That explains the monkey suit." He turned his eyes to Caro. "And you say you're a Whittaker? Any relation to the New York Whittakers?"

This conversation was going downhill quickly, and Caro could feel the eyes of Britney's mom weighing and appraising the diamond studs she wore in her ears. "I am originally from New York, yes, but I'm sure there are plenty of Whittakers there." She suspected the man knew exactly who she was, and she was not about to get into a conversation with him about her family. She could have said she was from Kentucky but knew her accent would give her away if she tried that. "Could you possibly direct Nash to where Greyson is getting ready? I'm sure the groom would like some company. You know… best man duties and all that. Nash will need to hang on to the ring for Greyson."

"Oh yeah, maybe so. If you take that hallway over there, you'll find him."

Caro wasn't sure of what to do with herself, so she went with Nash to find the right room. It had a piece of paper taped to the door proclaiming GROOM in marking pen. She assumed that if she kept looking, she'd find another one that said BRIDE, but she wasn't too anxious to go offer Britney any support. "I think I'll just leave you two to do your manly thing and go find a good seat. I want to be close enough that I can admire you." Nash was already slipping through the door when she left to go find herself an aisle seat close enough to the front so she wouldn't miss a thing. *Thank heaven I brought my phone,* she thought. *I'll turn off the ringer, but at least I can read a book on it while I'm waiting. This is going to be one helluva long day.*

A few people were beginning to show up by the time she reached the sanctuary again, and two bored-to-death-looking ushers were seating folks. Caro wondered if they were friends of Greyson's. If appearances proved anything, she'd have guessed they were either more of Britney's cousins or guys her dad knew. They were definitely on the old side to be average groomsmen. This was proving to be such a mindfuck of a day. Even the flowers were odd. Where did anyone get camellias and poinsettias this time of year, and why would they want it to look like Christmas? Then, as if on cue, she overheard one of the florists who was on her way out the door whisper to her co-worker, "These people have such bad taste. I swear they just wanted the flowers that were the most impossible to get this time of year, thinking they'd impress their guests that way."

The other woman snickered and added, "We tried to talk them out of it. And who does a red-and-pink color scheme anyway? It's awful. They may as well have added balloons and glitter to make it look *fancier*!" She used a nasal voice for that last word as if she were imitating someone. Then she added, "Or maybe she wanted her daughter's color scheme to match that god-awful dress of hers."

Caro glanced at Britney's mother across the way. The woman was dressed in a garish pink and red dress. *Yep. Guessed it. I wonder how I missed that before.* She tried not to make a face, and just then a surly usher stuck out his arm and asked, "Bride or groom, miss?"

"Groom," Caro answered decisively. "We're very close. I'd like to sit near the front if you don't mind."

"Suit yourself. I don't think he's going to have many people on his side of the aisle except for the bride's overflow." And off they went.

"Are his parents here?" Caro whispered... and then wondered why she was whispering.

"Not that I know of. Sit here." He abruptly turned away as he left Caro standing next to the second row, center aisle. Then, just as abruptly, he turned back to her. "You have a date?" he asked with his eyes fixed on her cleavage.

She narrowed her eyes at him and answered frostily. "Yes. The best man."

"No way. Lou got married to that ball and chain of his three years ago."

"Not Lou—whoever he is. Nash. Greyson's *best friend*."

The clod shrugged and muttered, "If you say so. Too bad for you though. I could have shown you a good time." He gave her a smarmy wink and walked away.

*Ugh,* she thought. At least she'd be able to see, especially if the front row was going to be empty. *How sad. This whole wedding makes no sense to me. Where are Grey's parents?* Then, on an impulse, she stood up and moved into the front row. *Now he has some* family *here, at least. Grey shouldn't feel alone at his wedding.*

♡♡♡

IN ANOTHER PART OF THE BUILDING COMPLEX, NASH STOOD staring at Greyson. Neither knew what to say to each other. Finally, Nash broke the silence and offered, "We didn't know what to get you for a wedding gift, so we haven't done it yet. Any ideas? Caro looked at the registry and didn't see anything she thought you'd like."

"I don't even know what kind of crap Britney put on it. A bunch of ugly towels or something? A solid gold croquet set?" He ventured a small laugh.

"Are you nervous, Grey?"

"Petrified. You have no idea."

"You can always make a break for it. I'll grab Caro, and we can be out of town before the organist starts to play. Oh…

Oops. Too late. I hear music. Well, before the bride makes her grand entrance maybe."

"Nash, you're supposed to be here to support me!"

"I am supporting you, Grey. I fucking love you!"

"Lower your voice!"

"Sorry. *I love you,*" he rasped out in a broken whisper.

"It's too late. I made a promise to Britney. And her father just might kill me if I backed out now."

"That seems a bit extreme."

"You don't know the guy. I suspect he has connections to the mob. Or, if he doesn't, he knows some very unpleasant characters."

"Grey! Come to your senses, man. Get out now."

"No."

Nash swore and threw himself into a chair with a massive sigh. "Gimme the ring then. I'm supposed to hand it to you during the ceremony."

Greyson plopped down next to Nash and handed over the wedding band. Nash didn't even look at it as he stuffed it into his pocket.

"Just out of curiosity, what did your parents say when they met Britney?"

"They haven't met her."

"Why not?"

"I never actually told them about the wedding."

"They aren't even here? What did you tell Britney about that?"

"She never asked, so I never said anything."

"Why don't you want them here at your wedding? Are

you on the outs with them or something? I don't get it. None of this makes sense, Grey. And how could she not even *ask* about your family?"

Greyson rubbed his hand over his face and looked at the floor. "I know. It's all wrong. I... I guess I never thought it would go this far. I can't believe we're here at the church, and I'm supposed to go out there and promise to love and honor Britney in front of all of her family and friends."

"And your friends...?"

"You and Caro are it. I didn't invite anyone else."

"Grey, you need to explain yourself. I'm completely lost. I thought you'd have relatives, maybe the other guys from the band, and whatever friends you've been making over the past ten years. I was actually looking forward to seeing the guys and meeting some people. And now it sounds like you've just let Britney turn this into her show with you paying for it. What the fuck, man? What does she have that's making this happen to you?"

"Her f—" Greyson began to explain, but just then the door swung open and two men in tuxes barged in.

"**H**ey, Greyster, my man. Chase sent us in to see if you needed *anything* to get you through the ceremony," one of the men offered with a wink. "I have some blow, pills of all types, or the ever-popular tequila." He patted a flask in his pocket. "Name your poison."

"Thanks, but I'm good," Greyson answered stiffly and glanced nervously at Nash—pleased to see that Nash showed no interest whatsoever in what these two scumbags had to offer. "You can leave," he told them.

"Suit yourself. He's trying to be a good host. You're missing out if you ask me, and you're not much of an ex-rocker, are you?" He fake-coughed into his fist, but it sounded a lot more like he was saying, "Pussy," while his buddy smirked. The guy then proceeded to prepare a couple of lines that the two of them snorted up with relish. They wiped their noses with their fingers, and one said, "Back to work seating the guests." He turned to the other one and chuckled nastily. "Did you see the tits on that tall brunette? Yow!"

"Friends of yours?" Nash asked in a flat voice. "Oh no, wait. They must be part of Britney's crowd because you *didn't invite anyone.* And who the hell is Chase?"

"Britney's dad."

"Grey, what the fuck are you getting into with these people?"

"Chase Hunt scares the crap out of me if you must know. He's more than just obnoxious—he's frightening. I didn't invite my parents because I didn't want them to meet him, and I thought that they'd think I was making a mistake." Nash started to interrupt, so Greyson put up a hand. "My thinking was that we'd get to know each other better and, if we make it, after a few months, I'd take her home to Indiana to meet everyone, and it would all be fine. I'd tell them we eloped or something. I know it's a dumbass thing to do to lie to your parents, but it was to spare their feelings more than anything. Britney's a good kid. I think we can get along. I thought I'd finally buy a house that's not so close to her mom and dad, and we wouldn't have to see them too often." Greyson rambled on, "I made her a promise, Nash. I told her I'd marry her and care for her always. If I back out now, I'd be a horrible person. I'm not that kind of guy. She'd be devastated if I left her right before the ceremony."

"So you're going through with this to spare her feelings, and you're ignoring your parents to spare their feelings, and you're not thinking one iota about your own needs. It's time to wake up, Grey. You're going to end up hurting everyone anyway even if you go through with this charade."

"You think so?"

"I bet if you looked out there right now, Caro's trying not to cry. I know I am."

Greyson's expression simply melted then. He stared into Nash's blue eyes and saw the love there that he so desperately wanted. Immediately he thought of Britney's eyes and wondered if he'd ever seen any emotion in them that floored him the way Nash did. Greyson stormed out of the room and headed down the hall toward the sanctuary.

Standing just inside the hallway, he peered out and zeroed in on Caro. He was surprised and touched to see that she was taking up the role of family in the front row. He'd expected to feel lonely without his parents, his sister, and her family there, but the idea of subjecting them to the Hunts was also intolerable. *Nash is right,* he realized, *Caro does seem to be holding back tears.* Caro dabbed below one eye and wiped her nose quickly. Or maybe she wasn't holding them back all that well after all.

Greyson turned abruptly and almost smacked into Nash, who'd followed him down the hall. "What are you doing, Grey?" Nash asked softly.

"Just looking. I need to find Britney."

"I doubt you'll be able to see her, and they look like they're about to start any minute. The place is really filling up."

"Tough shit. I need to talk to her."

"Well, okay then. Far be it from me to stand in your way. Let's go look for the bride's room."

They wound around the building through the long hallway and came to what seemed to be the other side of the church before they found it. Greyson knocked politely on the door, and an overly made-up face appeared in the partially opened doorway. "Greyson! Get out of here! You can't see Britney until she walks down the aisle with her dad," scolded one of the bridesmaids.

"I need to talk to her."

*"Go away! I'll see you at the altar! Don't you know anything about traditions?"* Britney squawked from somewhere behind the door.

Ignoring her attitude, Greyson soldiered on. "Hey, Brit, do you love me?"

"That's a dumb question. I'm marrying you, aren't I?"

"Yeah, you're right. It's a dumb question. I'll see you at the altar." He turned to a baffled Nash and said, "Let's go." He led Nash out to where the wedding planner was still sweating and bossing, only in a quieter voice finally.

She glared at the two of them and hissed, "Where the *fuck* are your boutonnieres?"

"Hell, if I know. I'm just the groom. I was told to go wait in that stuffy office until now, and here I am. This is my best man…"

"Well, *obviously* he's your best man, but where are the flowers?" she fussed. Off she went in another direction, muttering, "I have to do *everything* myself!"

Nash and Greyson stood silently waiting for someone to

tell them what to do as people swarmed past them looking for a seat. The rows of pews were filling up quickly now, and the organist played on. The music selection could not have been worse to Nash's way of thinking. There were some traditional hymns, and those were fine, but the organist also apparently had orders to throw in some show tunes and was doing a terrible job of adapting them to a pipe organ. That, and the wrong notes, had Nash's skin crawling under his tux. He suddenly wanted a cold beer in the worst way.

Finally, the wedding planner appeared with two bouton-nieres in her hands. "Some idiot left these with the bride. Here. Put them on." She handed them both enormous pink camellias, and both men couldn't help but stare at them and then burst out laughing.

"Seriously?" Nash asked with an undignified snort. "We're going to look like old ladies with corsages… or clowns. See if yours squirts water, Grey."

"Brit likes pink. Here, I'll do you, and then you can do me." Greyson reached for Nash's lapel as Nash cracked up.

"I'd love to *do you*." Nash wiggled his eyebrows up and down.

"Oh, shut up and hold still."

Once they were properly adorned with their dumb blooms, they gave each other a serious look. Nash said quietly, "Last chance, Grey."

"Let's go," Greyson answered solemnly. They took their places at the groom's side of the altar, and then a few more groomsmen—or *goonsmen*, Nash thought to himself—came and stood next to Nash.

Greyson looked at Caro and gave her what he hoped was a friendly smile, but the tears were now flowing freely down her cheeks. She looked devastated as she squared her shoulders and tried to smile back—unsuccessfully.

But he didn't have time to dwell on Caro because just then the bridesmaids were beginning their procession down the center aisle to the tune of "I've Never Been in Love Before" from *Guys and Dolls*. Greyson tried to keep a straight face— the music was *so bad*. He glanced at his soon-to-be mother-in-law and noticed the rapturous look on her face. *She must have picked the music,* he decided.

Each poor woman was attired in the most god-awful costume he'd ever seen. The fabric was stiff-dotted Swiss, and the dresses had ruffles everywhere. They were Pepto-Bismol pink with cherry-red dots and frilly trim and were the least figure-flattering things he could imagine. The bridesmaids were probably all beautiful, but they looked like idiots with their hair in ringlets and sporting big, goofy red hats with pink feather plumes. Bad taste didn't even come close to describing these tragedies. One after the next, these poor girls paraded down the aisle with expressions that varied from grim to angry, amused to acceptance. No one looked happy or proud to be there.

Finally, the music changed to "Here Comes the Bride," and everyone stood. The organist seemed finally in her element and added many trilling flourishes and unnecessary blasts of earsplitting wrong notes. Greyson idly hoped that he hadn't paid much for her services.

Chase Hunt had a firm grip on his daughter as he

marched her down the aisle toward her (supposed) beloved. He had a self-satisfied look on his red face. *How nice that he matches the color scheme*, Greyson thought idly.

Greyson's eyes focused on Britney. Unlike her attendants, she was dressed like an exquisite little princess—including a glittering tiara. There was no denying she looked gorgeous, and there were plenty of oohs and aahs from the congregants. However, as Greyson stared at her, he realized she was not even looking back at him. She was looking at... Nash? She even winked at him and licked her lips!

Feeling invisible, Greyson narrowed his eyes and turned to look at Nash. His best man's face looked like a thundercloud. Obviously, he was not flirting back with Britney.

As the bride and her father approached the altar, the minister beamed at them. The music died down—thankfully—then her father handed her off to Greyson and whispered, "Take care of her, or you'll be sorry. Got it?" Then he burst out laughing like it was a cute joke. The congregation took their seats.

"Blah, blah, blah," was what Greyson heard from the minister after that. He tuned the man out as his mind spun in a million directions at once. But he finally did pay attention when the man asked the congregation, "Does anyone know a reason these two fine young people should not be joined in holy matrimony today? Speak up now or keep it to yourself forever." He paused, and the air felt electrified for a few seconds. Greyson whipped his head around and stared at Caro, but she just kept weeping silently. His heart rate sped up so badly he thought he might faint. He turned the other direction and stared at Nash. His best man was still glaring at Britney. He turned to Britney, who finally tore her eyes away from Nash long enough to look at Greyson and appear embarrassed. She gave him a weak smile.

No one spoke.

The minister then went into another florid, impassioned speech about who knew what. Greyson's heart pounded so loudly he didn't think he could hear anything over it. He swayed on his feet, and Nash caught him by the elbow. There were a few gasps from the guests, and one loud whisper of, "Is the groom drunk?" But Greyson seemed to rally quickly.

More *blah, blah* went in and out of Greyson's ears until the minister looked him in the eye and said, "Repeat after me. I, Greyson Foster…"

"I, Greyson Foster…"

"Take you, Britney, as my wedded wife…"

"Uh…"

Greyson swayed again, looked at Britney straight in the eye, and said, "You need to figure out how to behave more like someone who is supposedly in love." He spun around and grabbed Nash by the shoulders. He stared into his best man's eyes for a moment and then planted a huge kiss on Nash's lips. "Let's blow this pop stand," he muttered, and latched on to Nash's arm, dragging him down the aisle to where he reached for Caro in the front row. He hauled her out of her seat, kissed her, and yelled, "Run for your lives!" Then he burst into maniacal laughter as the three of them high-tailed it down the aisle. They exploded through the front door and flung themselves into one of the waiting limousines.

"Take us to the Beverly Wilshire please! And hurry!" he ordered the astonished driver. "Step on it, man! I'm the groom, and I forgot the wedding ring! We have to get there and find it right away!"

Off they zoomed. Fortunately, the driver was new and somewhat gullible. When they reached the hotel, Nash flipped the guy a wad of large bills and said, "Thanks, man. We won't be needing you now, but if anyone asks, you took us to the airport, got it? You might want to drive around a little before heading back so it'll seem more believable. Or just go turn in this car and find another company to drive for… right away."

Once they were back in the suite, Caro burst out laughing. "I feel like Bonnie and Clyde and Clyde making our getaway!" She looked at the two men who stood staring at her. "Now what?"

"Now we get Grey to hightail it back to Kentucky with us and never look back, right?" Nash looked at Greyson.

"Uh… sounds as good as any plan I can come up with. I sure as shit don't want to stick around here and let any of Chase Hunt's goons find me. I value my body parts too much for that."

"So do we," Caro replied with a smile. "Grey, when did you finally know that you weren't going to go through with the wedding? You had us pretty convinced."

"It just all added up that Brit never loved me. I saw her making eyes at Nash and ignoring me, and I thought to myself that it would be awful to be married to someone you'd never be able to trust. Then I thought about her mom and dad, and as scary and obnoxious as that man is, I couldn't inflict him on my family... ever. I had to make a run for it. So it was pretty much an in-the-moment kind of decision. I'm sorry I didn't do it before today, but... it is what it is."

Nash put his arm around Greyson in a comforting hold. "Just to be clear about this, Grey, do you have any teaching you need to do now?"

"No. We're off for the summer."

"Any gigs scheduled?"

"No. I planned a few weeks off for the honeymoon. I'm not busy with anything at all now since the farce of the century has been abandoned."

"Caro, can you schedule us a plane again? Right away?"

"On it already," she answered as she made some entries into her phone. "Sounds like a good plan to me. Grey?" Caro regarded him hopefully.

"Um. Sure." He looked at their eager faces and said, "Yes. Let's go."

Nash was divesting himself of his tie and asked, "Do you need anything from your house before we head out?"

"I need my computer and my piano. The rest of the stuff can all burn to the ground with the house as far as I'm concerned." Greyson suddenly wanted to get out of LA as fast as possible.

"Okay, the plane will be ready for us in three hours. Thankfully it was still here and ready to go. In the meantime, I can schedule an emergency company I know to move your stuff, Grey. Would that work?"

"The piano too?"

She nodded, "The piano too, although Nash has a pretty sweet setup in his recording studio already."

Nash interjected, "That's fine. We can put the piano in the living room and class it up if you want." He ruffled Greyson's hair. "This is going to be great."

Greyson's head drooped, and he slung his arms around both of them. "What would I do without you guys? You're amazingly organized and efficient, Caro. Thanks!" He guessed that having billions at your disposal meant you could hire just about anyone you needed to do your bidding—even on a Saturday night.

"It comes from working with the governor and his wife for so long. Efficiency and organization are my top skill sets."

Nash laughed. "You have plenty of more exciting skills than that, sweetheart." He approached her and nuzzled her neck while she continued to poke at her phone.

Greyson flopped onto the couch as if he couldn't stand another minute. He laid his head back and closed his eyes. "I'm so grateful you two showed up. I can't believe I almost let myself do… that thing."

"I'm sure every bride would love to hear her wedding be referred to as 'that thing,'" Caro said with a shake of her head. "We're just so glad you came to your senses."

Nash and Caro started cramming their clothes back into their bags, and Nash looked at Greyson. "Do you want to borrow some normal clothes?"

"I'm good. I'll just take off the jacket and vest and wear the shirt and pants. I would actually like to stop by my house though and pick up a few things and my laptop, if you think we have time. I was kidding about burning the place down."

"We can do that if we leave right now," Caro said.

"Let's do it," Nash agreed.

A driver was waiting for them out in front, and they were already checked out of the Beverly Wilshire by the time they stepped into the back of the car. Caro's efficiency was a thing to behold.

"I'll leave the keys with the next-door neighbor and tell her she can have my stupid car as a thank-you. I always hated that thing. The neighbor lady has always been nice. You can tell the movers to get the house key from her, and this way I can say goodbye to her too," Greyson explained. He nodded to himself thoughtfully.

"We need to make it quick, Grey. Even if the limo driver sent them on a wild-goose chase to the wrong airp... uh, place, you don't want to stick around your house for any length of time in case of unwanted visitors." Nash noticed their current driver was giving him a funny look in the rearview mirror, so he tried to sound as vague as possible.

The driver, however, blurted out, "Hey, aren't you that guy with the famous horse—Pippi Longstocking or something like that?" He laughed and added, "My grandmother has the biggest crush on you."

Nash rolled his eyes. "You must be thinking of someone else."

"Right," the driver muttered and furrowed his brow. *Weirdo.* "You know, if you gave me an autograph, it would make my nanna's day."

Caro squelched a giggle and covered it up with a fake cough.

Nash pulled a pen out of his carry-on bag and asked with a sigh, "Anyone have a piece of paper?"

"Who uses paper anymore?" Greyson asked. It was a reasonable question.

"Here!" The driver thrust a small tablet over the seat back. "You never know in this town what famous person you'll run into."

"Just don't tell anyone you drove us, okay, buddy?" Nash scribbled his name and dumped the tablet back into the front seat. "We're on kind of a top secret mission right now, and the less you know about it the better. It's for your own safety."

*Rich people are so weird,* the driver thought. "Sure, man, whatever. And thanks. My nanna's going to love this."

*Sixteen*

Making a pile of Britney's stuff was easy enough, and Greyson crammed as much of his own stuff as he thought he wanted into a bag. He was in a hurry to get out of the house because it felt as if Britney could pop out from behind a corner at any moment, and the thought was like a bad dream.

Greyson was just about to call his landlord and let him know he was leaving for good… when a big bucketful of reason suddenly swamped his brain with doubt. His clear vision for a future with Nash and Caro fogged up. *What am I doing? These two broke my heart, and I'm jumping back in with them again like nothing happened?* He wandered out to the living room where Nash was playing something soft and beautiful on the piano, and Caro was looking at a file on Nash's phone. She hummed the melody as Nash played.

Greyson had never heard whatever it was, but he loved it instantly. *My perfect black and white keys.*

"Um…" Greyson hated to interrupt them. *God, they're beautiful.* "Guys?"

With matching smiles of pure delight, Caro and Nash turned to Greyson. "Yeah?" Nash asked. "Everything okay?" he added when he saw Greyson's expression. His hands fell away from the keys, and he wrapped one arm around Caro instead.

"Look, um…" Greyson plunked down onto the couch, staring at them. "I'm not sure moving is a good idea after all."

Like a choreographed dance, Caro and Nash rose from the piano bench and sat down on either side of Greyson, boxing him in. Caro immediately began to stroke Greyson's hair out of his face, and Nash grabbed his hand, scooting around so that his leg was crossed over Greyson's.

"What's going on in that exquisite head of yours, Grey?" Caro asked softly. "Are you worried about something?"

Greyson barked out a laugh. "I'm worried about *every-thing*," he choked out. "We've all been together about a minute, and you expect me to give up my life in LA and move to Kentucky with you?"

"Do you like LA?" Nash asked with raised eyebrows.

"No. I hate it here, actually. But it's good for business."

"I call BS on that one. You can make music in Kentucky. The music scene there is legendary. What else? Are you worried about Britney?"

"No! Well, maybe a little. Her dad's a creep."

"Not your problem, dude. You know you're lucky to be rid of her, right?"

"Yeah." Greyson looked at the floor. "I did have *some* feelings for her though, and it's not like I can suddenly just turn them off like a light switch."

Caro looked at their stubborn faces and smiled sweetly. "Grey, that's because you're such a good guy. You know in your heart that she isn't worth it. So what is this really about? Are you worried that we'll make a mess of things again?"

"Of course I am! Do you know how hard it's been for me the past several years? I wanted you both so badly. And I left Nash just like you did! I was afraid you'd never speak to me again if I tried to come back. When I heard from Nash's dad that he got some psychotherapy, I was so proud of him. I tried it too, but the only advice I got was from a wacko who offered to detoxify my life by fucking away my troubles. I quit after that." He let out a long sigh. "I was mad at myself and disgusted, so it didn't do much to get me into a positive headspace. I can't go through that again, you two!"

"We can't promise everything will be perfect, Grey, but I can promise to try as hard as possible," Caro vowed. "No more disappearing into the night for me."

"Me too," agreed Nash. "You grew up in Indiana, so wouldn't it be nice to be closer to your family finally? They must miss you."

Greyson sighed. "Yeah, there's that. My sister had a baby a few months ago. She lives in Carmel just north of Indianapolis, and I'd love to see the little squirt. But let's be real here. When we were together before, we were in Chaos, and we lived, worked, and played together *all* the time." He looked at Nash. "Now you have some humongous farm to run, and Caro has her job she was telling me about with the governor's wife, and where does that leave me? You'll both be out riding your horses, and I'll be twiddling my thumbs all day, waiting for you both to come home."

Nash started to laugh, and Greyson glared at him. "Look, Caro and I have things to do, true, but so will you. You can compose and collaborate just as well from Kentucky as you can from California. How much of that work is done virtually anyway?"

"Well… lots of it, I guess," Greyson admitted.

"Then that won't be any different. And if you want to keep teaching, there are plenty of folks in Lexington who want to learn music." Nash was happy to see Greyson relax a little. "We're older now, buddy. We have other responsibilities, and we don't have to be together twenty-four seven to keep our relationship intact and healthy. No one does that. And as you can see since I'm here right now, I have a staff that takes care of the farm extremely well when I have to leave it."

"And Zoë doesn't need me at her side all the time with her literacy foundation. She has her four kids to raise, and her two…" Caro winced. "I mean her *family,* so our job together is just a part-time thing."

Nash's eyes narrowed at Caro, and he asked, "Zoë's two what? Dogs?" The pinkness of her cheeks made him think she was talking about something else.

Caro looked as serious as a judge suddenly, and her eyes

went back and forth between Greyson's and Nash's for a drawn-out moment before she answered. "This is something huge, and I have to have both of you promise on your eternal souls that you'll never speak of it to anyone who isn't in this room right now. If I could, I'd have you sign a notarized NDA."

Greyson looked baffled, and Nash looked amused, but they both said, "I promise."

"You'd have had to find out sooner or later anyway if you plan to spend your time with me as my two boyfriends and as each other's boyfriend at the same time. In other words, if you look at us like a throuple or a triad—"

"We get the picture, Caro," Nash interrupted with a soft laugh. "If Grey agrees, we're all in this as equals, so what has your panties in a twist?"

Caro gulped. "Zoë is blissfully, happily married to both Tanner, the governor, *and* my brother Eli." Her words spilled out rapidly. "No one is supposed to know because originally Tanner wanted to run for president when his term as governor was over. He's since changed his mind—thank heaven—but they've worked extremely hard to keep their relationship private. They aren't ashamed, but back when the two guys got together, gay marriage wasn't even legal, and Eli wanted Tanner to have the best chance to succeed in becoming governor and ultimately president. Things are a little better now, but not necessarily for a public figure in a three-way relationship. It's up to them when or if they ever go public with the information."

The men stared thoughtfully at Caro as she continued,

"Being so close to all of them has been both wonderful and difficult. I love that they're so happy, but I have to constantly be aware of what people see and hear. And I've been mistaken for Eli's wife many, many times—something I never dissuaded anyone from thinking because it gave him a cover. In a lot of ways—that I'm glad for now—I put my personal life on hold to help them out. If I'd pursued any of the boring relationships I've had over the past few years, I wouldn't be here now with the two men I've loved for so long."

"Thank you, Caro, for trusting us with that information. It is a big secret, but you can count on our discretion," Greyson assured her as Nash nodded.

She looked at Greyson's sincere expression and said, "We've all had our challenges, Grey. I didn't seek counseling, but I've been just as miserable without the two of you. Please understand that. Now I firmly believe that life is too short to be afraid of loving whomever you love." She stroked his arm soothingly and added, "It's been, as I said, both wonderful and challenging to watch their relationship grow and blossom. It hasn't always been easy for them, and as the children get older and go to school, there might be new obstacles they face. However, as I've watched the way they all love and support each other so beautifully, it made me crave what the three of us had and could have again. It was like torture in some ways, and in others it gave me hope. I'm just glad that Nash and I finally ran into each other and cleared the air so we'd all have this chance again."

"One of the best things that's ever happened to me," Nash added as he rubbed Greyson's back.

"So Grey, please take a chance on us again. We won't let you down," she said, squeezing his hand.

Greyson nodded thoughtfully but said nothing.

Regarding Greyson with a smile, Nash asked out of the blue, "Have you ever ridden a horse?"

"I visited Elvis once before I bought him, but the only horse I've actually been on is the kind you stick a quarter in out in front of the grocery store. I was probably about four," Greyson answered with an embarrassed look. "Why?"

"I think you'd get along well with Gene Simmons."

"What?"

Caro laughed. "Gene Simmons is one of Nash's horses. He's a big, sweet pinto with a white face and black around his eyes, so he looks like the Demon from Kiss. It would be a blast to teach you how to ride him. But only if you want to. No pressure."

"Um. I guess I could try. But I might need a seat belt or an airbag, or at least a crash helmet." He looked nervous.

"We'll take care of you," Nash promised. He ruffled Greyson's hair and kissed his neck. "If we get to have you back, we'll make sure you're safe. Gene Simmons is a big softy. Smooth gaits too."

"What does that mean?"

"It means he won't rattle your bones when he moves."

"So will you stop worrying and come home with us?" Caro asked.

He closed his eyes, took a deep breath, opened them again, and answered, "I'll come."

"A lot, I bet." Nash laughed and squeezed the bulge in Greyson's pants. "Thanks, buddy. We'll be good."

"So good," Caro agreed with a sparkle in her eye. "Why don't we prove that to Greyson right now, Nash?"

Nash removed his leg from atop Greyson's and quickly whipped the shirt off him. Greyson sat mildly stunned and amused as Caro hastened to unzip his pants and pull them down with his boxers. When the pants were pooled around his ankles, both Nash and Caro went for Greyson's rapidly expanding dick. Like a perfectly planned move, they tilted their bodies and bent over it, licking, and kissing his length. Intermittently, they alternated kissing each other and stroking Greyson. Their free hands roamed around his bare chest, where they pinched his nipples or reached down to stroke his thighs. Caro nibbled on a nipple while Nash tugged gently on Greyson's balls, and then she bent to engulf him deeply as Greyson hissed and moaned. The onslaught of their hands and mouths together was merciless. Stroking, pinching, caressing, tweaking, licking, sucking, and biting. Greyson became a quivering mass of want. Bright blond waves spilled over him on one side like a silken veil, and shiny black locks slid over his other side in a cascade of dark delight.

*So beautiful. All mine.* Greyson plunged his hands into their hair, gently guiding their movements over him. His hips began to lift rhythmically as if he had no control over them.

Caro's mouth retreated, and she took a deep breath, but Nash took her place immediately, swallowing Greyson down, and scraping him gently with his teeth.

"Ahhh," Greyson moaned until Caro sealed his mouth

with a kiss. She sucked his tongue into her mouth, exploring and teasing. The sensations coming from what Nash was doing to him became too intense though, so Greyson had to pull back. He was afraid he'd bite her as he panted and shook. Caro slid her mouth to Greyson's neck and licked him, causing him to shiver.

All at once, the blitzkrieg became too much, and Greyson shouted, "I'm gonna blow!"

Nash just chuckled, causing Greyson's dick to vibrate with even more sensation, and Nash doubled his suction. Caro slid off the couch and knelt in front of him, where she lifted his balls and reached between Greyson's legs. She sucked a finger into her mouth, then she shoved the tip of her finger into Greyson's butt at the same time that Nash bottomed out, deep-throating him.

The shout that accompanied Greyson's climax rumbled up from somewhere down around his knees before it completely erupted out of his mouth. It was an unearthly sound of relief and sublime pleasure. He was sure that no one in the history of world sex had ever come as hard as this. It must have taken all his bones out with it. He gushed into Nash's mouth —Nash moaned against his shaft as he swallowed and swallowed, finally pulling back to watch another enormous rope of cum paint Greyson's chest. It was a magnificent mess.

"No more doubts, Grey," Caro whispered. "We love you so much."

"Yeah," Nash agreed.

Greyson's eyes looked unfocused when he asked, "Can I

get a bottle of water please? I don't think I can move." His chest heaved as he panted. "Holy mackerel."

# Seventeen

Shortly after reviving Greyson, they made it to the charter airport with no hitches. They assumed the Hunt family was either on a wild-goose chase or had decided Greyson wasn't worth the bother to find and rough up. It was then, however, as they sat and waited to go aboard, that Greyson's phone finally rang. He swore colorfully.

"Problem, Grey?" Nash asked—knowing full well the source of Grey's displeasure.

Making a grim face, Greyson answered his phone. Immediately a shrill voice berated him for running out on her and shaming her in front of hundreds of her closest friends. She said her daddy expected an apology and for Greyson to return immediately. Apparently, the guests had all insisted on staying for the reception even without the groom present, and there were a lot of inebriated people ready to castrate Greyson if he didn't show up and marry her.

"Britney, *stop*," he commanded. "I'm not coming back and we're *not* getting married, and that's final." He listened a moment and said, "*You're* embarrassed? How do you think *I* felt when you were making kissy faces and drooling over my best man during the ceremony? Do you think I was the only one who saw that? Look, just give me a list of the people we were doing business with, and I'll take care of paying for everything myself that hasn't already been paid. If you text it to me, I'll do it right away." He knew that dealing with the vendors would be difficult for her, and it was typical of his kind nature to spare her that embarrassment.

Nash could hear some loud whining but couldn't make out the words.

"Why? Why do you *think* I don't want to marry you? You're so into yourself; you don't give a flying shit about me! Don't even pretend to be brokenhearted. And I heard about your offer to Nash." There was more whining. "Of course I believe him. He's right here. Listen, I'll put you on speaker." He poked a button angrily. "Go ahead, Nash. Repeat what you told me."

"Hello, Britney. Do the words *ya wanna have a blowie* ring any bells? An offer to hit the alley with you while Greyson was in the john? A reassurance that we'd have plenty of time 'cuz he was *constipated*?"

Greyson's face went red. That was more than he'd known, and it was mortifying. He knew Britney used the term *blowie* fairly often, and it sure as hell wasn't a word in Nash's repertoire, which just confirmed what he already knew to be true. Grey also knew he often spent too long in the bathroom when he was with Britney, giving himself time away from her. If he'd had even a glimmer of doubt about their conversation, it was gone for good.

Britney made a lot of fake-sounding crying noises on the other end of the line, but she had the sense not to deny anything Nash said.

"You can stop by my house tomorrow. Actually, now it's my ex-house, kind of like you!" Greyson gave a satisfied sigh. "I left a pile of your stuff on the back porch, and I can't be responsible for what happens to any of it. So if you don't get it right away, you'll have to deal with the landlord. And don't go trying to make it sound as if I tried to steal some of your damn leotards or nail polish. All of your shit is there."

More whining.

"I'm leaving town. Don't call me again. Goodbye." He hung up. "Well, that was pleasant."

"Grey, this is just a wild-ass guess here, but have you had sex with anyone else besides Britney since we split up?"

Greyson hung his head and muttered, "Um… no."

"Well, no wonder you thought you were in love with her. Sex doesn't always mean love, you know? I think you're such a good guy your sense of reason got mixed up somewhere in your pants." Nash laughed softly. "I can imagine how horny you must have been after all that time."

Greyson didn't look up when he admitted, "It wasn't even great sex, but you're probably right. And I just kept thinking that things could be so much better for her if she didn't have to be around her father and all of his crap."

"You were marrying her to save her?"

"Maybe… in a way."

Nash said softly, "Grey, sometimes your heart is just too big. You're so kind and trusting. That girl has had a lifetime of her father's crapola. It wasn't going to get fixed just because she had a new address."

An airline employee entered the lounge and announced that they could now board the plane.

Glad to be done with this conversation, Greyson jumped up to go.

When the plane finally lifted off California soil, they all breathed more easily.

♡♡♡

Hours later they touched down in Kentucky, and Caro suggested, "Let's all go to my house. It's closer, and I think we could all use some rest. We can go back to Lexington tomorrow. Would that be alright?"

After a quick drive over to Frankfort, they made it to Caro's place where they all dove for the shower. They couldn't wait to clean up and relax.

Nash was the last one out, and he found Caro and Greyson sitting next to each other on the edge of her bed. Their robes had been discarded somewhere. *This has great possibilities*, he thought as he watched them kiss each other hungrily. Chuckling and shucking his towel, he crawled behind them where they sat.

With a gentle finger, Nash caressed a line down Caro's

spine and asked Greyson. "Front or back?" Caro shivered at his touch and thought about what Nash was suggesting. It was something they'd asked each other back in the day. She could already feel herself getting swollen and wet.

"It's been so long; I'll take the back please," Grey whispered and kissed Caro's bare shoulder. He slipped a hand between her legs and stroked her. "She's so wet, Nash. Our lady wants us badly. Just like she always did." He bent down and flicked his tongue over her nipple as Nash reached around her and tweaked the other with his fingers while Caro made a happy humming sound. With his other hand, he reached around and did the same thing to Greyson's nipple, causing him to shudder.

Greyson dropped to his knees beside the bed and told Nash, "Take my place where I was sitting. I need to enjoy both of you for a while."

Nash complied as Greyson buried his face between Caro's thighs. With one hand, he pushed his finger inside Caro as he sucked her clit into his mouth. His other hand grasped Nash and stroked up and down his length. When Caro's moans filled the room, he kissed her thigh and leaned over to suck Nash, still pumping in and out of Caro with his finger and using his thumb on her sensitive nub. Now both his partners were moaning in a blissful song without words, kissing each other at the same time. He added another finger, making Caro change her tune slightly with a little hitch in it. Nash went stiff all over and warned Greyson, "This is going to end too soon. Grab a condom, Grey."

As Greyson sat up and went for the box of rubbers, Nash

grabbed Caro and positioned her on his lap, where she straddled him face-to-face. Quickly he slid into her, making them both sigh in happiness. Then he leaned back and scooted more to the middle of the bed while Caro stayed on her knees with her bottom freely exposed to Greyson.

"So beautiful," Greyson whispered, admiring and rubbing her round bottom.

Thwack! He slapped her right butt cheek, causing her to cry out in shock and stare at him over her shoulder.

"What was that for?"

"For years of making us all miss this! And… because I felt like it."

"Do it again, Grey," she pleaded.

Thwack! This time, as Caro flinched and hissed, he left a big red handprint on her left cheek, and then he kissed away the sting.

Nash just chuckled. "Play nice, kids."

"No! I like this not-so-nice stuff," moaned Caro in her sultry voice. *Who knew?* She was flush with endorphins from the slaps, and that made her feel warm and fuzzy all over. She squirmed against Nash, pressing herself against his pubic bone for maximum friction. She craved more and more of… everything.

"So you two are bareback riders now?" Greyson observed. "I'll get tested right away, even though I always used a condom despite the fact that you-know-who was on the pill. I'd hate to think that the little bitch had any extracurricular activities." He rolled on a condom and began to prepare Caro's hole. First, he painted her with a dollop of lube, then he slowly and gently began to insert his pinkie finger. When that met with no resistance, he switched to his index finger.

Caro squirmed against Greyson's probing finger as she slid up and down on Nash. "I like some pain, Grey. It turns me on, so you can go a little faster," she explained encouragingly. "Use another finger." He did, and she gasped. His fingers were actually larger than she'd remembered.

"Are you all right?" he asked.

"Keep going like that. I love it. Nash, are you doing okay?" She cocked an eyebrow at him playfully.

"Never better." He captured her mouth with his and silenced her for a moment with his tongue. Finally, he pulled away and ordered Greyson, "Fuck the woman already, man!"

Greyson lubed himself and realized how good just the pressure of his light strokes felt on his dick. He was so aroused he could barely remember feeling this excited. Positioning himself behind Caro, he slowly entered her ass. Sheer bliss. It was magic. Caro was tight and hot around him, and he could feel the ridges of Nash's shaft moving deep inside her. His eyes nearly rolled back, but then he felt Nash's strong hand grab the back of his head and pull his face down to kiss him. Their tongues battled each other, and they swallowed moan after moan of total delight.

Deeper and deeper, he probed her, bottoming out as his groin met her body. His balls dangled and swung, smacking against Nash as he went as far as he could go. Pound, retreat, pound, retreat. Over and over, he thrust, faster and faster, feeling the tension grow in Caro's tight body. He smoothed his hands over the fading redness on her cheeks and then whacked her a good one on both sides once again. Right, then left—thwack, thwack!

Caro let out a protracted moan so long and deep it seemed to be drained from the depths of her soul. She came, and her body clenched so tightly around both men that they thought their dicks might break off. This was pleasure beyond reason. The chorus of masculine sounds they made was like nothing any of them had ever heard as they emptied themselves into her body. Caro collapsed onto Nash, and Greyson flattened her with his body for a few moments until he decided he really needed to get rid of the condom. Reluctantly he pulled away and cleaned himself up. Wordlessly he brought a wash-cloth to Caro, who still had not moved, and cleaned the lube off her. He tossed the cloth toward the bathroom door and lay down beside them where he could touch them both at the same time. With Greyson's arm wrapped around his lovers, they all drifted to sleep for a little while. Nash was still buried inside Caro.

♡♡♡

NONE OF THEM COULD HAVE SAID HOW LONG THEY SLEPT, BUT they all seemed to rouse at the same time. Nash had not removed himself from Caro, and he was growing hard again. This time, he rolled Caro over and began fucking her from above, so Greyson grabbed another condom and quickly gloved up. He admired the sight of Nash's toned ass cheeks clenching and releasing as he slid in and out of Caro.

Nash looked over his shoulder when he felt large hands on his backside and laughed at Greyson's questioning look. "Fine, but don't get any dumb ideas about *spanking* my ass." He continued to make love to Caro, who purred in happiness beneath him. They kissed deeply while Greyson prepared Nash for entry. Nash didn't rush Greyson along as he had when it was Caro's butt getting prepared, and Greyson had a private laugh with himself about that. *This is going to be a first for him, so I need to be careful. I want him to enjoy it. In fact, I want him to crave it.*

"Grey is going to make you feel so good. You'll love it," Caro crooned to him with gentle conviction. She knew this was a big step for Nash.

Nash seemed to relax in slow increments as Greyson prepped him carefully with his fingers and plenty of lube. But finally, Greyson was pushing against Nash with the head of his dick, causing Nash to gasp as Greyson breached the entry. At first Greyson slid in slowly, letting Nash adjust, but eventually he began hammering—driving Nash into Caro at the speed and tempo he created. He felt like pounding his chest and shouting, "Mine! They're both *mine!*" He kept his mouth shut, but Greyson felt on top of the world at that moment.

Nash was initially shocked—though in a good way—at the sensation of having Greyson inside his body. He'd always been the top when they'd fucked in the past. But as he relaxed and Greyson hit that magic spot deep within him, Nash closed his eyes and decided this was the best way to have sex in the world—sandwiched between the two people he loved the most. Greyson gave him pleasure so profound he could hardly believe it, and Caro's delicious body simultaneously clamped his dick in a paradise vise. When Greyson hit Nash's prostate and bit the back of his neck, Nash rasped, "Right there! Fuck!" and shuddered.

Shock waves rippled through Caro as she relished the sight of her men loving each other. She'd always wanted this for them. Now that they could do it to each other, their sex life would only get any better—she was sure. The expression on Nash's face as Greyson penetrated him made her toes curl. In their previous encounters, Greyson had always been the softer lover, whereas Nash was the take-charge, aggressive guy, and from what Nash had told her, after she'd left them, he was always the top until they split up. Experiencing this was *hot*. She felt as if any barriers were finally obliterated. It seemed to her they were all equals now.

They had all just finished and were luxuriating in a blurry postcoital fog when Greyson's phone rang. It was a distinctive ring that he recognized immediately.

"Ugh. Sorry. I should have turned it off or blocked her. I better talk to her now though, or she likely won't stop calling." He peeled off his condom and tossed it away, picked up his phone and asked in a flat tone, "What?"

There was a lot of loud feminine whining on the other end, and Greyson said, "Hurry up and spit out whatever it is you want, Brit. I'm busy." More whining. "Busy fucking, if you must know." Nash and Caro tried to muffle their snorts. "None of your business who, that's who! Now what do you want?" He listened for a while and scrunched up his face. "That's not gonna happen." More noise. "No. Look, if you're pregnant, it would be a miracle, so don't try to pull that shit on me. You're no more pregnant than I am. And if you were, I know you'd just go out and take care of it like it was nothing, so you wouldn't have to give up your dancing for five minutes." The sounds got louder. "Look, if I thought for a millisecond that you were pregnant, I'd take care of you as long as it took to pop out the kid—*full-term*—and then the kid and I would be long gone. But I'm not going to sit around and listen to you moan nonsense about what-ifs that would never be true, so you're going to have to try a lot harder than that one. I told you not to contact me again, and I mean it. You broke my trust. Text me the list of people to pay. That's it." Greyson smashed his finger on the disconnect button and slumped down onto the bed with a heavy sigh.

♡♡♡

LATER THAT MORNING, THEY WERE WAITING FOR CARO TO PACK up more of her belongings to take to Nash's house. Nash was reading a book, and Greyson was scrolling through something on his laptop when he asked, "Hey, Caro, how many florists do people usually hire for a wedding?"

"One, why?"

"Not different ones for bouquets and centerpieces?"

"Well, I guess you might if the wedding were huge or something, but usually people want to carry the color theme and style throughout the whole celebration."

"Hmm. Interesting. What about wedding planners? How many do you need?"

"One company might have a couple of people work together, but generally it's one person, and definitely in that case it would be just from one business."

"Fuck," Greyson muttered under his breath. "I need to make some calls."

"What's going on, Grey?" Nash asked, pulling his attention away from his book.

"I've been paying bills that Britney and her parents have given me for the wedding, and frankly, I wasn't paying a lot of attention. But the list of the people she gave me to pay doesn't coincide with some of the bills I've already paid, and I think something weird has been going on."

"Uh-oh," Caro breathed.

They both went to look over Greyson's shoulder at his bank statement. There were multiple checks written, but there were also several automatic withdrawals that did not look familiar. Greyson felt his blood run cold.

"I'm calling the police. Is that what you do? I don't even know!"

Caro was explaining that he needed to report this activity to the fraud divisions when Nash interrupted, "Look! There was a $20,000 withdrawal made today by some travel company. On a Sunday? Did you book a honeymoon with someone?"

"Yes, but that name isn't familiar. And we booked and paid for the honeymoon weeks ago. Or so I thought."

"How much do you know about Britney's dad?" Nash

asked. "She mentioned how he liked to bet on the horses. I wonder if he has some gambling debts."

"I wouldn't put it past him now that you mention it. The guy is a class A sleazeball." Greyson immediately called his credit card companies, requested new cards, and alerted them to possible fraud. Then he called the twenty-four-hour emergency number for bank fraud and reported suspicious activity. By the time he was done making his calls, he was shaking and pacing around the room. "What a nightmare. I've been such an idiot!"

♡♡♡

ACCORDING TO HIS FORMER LANDLORD, BRITNEY NEVER SHOWED up for her belongings. Apparently, the stuff she'd carelessly left at Greyson's house wasn't worth all that much to her after all. The local organization that raised money for victims of domestic abuse benefited from her lack of concern. When her last-ditch, asinine effort to fleece Greyson out of potential child support for a nonexistent baby failed, she and her parents took off and got out of Dodge.

"I think we've bled this turnip dry," Chase Hunt told Britney. "Time to find a new cash cow." Mixed metaphors had always been her father's thing. "Yeah, time to go prospecting again while you still have your figure, baby girl." *First things first, however. We have business to attend to,* he thought deviously. He wanted to get on the road right away.

Britney pouted in the back seat of her father's leased car.

"I liked him. Greysie is cute and has a really big... uh..." She sighed, and a crocodile tear slid down her cheek as she realized she probably shouldn't mention her favorite attribute of Greyson's to her parents. "*And* I never got to smoosh cake into his face at the wedding reception. I was really looking forward to that. I'm so mad at him for wrecking everything."

Her mother glared out the window, thinking about how stunning she'd looked as mother of the bride and how it was all ruined. No one had paid the least bit of attention to her—in her knockoff designer gown—once the groom skipped down the aisle with his two weirdo friends. They were both, she had to admit, extremely attractive. That fiasco was all anyone wanted to talk about. And it was going to take a lot of research and work to find another sugar daddy for her daughter now. *How could everything go so wrong overnight like that?* "Britney? What asinine thing did you do or say to Greyson that made him dump you?" Her voice made it clear she was ready to strangle someone.

Britney knew perfectly well what she'd said and done, but she answered, "Nothing, Mom! I didn't say a thing to Greysie." She had her fingers crossed. "He has those friends who blew into town though, and they must have turned him against me for some reason." She sniffled and then blew her nose with a big honk. Then, just to be conversational and change the subject, she said, "Greysie's friend is the guy who owns that racehorse everyone's so interested in. I bet they'll be at the Belmont Stakes."

"Precisely why we're heading to New York. Wouldn't you ladies enjoy seeing history made if there's a Triple Crown winner this year?" He chuckled as his mental wheels began to spin. He desperately needed to make a killing somewhere before he ended up at the bottom of a lake wearing cement shoes. *Loan sharks are such unreasonable jerks. I just need to figure out exactly how to play this.*

His wife looked at him with lustful pride. She had a good idea of what he was up to. She loved a man who could scheme. She knew just how she'd congratulate him when his plans came to fruition. It had been far too long since she'd put on her boots, fishnets, and black leather bustier and brought out some of her toys. She knew how to bring Chase to his knees with some clamps, plugs, a whip and... well, the possibilities were endless. Her mood elevated immediately. Punishing her bad boy, the way he loved it, was going to be fun. Just thinking about it made her squirm in her seat. He just needed to earn this reward first.

# Eighteen

Later that day, the three lovers took off for Best Life Farm in Lexington. Greyson admired the scenery, and it reminded him how much closer he was now to his own family—just one state north of Nash's place. He was surprised at how much this comforted him, and he was anxious to see them as soon as possible.

Greyson's piano and the rest of his stuff would arrive in a couple of days. Their plan was to get Greyson settled and then head off to New York for the Belmont Stakes. Caro also needed to make some kind of arrangement with her house and her staff.

"I definitely want to live on the farm with both of you, but keeping the house in Frankfort makes a lot of sense. I'll still need to be there some of the time for Zoë, Tanner, and Eli." Caro seemed to be thinking out loud and asked, "How would you both feel if I asked my cook Angela to come out here with us and continue working? She's amazing, and I don't want her to lose her job. Is there somewhere she could live, Nash?"

"Sure. That would be great. There's lots of room. And maybe we'll see more of my dad if we have someone cooking regularly. He gets by but isn't the greatest in the kitchen."

"I'm starting to feel like a kept man," Greyson mock complained.

"Don't worry; I'll be happy to put you to work as much as you like," Nash promised. He had spent a lot of time on the phone, checking his emails, and was obviously extremely busy, so this was no surprise. "With a place this large, there's always something going on. For now, let's go introduce you to Gene Simmons. The first time will just be from the ground, so no need for boots just yet." He looked at the Nikes on Greyson's feet. "We need to get you properly outfitted for riding anyway."

Nash led them through the kitchen again to pick up a baggie of carrots. Accompanied by Janis Joplin, Jimi Hendrix, and Sid Vicious, they all trooped out to visit the Mötley Crüe, again by taking the golf cart.

"Why carrots?" Greyson asked. He looked a little nervous.

"They like them, and carrots are better for them than apples or sugar cubes despite what people often feed horses. The carrots are just a special treat for getting you acquainted, and these guys don't get them very often. I don't want to just take one to Gene Simmons and cause hard feelings."

Caro then demonstrated to Greyson how to properly offer a carrot. "Hold the piece out like this in your open palm.

Keep your hand still and let him take it from you. If you pull away, you might get nipped, and their teeth are *big*. Just stay calm. He really is a sweetie pie."

"And here they come now." Nash laughed as they approached the gate. A small herd of horses trotted toward them, clearly expecting something tasty or fun.

"There're so many of them," Greyson exclaimed as each horse pressed against the fence for attention.

"Bunch of pussycats," Caro promised. "Just stay calm," she said in a deep, conspiratorial voice. "They can smell your fear."

"They can?"

She squinched up her face and laughed. "I'm just pulling your leg. They see it more than smell it." She snorted when he blanched. "Relax, Grey. They're a gang of big pets. Just watch out for your toes."

"Here's your guy, Grey. May I introduce you to your new horse, Gene Simmons?" A tall, somewhat chubby black-and-white pinto was nosing into Nash's hand. "He loves his food." Nash laughed. He then passed a piece of carrot to Greyson and said, "Go ahead and say hello. Stick it out there for him to eat."

Stepping closer, Greyson muttered, "He's enormous." However, he raised his carrot-laden palm to the horse's mouth and gasped when Gene Simmons ever-so-gently plucked it up with his lips. Then they could hear a lot of satisfied crunching as the horse enjoyed his treat. "Wow." Greyson breathed out. Gene Simmons then started nosing around at Greyson and nudged his arm. "What does that mean? Does it mean he likes me?" Tentatively Greyson raised a hand to pet the horse. "Can I give him another one?" Nash handed another chunk to Greyson, and the process was repeated. "His lips sort of tickle," he said in wonder. "I've never even had my own goldfish. Thanks, Nash!"

Stroking Gene Simmons' muscular neck, Greyson shifted closer to the horse and began to murmur to him. Eventually, he leaned his head against the horse, and the two of them appeared to be sharing a private moment.

Nash and Caro stood silently, watching this sweet scene unfold. They didn't want to break the mood, but eventually, a little mare with her distinctive roan coat butted in and started begging for a treat too. Laughing, Caro gave her one and said, "Tiny Dancer, you're a pest. You're lucky you're so cute."

"I have an idea," Nash announced. "Wait here with Grey, and I'll be right back." He took off in the golf cart for the tack room.

In less than two minutes, Nash returned with a halter and a lead line. "Grey, how would you like to take Gene Simmons with us and go visit Elvis?" He slipped the halter onto the big guy's head and clipped on the rope. "Y'all can get acquainted on the walk over there. And the horses can say hi." Greyson looked receptive, so he explained. "Horses like to be handled on their left sides. So when you get on and off or lead them around, it's all on their left. Got it?"

"Um, okay."

Nash maneuvered the horse over to the gate and opened it just enough for him to go through but not so open that he had a loose herd of horses running around his farm. Gene

Simmons waited patiently for Nash to close the gate and hand over the lead line to Greyson.

"Hold it like this, and just walk at a normal speed with his head next to you. If he spooks at anything—which I sincerely doubt that he'll ever do—just let go. I don't want you to get hurt. He can't get into too much trouble if he's loose. And knowing him, we can get him back right away with a carrot."

They left the cart and took off walking toward the barn where Lady G and Elvis were stabled. Nash and Caro led the way, letting Greyson get acquainted with his new horse. As predicted, Gene Simmons didn't cause any trouble and seemed as happy as could be to have a new friend. "Good choice for them, Nash," Caro said softly. "Grey's having a great time. He's even singing to his new buddy now."

Sure enough, they could hear Greyson's deep voice crooning "Ghost Riders in the Sky" to Gene Simmons. He sounded remarkably like Johnny Cash at that moment.

"I just hope the horse likes country." Nash snickered. And then Greyson broke into a much louder version of "Save a Horse, Ride a Cowboy." When Nash turned to look back at them, Greyson winked at him and did a little two-step. Gene Simmons didn't break stride; he just plodded along politely.

"Here we are, Grey. Elvis is right over here." He led them to Elvis and slid the door open, leaving a stall guard in place. Elvis came to say hi right away, and Nash handed him a carrot. Elvis looked politely at Gene Simmons and gave him a friendly nicker too. "They've met before. In fact, the stall next to him is available, so we can keep Gene Simmons in here with Elvis and Lady G." Looking at Greyson's horse, he said,

"You're moving up in the world, big guy. We'll just have to make sure you get plenty of exercise now so you don't get any fatter."

"Hey, my man here isn't fat," Greyson protested. "He's just… big-boned." He was already in love with the horse.

"Well, haul your big-boned best friend over to meet Lady G then. She's not always as accepting as Elvis, so don't get too close at first. She can get bossy, so that's why she's been in here instead of with the rest of the Mötley Crüe. She adores Elvis, but she doesn't know Gene Simmons yet." Nash also opened her door, and the mare stuck her head over the stall guard to say hello.

Caro fed Lady G a carrot and said, "Here are a couple of guys we'd like you to meet, so be nice."

Lady G munched her carrot and then raised her head. Her eyes looked a bit wild, and she blew a big huff out of dilated nostrils. She pawed the ground and then whinnied loudly. Gene Simmons took notice of her and all but dragged Greyson over to her, but as soon as they got close, Lady G whipped around and presented her butt with her tail in the air. She backed into the webbed gate, straining to get through it backward.

Caro started to laugh her head off, Nash said, "What a hussy," and Greyson looked confused.

"What's going on?" Greyson asked. "Why is she acting like that?"

Through her laughter, Caro explained, "She's apparently in season and thinks Romeo here is hot stuff. Look underneath him, Grey." She slid the stall door closed on Lady G's rump, hiding her impassioned display. "Knock it off, you harlot." She laughed.

Grey's brow furrowed as he stepped around and bent down. His eyebrows shot up nearly past his hairline when he asked, "Is that normal? Good Lord!"

Nash also took a peek belowdecks and muttered, "Just what I thought. He's proud cut." Then he turned to Greyson's baffled expression and asked, "Have you ever heard the expression 'hung like a horse'? It's an impressive sight when they're breeding, I can assure you. In this case, Gene Simmons here isn't fully equipped to breed, but he probably has enough of his testicles left to make the mares think he can, and he does love the ladies. If he were a stallion, that hard-on would be even more impressive."

"They cut off most of his balls?" Greyson asked anxiously. "Why?"

"Unless a male horse is expected to be used for breeding, he'll be gelded at a fairly young age. Otherwise, the worry is that they'll be too hard to handle. Once in a while, a horse is left 'proud cut.' That could have been done for many reasons, but we'll never know the specific reasons in this case. It could have been done on purpose or as a mistake, and it probably accounts for his rather large neck, but at least this horse is polite about it. Sometimes they can be a real pain in the ass."

Greyson had to resist the urge to cradle his own sack protectively at this news. "What about Elvis?"

"He's a gelding. Fully castrated."

"Oh! So that's what that means." Greyson's face suddenly looked like the lights went on inside. "When I bought Elvis, I thought they were saying he was like gelt. You know… gold candy. I thought it was a compliment that he was so sweet. Boy, was I dumb!"

Nash swung an arm around Greyson's neck and murmured in his ear, "Not dumb. Just inexperienced. We'll make a horseman out of you around here, Grey. Believe me. And Elvis is as sweet as candy. He's the best gift I've ever received." He gave Greyson a kiss on the cheek and patted his ass. Then he stepped away and asked Caro, "Can you show Greyson how to put Gene Simmons into the stall down there next to Elvis please? I'm going to go look for a pair of chaps in the tack room."

So Caro and Greyson settled Gene Simmons into his new digs and made sure he knew how to operate the automatic waterer. "Did you know," she asked, "that horses drink by pursing their lips and using their tongues like a straw? They don't lap up water like dogs and cats, but I bet most people think they do. Watch closely, and you'll see."

Greyson watched spellbound as Gene Simmons dipped his mouth into his bucket of water, and there was a faint but audible sucking sound. "Fascinating."

Caro showed Greyson how to take off the halter, and they both gave the horse some friendly pats before closing him into the stall. Turning around, they saw Nash walking toward them with some weird-looking leather pants in his hand. "These are for you," he told Greyson. "I'm pretty sure they'll fit."

"Cool. Assless pants. Just what I've always wanted. Great for hot days when free balling is the only solution."

Nash rolled his eyes. "The chaps go on over your jeans, Mr. Free Baller. The suede will help you stick to the leather of the saddle. It's a safer, more comfortable way to ride, and they also help prevent saddle sores. The leather pads on breeches act pretty much the same way, so that's what Caro and I wear. I think you'll be happier with a Western saddle on Gene Simmons though, and the chaps are appropriate."

"I know what chaps are. I've watched a few rodeos on TV." He tried them on and swaggered around the barn, trying to look bow-legged. "I like 'em!" he exclaimed.

Nash gave Caro a look and whispered, "Don't tell him. We'll deal with it later."

Squelching a fit of laughter, Caro exclaimed, "Now you just need a decent pair of boots. Nash, do you have any that will fit?"

"We can check back at the house, but I don't think so. What size shoe do you wear, Grey?"

"Twelve. Narrow."

"Yeah, unless a few pairs of socks would work, mine will be too long and wide. Looks like we need to do some shopping." He looked at the end of the barn, where a man was silhouetted in the sunlight as he entered. "Hey, Benny." Turning to Greyson, Nash explained, "Benny is the stable manager." Looking back at the newcomer, Nash went on, "You met Caro already, but this is our friend Greyson Foster. He's moving in, and he'll be riding Gene Simmons from now on. We've moved the big pinto into the empty stall next to Elvis, but when you feed him, be careful not to overdo it. He needs to be on a diet for a couple of weeks. Regular exercise will help, but he still needs to lose a bit of that chub."

"Yessir, Mr. Keating. I'll take care of him. I always liked that horse." Turning to Greyson, he stuck out his hand and shook. "Pleased to meet you, Mr. Foster. You'll be satisfied with Gene Simmons. He's a character but as gentle as they come."

Smiling, Greyson answered, "Nice to meet you too, Benny. Call me Greyson. But why do you think I'd be happy with a gentle horse?"

"Just a feeling I have. And you have your chaps on backward."

# Nineteen

Caro spoke to her cook Angela that night, and it turned out the woman was thrilled with the prospect of cooking for more people and moving much closer to Lexington, where she had family. Caro also promised her a raise because she'd have more work to do. So it was settled. The next afternoon, Angela arrived with her things, and they all helped her move into the cook's quarters off the kitchen. It was a nice little apartment, already equipped with the essentials. Nash made sure to tell her that she could decorate in any way she saw fit.

The first thing she did once she was unpacked was take stock of the contents of the kitchen, and she ordered a delivery of what she called the basics. They explained about Greyson's corn allergy, which she took in stride, saying, "I know how to handle that—no problem," and then she said she'd like to take a walk around the property. "I'll be back in plenty of time to put the delivery away and get dinner ready," she assured Caro, and then she took off with the trio of Rottweilers following close at hand.

"Those traitorous brats," mumbled Nash as he watched his goofy, smiling dogs follow Angela out the door.

Caro snickered. "Apparently you missed that she had a pocketful of cheese squares. She loves dogs and was always sorry I didn't have one. Now, do we need to discuss our trip to New York? Where's Grey?"

Nash shook his head smiling. "The big softy took off to visit Gene Simmons. He didn't want the horse to get too lonely in that stall all by himself. He ought to be back soon. He took the cart. Then again, maybe he'll stay there and sing to the big guy some more."

Smiling with fond understanding, Caro said, "Okay, well, I need to go call Eli anyway and fill him in on my life. Can we have them all out here soon? I'm sure they'd love it."

"Absolutely. I want to get to know your family, Caro. All of them. You don't even need to ask. This is your place too now." He pulled her into a warm hug and kissed the top of her head. "Now it makes more sense that you said you sometimes head over to Eli's house for family brunch on Sunday. I imagined it was just the two of you with your mimosas and eggs Benedict or some shit. You meant the whole, entire Whittaker-Lassiter clan, didn't you?"

Smiling, she answered, "I did, but in the future, I need to be more careful not to make slips of the tongue like that. You're very perceptive, Mr. Keating."

After a few lovely kisses, Caro went outside and dangled

her feet in the pool while she spoke to her big brother, and Nash called his dad to check on things in New York. He also had to make sure they had enough seats in the owners' box for everyone. The big race was in just a few days now, and he felt butterflies just thinking about it.

The paparazzi had let up a little, but there were still a few camped out in the front by his gate, and he expected it to get worse as the race approached. Nash shook his head and thanked the stars above for the security fence around his property. He knew if they caught wind of his relationship right now, they'd be relentless. On one hand, he never intended to live in secrecy, but on the other hand, his love life was no one's business but his, Caro's, and Greyson's. Realistically, however, he appreciated what a juicy story their lifestyle would make. Famous horse, famous entertainers—even if they weren't currently performing—and a polyamorous arrangement that the paps would surely make to sound naughty no matter what. He didn't feel naughty. He was just doing what came naturally to him.

Settling into his favorite chair, Nash dialed his dad. "Hey, how's it going?" he greeted the older man cheerfully.

"Great, son. Just great. Pip's looking terrific, and Jorge's in good health and thinks the colt is storing up for the long one." Nash knew that the Belmont was the longest race most Thoroughbreds would ever run, and the majority of them just weren't built for that distance. "Jorge is such a typical jockey. The man is completely fearless, skinny as a rail, and is as happy as a clam. Those guys just love their job." He chuckled.

"Good to hear, Dad. I'll be there the day after tomorrow, and I'm bringing two people with me this time."

"Oh?"

"Yeah." Nash couldn't stop smiling. "Caro and Greyson are coming. And they are both, um… living here at the farm with me now."

After a silent pause, his dad answered softly, "Well, that's just great news, son. I'm happy it's all worked out at last."

"You're not surprised?"

"Hmm. Not terribly. That boy called me constantly when he was worried about you. I knew it was more than a former bandmate's concern. Caro is more of a mystery to me, except that you told me you and she were patching things up. I'm looking forward to getting to know them. Oh, gotta run, Nash. I'm needed at the barn."

"Okay, Dad. We'll see you soon, and please make sure we have enough seats in the owner's box."

"Will do, son. Don't worry. There's plenty of extra room. We have tickets for six."

"I love you, Dad. And I'm sorry I don't tell you that more often."

"I love you too, Nash. Have a safe trip here. See you soon." And he was gone.

Looking outside, he could see that Caro was still deep in conversation with her brother, so he surveyed the living room and tried to decide on the best place to put Greyson's piano. He paced around and then began to slide furniture into new places. Satisfied finally, he was pleasantly surprised to feel a pair of arms wrap around his waist from behind. "Good talk with Eli?" he asked as he turned around.

"Yes, he's the best. And he's happy for us in a way that not too many people will ever understand. He said to tell you that if you or Grey ever have any questions, he's there for you, and he's a vault. He also sends his good luck wishes for Domino Pip and said the Challenger 300 is ours to get there and back. I think he was a little sorry they won't be able to make it, actually, but Tanner has some important function to attend with Zoë. He says he's just sitting this gala out and staying home with the babies and their manny, Dante. Eli is such a great daddy, and he's so happy."

"Glad to hear it. I'm looking forward to getting to know all of them." He gave her a quick smooch. "Feel like taking a walk? I thought Grey would be back by now, and he has the cart, so let's go see if we can find him, okay?"

"Good plan," she agreed.

And off they went toward the barn.

Eventually, they passed Angela on her way back to the house with the dogs, who appeared to have fallen in love with her, and as they neared the barn, they could hear Greyson's deep voice belting out "Wild Horses."

Nash laughed out loud, saying, "At least you're teaching that horse to be a rocker finally and not bending his ear with all of that country stuff," as they entered the barn.

Greyson turned around with an enormous grin on his face. He had Gene Simmons in the cross ties and was carefully combing his mane. "Remember what Professor Jensen used to tell us at Berklee? *All* music is good music. And this big guy likes some variety. Benny taught me how to clean his feet with a hoof pick and use the different grooming brushes on him," he added proudly. "He likes the currycomb the best. He makes goofy faces when you rub him with it just right."

"As long as you're both happy," Caro said as she wrapped Greyson in a hug. "Feel like having your first ride now that you have Gene Simmons all spruced up and we're all here?" She looked down and was pleased to see that Greyson was wearing his new boots. Nash had told him that they would need a bit of breaking in.

"Sure!" Greyson laughed and added, "I'll even wear the assless pants the right way this time."

"Chaps," Caro explained with a giggle. "It's spelled like chapped lips, but pronounced *shaps*. It actually comes from the Spanish word *chaparreras*. They were originally designed to protect riders' legs from getting ripped up riding through the chaparral. Very practical."

"And sexy," Greyson added with a wink.

"And sexy," she agreed. "There will always be some lunkhead around who swears it's pronounced like chapped lips, but don't believe him."

Shaking his head and laughing, Nash went to the tack room and came back with a Western saddle and bridle. "These will work," he explained and proceeded to show Greyson how to put the saddle on and do up the cinch. "This is another thing we do from the horse's left side. More importantly, however, don't expect the cinch to be tight enough to get on immediately because a lot of horses will take a deep breath and expand their chests so you can't put it on properly until they relax. Some of them even need a friendly little poke in the belly with your knee to encourage them to exhale." Then he showed Greyson how to hold the bit and slip it into Gene Simmons' mouth as he tucked the headpiece behind the horse's ears. "Gene Simmons is always polite about this, but not all horses are as congenial." Nash also checked the fit of the bridle, making a small adjustment, so the bit wasn't too high and pulling on Gene Simmons' lips.

"How do you happen to have him anyway, if he's such a great horse?" Greyson asked as he stroked the horse's neck.

"Oh, he was purchased for a family's daughter, and then the parents split up. No one wanted the financial responsibility, and the daughter was getting to be more interested in boys. It happens all the time. The asshole father wanted to get rid of him quickly and was about to send him off to... you don't want to know. We heard about it and stepped in." Then he added in a grim voice, "I paid for him by the pound."

Greyson looked sad and patted the horse. "Poor guy. You came from a broken home. I'm sure glad Nash found you, buddy."

Nash brightened up and said, "Maybe it was fate. I knew you'd come back, and I'd need the right horse for you when you did. I didn't even have to ride this guy to see that he's special. But once I did, I knew I had to find the right person to appreciate him. And then you arrived. I couldn't be happier for both of you."

Once Greyson was properly suited up in his chaps and wearing a helmet, Nash showed him how to check the cinch one last time. "Stick your fingers in here, and if it's loose, you'll need to tighten it." He watched and said, "Good. It looks fine, but still make a habit each and every time you get on a horse to check first. It looks really bad when someone steps into the stirrup and ends up with the saddle spinning half the way around the horse, or worse yet, you end up half the way around the horse *in* the saddle." He held onto Gene Simmons' reins and instructed Greyson, "Okay, now put your left foot into the stirrup and step up. Swing your right leg over his back without touching him. You certainly don't want to kick him in the rump. Ease onto him now. Don't just flop into the saddle. Good."

"Ugh! This is going to take some getting used to," Greyson said with a laugh. "And how do you ride a horse without smashing your balls?"

"Scoot up a bit and roll your butt under you a little. Sit up tall. You'll get used to it. Now remember, you're going to stay atop this horse by using your sense of balance. Don't try to squeeze Gene Simmons with your legs. That's how you'll tell him to go faster. And don't hold on to the saddle horn like that. It's not a handle. It's used for roping steers. If you're in danger of falling off, of course you can grab it, but only then."

Nash put the reins in Greyson's left hand. "This horse responds to neck reining. You'll change his direction by putting pressure on his neck, and he'll turn away from it. A lot of this is different from the way you'll see Caro ride. She uses different tack and different cues for her horse." He looked at Greyson's face and noticed a loss of color there. "Are you okay, Grey? Second thoughts?"

Clearing his throat and blinking, Greyson answered, "It's

just so *high* up here!" Then he laughed and patted Gene Simmons. "Be good to me, big guy."

"You won't have any trouble there." Nash laughed. "He's as gentle as a lamb."

They both heard some tiny clicks and realized Caro had her phone pointed at them, snapping photos of the event. "It's a momentous occasion, guys. Grey's first ride on a horse! Looking good, Grey! I do love a cowboy." She looked at Nash, "And I do love a man in breeches too."

"Why don't I get to wear breeches?" Greyson wondered aloud.

"You can eventually if you want to. We just think this is the fastest and safest way to get you used to riding. The saddle will also help you stay on a little better than a flat English saddle. Later, if you want to try jumping, we'll find you a different horse. Gene Simmons is a little too old and chubby for that activity, and he wasn't bred or trained for it. The whole idea is to get you as comfortable as possible. Okay, let's head out to the small ring over there. Be sure to keep your heels down and your toes up so your foot doesn't get caught in the stirrup if you lose your balance."

"How do I get him to move?"

"Touch him lightly with the insides of your legs and give him his head. Don't pull back on the reins unless you want him to stop. Good. Now you're riding, Grey."

Caro switched over to video mode with a huge smile on her face while Nash opened the gate and directed Greyson to turn right and walk around the perimeter of the ring, getting the feel of his mount. "Just walk a while, Grey, and loosen the small of your back. That is critical for your balance and comfort on a horse. Roll your butt under you again and sit up tall in the saddle. Good! Let your back muscles stay loose so you'll move with the horse and won't bounce around. Are you wearing boxers?"

"Uh, yeah."

"Next time you'll chafe less if you wear tighter underwear. They call them jockey shorts for a reason."

"Great, now you tell me."

"Sorry. This was an impromptu ride, and I won't make you stay on very long. You'll feel it in your muscles tomorrow in any case. You're looking more relaxed now. Are you ready for a slow jog?"

"Um…"

"Shorten up the reins a little so they don't flop around but not tight enough to cause pressure on his mouth, then go ahead and give him a little chirp."

"Chirp?"

"Make a kissing sound," Caro said with a laugh.

Greyson took a fortifying breath and made a big smacking smoochy sound, causing Gene Simmons to lumber into the slowest, smoothest jog ever. Immediately, Greyson grabbed for the saddle horn as his eyes went wide, but just as quickly, he smiled broadly and put his hands back the way Nash had shown him—one out in front and the other resting on his thigh. "Wow! This is cool! Good boy, Gene!"

Caro cracked up and said, "He's not a dog, Grey. You don't have to praise him verbally like one." She looked at Nash and said quietly, "That horse is going to take care of him, isn't he? What a sweetie. Wait until Grey rides someone with a fast trot and rough gaits. He won't know what hit him."

They put Greyson through his paces for a while, getting him to neck rein the horse to go in different directions, stop and start, and had him dismount and mount again without any help. Finally, when they decided he looked calm enough, Nash asked, "Are you ready to go even faster?"

"Ready."

"Okay, now you're going to lope. It's a very smooth gait, and my guess is you'll like how it feels. It's a three-beat count, unlike the jog which was a two-beat count. You're going to cue the horse with your outside leg so he takes the correct lead. Don't worry about that part now because we'll deal with leads later on. If you get nervous, just plant your feet, sit back a little and say, 'Whoa.' Gene Simmons will do the rest for you. Okay, ready? Cluck to him this time and cue him with your outside leg. Do not wrap your legs around him or you might end up at a gallop. Try to stay loose, Grey. Keep your shoulders down and relax your back."

The look on Greyson's face morphed from instant horror to sheer pleasure as Gene Simmons broke into a smooth lope. Except for a bit of extraneous flopping around, Nash and Caro could see that Greyson was trying hard to follow instructions, and he was naturally quite coordinated. After a few minutes of loping around the ring, Nash announced, "Okay, it's time to call it a day. Pull back gently and tell him whoa and… Oops! You forgot to sit up." He watched as Greyson lurched forward over Gene Simmons' neck and grimaced as a sensitive area undoubtedly banged into the pommel of the saddle. "Let's try that again, Grey. Take a deep breath and get comfortable again. Now ease him into a lope and then sit up straight and say, 'Whoa.' There you go! Much better. Alright, let's take him back to the barn at a nice slow walk. Never, ever let a horse run back to the barn, or you'll create a monster."

"Great job, Grey!" Caro cried out to him happily. "Tomorrow we can all ride together if you're not too sore."

Greyson scoffed at her words until he stepped down from his horse and his legs wobbled, feeling like jelly. *Maybe I might be a little sore later tonight.*

# Twenty

While they waited for Angela to get dinner ready, Nash made a suggestion. "Let's go have a little fun in the recording studio. Caro and I were playing around with something at your house, Grey, and we think you'd like it. You can use the keyboard in there." He picked up his phone and sent some documents to his printer while they made their way to the music room.

"This is a great setup you have here," Greyson said, looking around with admiration at the array of recording equipment. Nash also had a full drum kit and a row of guitars lined up in all their shiny, colorful glory. After taking it all in, Greyson sat at the keyboard and warmed up his hands.

"Thanks," Nash replied. "I enjoy it. I had some excellent help setting it up. Like I said before, the music scene in Kentucky is legendary, and you can find great people to work with. Anyway…" Nash handed Greyson some sheets of music and lyrics. "Here you go. This needs some work, but I'm sure you can add your special sauce to it to make it better."

For the next hour or so until Angela called them in to dinner, they all gave their input into the song. It wasn't a masterpiece, but they had fun with it, and it came from the heart. Most of all, it felt so good to play and sing together.

THE PERFECT NUMBER THREE

*Nash:*

One and one was near nearly right.

But perfect three made hearts delight.

Then one left two to try and try.

Did you leave and never cry?

You made us worry. I made us sad.

Two left alone burned into bad.

CAROLINE:

I left the two to join the world.

I'd thought to be the proper girl.

We loved too hard, too much, too soon.

I had to leave to give you room.

You made me worry. You made me sad.

How could two loves turn out so bad?

· · ·

*N*ASH:

Come back to two or back to one.
Our story, love, just isn't done.
How could you go? Why is it so?
Look me in the eye and tell me no!
These two are too sad.
We've lost what we had.


*N*ASH AND *C*AROLINE:

We're two again like black and white.
Needing grey to blend it right.
Too flat, too sharp, we need the one—
The major third to make it run.
We're two again, still partly sad
Until we tune what we once had.


*N*ASH, *C*AROLINE, AND *G*REYSON:

We need to trust, to speak, to share.
To love the way few others dare.
We'll fight to drum the gloom away
As grey brings color to our day.
The perfect three will always say,
"This is our life, our love, our way."


*G*REYSON:

The perfect three will always stay.

This is our life, our love, our way.

# The Perfect Number Three

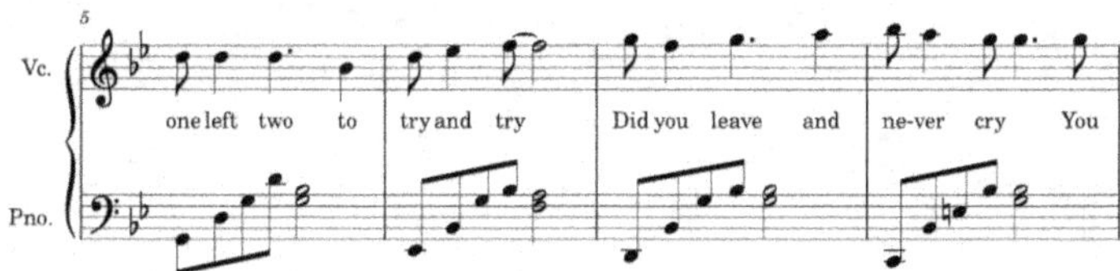

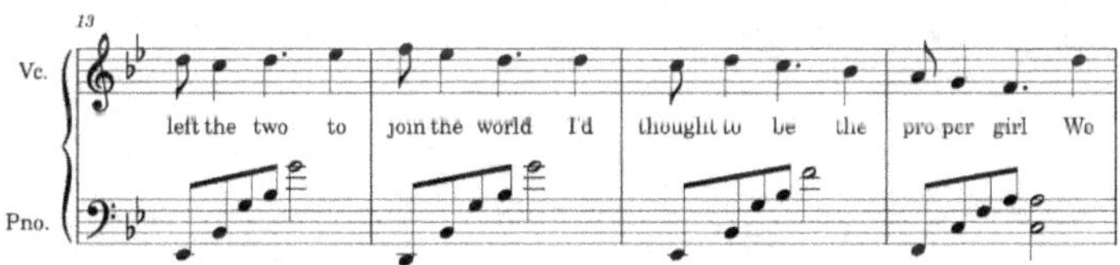

2
loved too hard, too much, too soon I had to leave to give you room
You made me worry You made me sad How could two loves turn out so bad?
N:Come back to two or back to one Our sto-ry love just is-n't done How
could you go Why is it so Look me in the eyes and tell me no! These
two are two sad We've lost what we had N+C:We're two a-gain like

Vc.
Pno.
black and white
Nee-ding grey to
blend it right
Too flat too sharp  We
need the one
The ma - jor third to make it
run
We're two a-gain    still
part-ly sad
Un - til  we tune what we once
had
N:We need  to trust
C:to
speak G:to share
N+C:To love  the way few  o - thers
dare
G:We'll fight to drum the

4
52
Vc.
Pno.
gloom a - way
N+C:As grey brings co - lor to our day
55
Vc.
Pno.
All:The per - fect three will al - ways say
This is our life, our love, our
58
Vc.
Pno.
way
G:The per - fect three will al - ways stay
61
Vc.
Pno.
This is our life, our love, our way

♡♡♡

LATER THAT NIGHT, GREYSON TOOK FULL ADVANTAGE OF HIS soreness by allowing his lovers to massage every inch of him. *Ah, heaven on earth.*

After massaging him everywhere, Nash and Caro's touch went from therapeutic to adoring. They sandwiched Greyson between them and rubbed him this time with their hot bodies. It was the most wonderful feeling he'd had in years. He groaned into Caro's mouth as she kissed him, rolling toward her in the bed. Her hands were all over him again, caressing him as if he were the most beautiful and cherished thing in the world. Firmer, rougher hands stroked him from behind, and he felt Nash's erection rub against his ass crack as he kissed Greyson's neck. "This has been one of the best days of my life, and it's just getting better and better." He moaned as Caro scooted down and kissed her way to his crotch.

Caro wrapped her hand around Greyson's rapidly thickening girth and stroked. She leaned in and licked the precum from his tip, then sucked him into her mouth. Greyson sighed with pleasure until Caro popped off and asked Nash, "Condoms?"

Nash leaned back and produced a box from the nightstand, so Caro grabbed one and swiftly rolled it onto Greyson. "Make love to me, Grey," she murmured. "We need you." She rolled onto her back, and Greyson entered her.

Nash, meanwhile, had also suited up and had a bottle of lube in his hand. He climbed over the others and positioned himself between their spread legs so he could access Greyson's backside.

Grey slid in and out of Caro and began to moan when he felt Nash spread his cheeks and paint his hole with lubrication. He gasped when Nash's large finger breached his entrance. "Careful, man. It's been a long, long time," he choked out.

"Too much?" Nash asked.

"Not on your life. I've thought about this happening for years. Do it. Just go slow."

Nash kissed Greyson's back and rubbed his stubble over the smooth skin, causing Greyson to shudder with pleasure. The feel of Nash's finger inside him, while he was inside Caro, was almost too much to comprehend. The perfection of this moment was beautiful and sublime.

Caro stopped any further discussion by seeking Greyson's lips with hers and kissing him deeply. Her hands never stopped stroking his body with infinite affection.

Feeling Greyson relax, Nash added a second finger, eliciting a deep groan from Greyson that Caro swallowed down.

Finally, Nash lubed up his own pulsating dick, hoping he could make this last. Happiness to have Grey back coursed through his veins along with desire so strong he was afraid he'd combust. Ever so carefully, he fed his steely erection into Greyson's body, and Caro was elated to see Greyson throw his head back and shout, "Yes, God, yes!" The last petered out into a long groan, and Greyson buried his face in Caro's neck.

Caro caught Nash's eye over Greyson, and the two of them shared a look of pure joy. They had their man back. Their beautiful Grey was part of them once again. And this time, it was without any of them holding back.

It didn't take long before Nash erupted into Greyson, and he in turn shuddered his release into Caro. Caro grinned to see her men so spent and happy, but she had not yet come herself. As soon as they pulled out, the men double-teamed her, however, and brought her to multiple convulsing orgasms with fingers, lips, tongues, and teeth. She was never to be denied her pleasure with these two.

The next morning, Greyson groaned, feeling the full brunt of those sore muscles as he crawled out of bed. It was worth it though, and a new song began to percolate in his brain. He called it "Bustin' My Ass for You," but he figured it might not have a very wide audience due to its references to chafed testicles in the chorus where he invited his partners to kiss them better. Then again… maybe he had a hit with this one. He could make a whole album and call it the *Not-So-Lonesome-Anymore Cowboy*. He'd dedicate it to Gene Simmons.

Stiffly, Greyson pulled on a pair of tight underwear as he watched Caro and Nash slip into their riding apparel. Everything they did was graceful and purposeful, and he especially loved the view of those shapely asses of theirs in breeches. Caro turned and caught him staring and gave him a saucy wink. "Looking good, Grey. Can you get back into the saddle again this morning? We can all go for a swim afterward and keep you loosened up."

"Absolutely. Gene Simmons will appreciate the exercise, I'm sure."

"Uh-huh," Nash said with a smile. "Let's have some breakfast! What time did you say our plane is supposed to leave, Caro?"

"Four o'clock."

♡♡♡

Angela proved to be worth her weight in gold in the kitchen. The night before, she'd served them a delicious dinner, and this morning she had yogurt, fruit, and granola parfaits for them and was standing by to fill them up on French toast as soon as they were ready. Caro skipped the French toast, but the men heartily tucked in, making happy, contented sounds.

"Angela, if I weren't already in love, I'd sweep you away," proclaimed Greyson, making her blush.

"Wait until my dad meets you," Nash told her with a wink, and her blush deepened. "Thank you for breakfast. We're heading out to go for a ride, and we'll see you later."

Caro and Nash echoed their thanks, and they all trooped out with the rottweilers on their heels. "Y'all're back to feeling loyal again, I see," Nash said to them as they nuzzled his hands for pats. "Good dogs."

Down at the barn, they took turns supervising how

Greyson saddled up Gene Simmons, and soon they were on their way. Nash started them on the same route he'd shown Caro when she first arrived. Lady G behaved and seemed to be over her infatuation with Gene Simmons this time, although she'd gone through the same shenanigans again when Caro mounted. It just made Caro laugh, but Nash had to warn Greyson to stand at least ten feet away.

Greyson looked aghast and asked, "Good grief, Caro! How come you don't end up on the ground when she does all that hopping around and making noise?"

"I was ready for it. The trick is to stay calm and loose." As soon as everyone was settled, off they went at a trot.

"Why do you guys go up and down in your saddles? Doesn't that wear you out?" Greyson asked.

"It's called posting and makes our ride smooth that way. You get used to it, so it becomes a natural part of riding and you don't even think about it. These horses would not be as comfortable as Gene Simmons if we just sat in our saddles at a trot. He's been bred to have a very smooth gait, where these horses are not. They're a lot springier and faster."

"Your saddles don't look like much compared to mine," he observed. "And not as comfy." He looked down and admired the padded suede seat beneath him.

Nash spoke up and said, "These are flat English saddles meant for jumping. There isn't a lot to them, so we can really feel the horse under us. And they're lighter weight for the horse. We'd never be able to rope livestock or carry a lot of gear the way you can with your setup. But on the other hand, you wouldn't be very comfortable jumping a bunch of obstacles in that saddle. A small one here and there would be fine if the horse is willing, however."

"I will never get enough of this sight," Caro exclaimed as they neared the pasture full of broodmares and their foals. "They've already grown. Aren't they wonderful, Grey?"

Nash stayed back next to Greyson and said, "Hold up here for a moment. Caro. How would you like to gallop by and give everyone a show?"

"Sure thing," she cried with a huge grin. She took off at a canter that turned into a gallop. Standing in her stirrups, she gave Lady G her head and led the broodmares and foals on a merry chase. Lady G had originally been bred for the race-track, so she was a fast one. She'd turned out to be better at jumping, however, and made a great hunter—much to Caro's delight.

"Gorgeous, aren't they?" Nash asked.

"The little babies or Caro and Lady G?"

Nash laughed. "All of them. This is like heaven on earth, Grey. We have our woman, and we live in paradise. Now we just need to start making some music again and life will be perfect." Then he added with a chuckle, "They're foals, not little babies. You'll learn." Then he sighed. "Just look at her. She's a natural—so completely fearless. By God, I love that woman. And I love you too. Come on, let's catch up to our wild woman up there. Ready for a lope? Just remember what I said about stopping. Don't let yourself pitch forward. Keep your heels down."

"Let's do it." Greyson was all smiles.

Caro was at the far end of the pasture waiting for them as

they took a leisurely pace up to her. She could see that Nash was holding Elvis back to a collected canter, and his horse looked anxious to run. Gene Simmons, on the other hand, loped along like he had all day and was content. She couldn't help but grin at them. As they got closer, Lady G gave a friendly nicker and pawed the ground. She was so ready for more fun.

The broodmares lost interest in their company and went back to grazing while their foals nursed.

"We're going a different way today, Caro. If you feel like jumping, we have another field of obstacles in this direction, and there's nothing particularly tricky about any of them, but overall, they're a little higher than the ones we took the other day. Grey, this course was designed with lots of space around the jumps for anyone who just wants to ride around on the flat. Caro and I will grab the obstacles until the horses start to look tired or we wear out… whichever happens first. Elvis is getting anxious, so I'll start." He turned Elvis into a different pass through a thicket of trees, not waiting to see if they would follow. He knew they couldn't resist.

Greyson was astounded by seeing Nash take off at a gallop on Elvis. The two of them exuded raw power and grace. Once they were all through the path and into the field, Greyson's jaw dropped as he observed Elvis sail over a fence and land smoothly on the far side, not even breaking stride as they headed to another jump. "Wow," he breathed. *It's giving me a boner just to watch that*, he thought. *Simmer down, or you'll hurt yourself on this saddle thing. Did Nash call it a pommel?* He squirmed a little in the saddle and thought about his sore muscles. *I wouldn't mind another one of their massages after today's ride.* He grinned.

"Nice sight, aren't they? Nash has so much fun with that horse, you have no idea, Grey. Giving him Elvis was not only generous of you but also a fantastic thing for Nash's morale. So anyway, I'm next. Just keep Gene Simmons to a steady lope, or if you need to slow down, that's fine as well. Just watch out that he doesn't take you under any low branches. Be careful!"

Lady G was ready to go, and they took off like lightning. Gene Simmons shook his head as if he wanted to follow his buddies, so Greyson gave him a cluck and a squeeze. As before, the pace was steady and comfortable, and Greyson really felt as if he was getting the hang of things. Trying to keep himself from flopping around while still staying loose, he watched breathlessly as Caro flew over the same fence that Nash had jumped moments earlier. *Nash is right. This is paradise. I don't mind riding on the ground though. I have no interest in flying over tall things like they do.*

Eventually, Gene Simmons seemed to be wearing out a bit, so Greyson pointed him toward the middle of the field and slowed to a walk. From there, he watched as Caro and Nash leaped over hedges, fences, fallen logs, stone walls, water hazards, and all sorts of crazy-looking jumps. Finally, when both the hunters were in a lather, and the riders' chests were all heaving from laughter and exhilaration, they decided to call it a day.

"Let's head back and give these guys a bath," Nash said.

"After that, we can all go swimming and then get ready to go. Did y'all enjoy yourselves?"

Caro beamed and laughed. "Of course!"

Greyson was still a bit goggle-eyed and answered, "That was one of the most beautiful sights I've ever seen. When you flew over that tall hedge thing, I thought my heart would stop, and then Caro did it right after you, and I almost fainted. How do you two have the guts to try stuff like that?"

"Lots of practice," Caro replied. "And it helps if you trust your horse. These jumps aren't particularly high, but in the beginning, you start with a cavaletti which can be just a pole on the ground—until you feel confident to jump over four, then six inches, then twelve inches, and on and on until you're ready for the real thing. It takes a while. And it's *so* worth it. You feel like you're flying. I do best on an eager horse like Lady G. Some horses need a lot of persuasion, and I'm not the greatest at that."

"Elvis loves to jump more than just about anything, so I feel like all I need to do sometimes is point him in the right direction and stay on board," Nash explained with a chuckle. "This horse has a lot of heart. I'm thinking of having our crew raise the height of a couple of these jumps a bit more so he has a little challenge. We'll see if we get around to it. Everyone is pretty busy with the mares and the breeding program we have. It's going to be crazy if Domino Pip wins the Triple Crown. I'm already getting hundreds of requests to use him." It was true that his inbox was filled with emailed requests and responses from their website, and the postman had dropped off a number of letters of the same nature. He needed to spend some serious time going through every-thing, and he would need help evaluating the feasibility all of that potential breeding. He was getting ahead of himself though. There were many decisions yet to be made regarding Domino Pip's future.

On the leisurely walk back to the barn, Nash's phone buzzed in his pocket. He fished it out and took a look at the caller ID. "Hmm," he said, grimacing. "Hey, Jerry. You have something for me?" He paused and listened. "Wow, okay. Look, I have to leave for New York this afternoon." Pause. "Yeah, the Belmont. Thanks. Look, do you think I could send Benny over with the trailer and he'll settle up with you? We'll take her for sure." He listened for a while and shook his head with a sigh. "Some people." Then he realized Caro was trying to get his attention. "Hang on a sec, Jerry." He looked at Caro expectantly.

"Do you need to pick up a rescue?"

"Yes."

"Then we'll all go unless it's too far away to make our flight. We can skip the dip in the pool, and the horse won't care if we all smell like horses. I'd love to see this happen. Grey?"

Grey nodded and shrugged. "Sure."

"Change of plan, Jerry. I'll be by in half an hour. We're just cooling down our horses right now, and they'll need a quick bath before we put them up. Benny and his guys can handle most of that."

♡♡♡

Just over an hour later they were heading back to Best Life Farm in Nash's truck with a trailer attached, a pretty little palomino inside. She wasn't much bigger than a pony at fourteen and a half hands.

"Wow. A twofer," Greyson exclaimed. "Why would someone give up a pregnant horse like this?"

"Two mouths to feed when they'd only budgeted for one, I guess. An awful lot of people underestimate the cost of taking care of a horse, and they don't realize how much work and expense horses create. My guess is they had no idea she was pregnant and tried to make her lose weight for a while. They were probably holding on by a financial thread and then discovered the pregnancy. I hope her foal is okay because there's no telling whether the mare has had proper nutrition. We'll have the vet check her out and do the best we can. Then we can just hope for the best. But don't be broken-hearted if it's a bad outcome. Sometimes that goes with the territory, unfortunately."

They unloaded her at the clinic, and the vet promised to keep a close eye on her while they were in New York. He'd proclaimed her dehydrated and too skinny.

"Poor little girl," Caro whispered and stroked her neck. "We'll see you soon, sweetie." She looked at the men. "What should we name her?"

Greyson answered immediately, "Dreamboat Annie."

"Aww. Perfect!"

## Twenty-two

When the plane landed in New York, a limousine sat waiting on the tarmac to take them to their hotel. However, as soon as everyone took their seats in the limo, they had a surprise.

"Hello, Caroline, darling. It's so good to see you. It's been too long."

"Mom! What are you doing here?"

"I found out just by chance that one of our planes was arriving from Kentucky today and gave your brother a call to see what time we could expect him. Imagine my surprise to find out it was *you* arriving without letting us know. I thought I'd give you a personal welcome, and I hoped there was nothing wrong that prompted you to visit unannounced. Anyway, I've had your room readied for you, but I see we have company as well. Please introduce me to your friends."

Caro tried to recover and closed her slack-jawed mouth.

Greyson took charge of the moment immediately by extending his hand. "It's nice to meet you, Mrs. Whittaker, I'm Greyson Foster, and this is Nash Keating. We're here in New York with Caro to watch the Belmont Stakes. Nash's horse is favored to win it. And if he does, he'll be a Triple Crown winner."

Smiling politely, Mrs. Whittaker released Greyson's hand with a nod and asked, "Well, isn't that exciting, Mr. Keating?" She shook Nash's outstretched hand. "Good luck in the race." Looking back at Caro, she continued, "You would all be far more comfortable at our penthouse than at a hotel, so I'll make sure we have rooms made ready for both the gentlemen as well." There was no question in her statement. Mrs. Whittaker was a woman who was used to having people agree with her.

"Mom, that's okay. We don't want to put you out."

"Nonsense, Caroline. It's nothing. That's why we have a household staff. Your father and I miss you and would love to get to know your friends better, so it's settled."

"Would you like to join us at the race?" Nash blurted out. "My father and I have seats in an owner's box."

Caro gave him a startled look, and her eyebrows shot up when her mother answered, "Why, yes. That would be lovely. Thank you, Mr. Keating. We're all horse lovers in this family. Well, except for Eli. He never took to riding the way Caroline did."

"It's Nash, ma'am," he said as he wrapped his arm protectively around Caro's shoulders.

Caro was trying her darndest not to whimper. This was a

train wreck. She knew she needed to let her parents know what was going on eventually, but she certainly hadn't expected to be ambushed by her mother at the very moment they set foot in her home state. *Why does being in a parent's presence suddenly make me feel like a naughty teenager? I'm a grown woman who makes my own decisions. But… in for a penny, in for a pound,* she thought and decided to forge ahead. "Do you remember back when I was touring as a singer with the band Chaos? Nash and Greyson are former members of the band."

"Yes, darling. I am fully aware of who Mr. Keating and Mr. Foster are."

Caro suppressed a gasp. "Did Eli say something to you?" She could *not* believe her brother would rat her out like that. If he had, he had some nerve exposing someone else's business when his whole marriage was a secret from the world—with the exception of the families of the two husbands. Her mother and father knew about Eli, Tanner, and Zoë and accepted the arrangement with grace. Caro figured it was because they'd treated Tanner like family ever since they'd met him as a freshman at Princeton and clearly adored him. On the other hand, they had never approved of Caro "running off to play rock 'n' roller" with Chaos, so her situation might not be as readily accepted.

Her stomach ached. She *so* wanted her family to like Nash and Grey.

"Mom, we've all become… reacquainted, and we're actually *together.*"

"You're singing again? I'm sure that's amusing, but please

tell me you're not going to go live on a tour bus and give eardrum-shattering concerts in dodgy cities. Didn't you get that out of your system?"

"No. I mean, not yet. Or maybe not at all. I don't know how to answer that, frankly. We haven't discussed performing together all that much yet. We've just been concentrating on our… relationship. For now."

Nash, who was sitting in the middle of the three of them, took his cue and grabbed Greyson's hand with his free one and held on. *No sense in sugarcoating. She'll either accept us for who we are or kick us out of her limo.*

Mrs. Whittaker's eyes flicked over the scene in front of her, taking it all in and skewered her daughter with a look. "Are you in some kind of competition with your brother, Caroline?"

"No! Of course not."

"Did Eli say something provocative that influenced your behavior?"

"Absolutely not."

Greyson's phone buzzed in his pocket, and he politely said, "Excuse me." He extricated his hand from Nash's and answered. It was the moving company with his piano, and they were apparently waiting at the gate to be let in. Greyson explained to them, "Angela will show you where to put it. I'll call her right now so she can keep the dogs out of your way and let you in."

While Greyson spoke to Angela, Caro's mother asked her, "When did you acquire dogs? Or does Mr. Foster also have an Angela who works for him?"

"Oh, um, no. We're all living together in the Lexington area at Nash's farm—and Angela moved there to cook for everyone," she said quickly. "Best Life Farm is where he has his racehorses—and his dogs. His father trains there, and Nash has a herd of broodmares and a whole slew of rescued horses he cares for and finds them good homes. It's a gorgeous place, and I've started riding again, and… it's all so wonderful." She ran out of steam while Nash squeezed her shoulder, and she noticed a smile on her mother's face finally.

"Caroline, if you think for a minute that your father and I would try to stop you from following your heart, you must have a very low opinion of us. I'm mostly just sad that you thought to come to New York and not stop in and at least visit with us. We see you so rarely anymore. We are fully aware that Domino Pip belongs to your long-lost love. And we are also aware that the man has graduated, so to speak, from making loud music to composing and producing. Furthermore, we know that he got an MBA in one year a while back from Northwestern and bought a bankrupt horse farm that he has turned around into a thriving business where they breed and train Thoroughbred racehorses." She looked at Nash. "Congratulations to you on your continued success, Nash." Regarding her daughter, who was blinking at Nash about the revelation about his graduate degree, she continued, "We were never opposed to a relationship with *him*. We just wanted you to settle down and complete your education. If you'd found a match within our circle, that would have pleased us, but it didn't happen, and we've never attempted to strong-arm you or your brother into marrying anyone. You know that. We merely presented a few men whom you summarily dismissed. I personally think that says a lot about your affection for the man. I did not, however, factor in Greyson. This is news, and I sincerely hope this arrangement has not happened simply because you want to do what your brother is doing."

Quietly, Caro explained, "We actually started well before Eli, Tanner, and Zoë married each other, and then we lost our way due to some unfortunate circumstances. But how did you know all this?"

"Certainly, you understand that your father has access to just about any information he'd like to hear about. And Nash called a few times with some very interesting and astute questions for your father. It piqued his curiosity about the young man." She regarded Nash again. "You've been pretty quiet, sir. What do you have to say for yourself?"

Nash cleared his throat. "The most important thing is that I love your daughter, Mrs. Whittaker. And we both love Greyson. I'm sorry we didn't contact you immediately when we knew we'd be coming to New York, but there's just been so much going on, we… Well, I'm sorry."

"Believe it or not, I understand. Sometimes things have a way of spiraling out of control when you least expect it, and I'm sure the possibility of a Triple Crown thrown into the mix makes things even harder to concentrate on. As for your rather unique relationship, I wonder what it is my husband and I have done to our children that they have both sought out such nontraditional matches."

Greyson chuckled, "Maybe your family has shown them that love can be infinite."

"Hmm. Am I to assume that you're all committed to each other the way Eli, Tanner, and Zoë are?"

"That's the plan, Mom."

"Well. I never. So at least you're not looking for *more* people to add to your… whatever you call it?" They shook their heads emphatically, and she looked out the window for a moment. "I used to wonder what I ought to tell our friends about Eli, but it seems everyone is far too interested in themselves to wonder overmuch about him. And he's all the way down in Kentucky, apparently for good." She looked back at each of them in turn. "I hope you know what you're doing. And I truly do wish you all happiness. This is even more reason to come stay at the penthouse, however. Not only will you have more privacy, but my husband and I also need to get to know you two gentlemen better. You are going to have to impress Mr. Whittaker, you know. He loves his daughter fiercely."

♡♡♡

LATER THAT EVENING, AFTER A DELIGHTFUL DINNER THAT WAS far less stodgy than Nash and Greyson expected, Nash and Caro's father had a quiet, but in-depth, conversation about strategies as well as the pros and cons of raising venture capital.

While they talked, Greyson gravitated to the Steinway

he'd discovered in the spacious living room. For a couple of hours and without ever opening a book of music, he played everything from classical pieces to movie themes to rock. He even threw in a couple of country songs just to be a little ornery and make Nash smile. As he performed, he looked sublimely happy and relaxed, and his mood seemed to cover everyone like a cozy blanket.

Caro and her mother sat and listened to Greyson play, chatting softly now and then. "You're so fortunate," Mrs. Whittaker said wistfully, "to live with music like this all the time. When you and Eli moved out, there was no one left to play. And neither of you ever had this man's gift on that piano. I am happy for you, darling, and I hope you enjoy singing again. That's your real musical talent. Your voice has a special quality that's not often heard."

Caro smiled, though inwardly she was surprised at her mother's compliment. It had never come up before. As a teen, Caro often sat and sang at the piano, playing whatever was currently popular rather than practicing the material from her weekly lessons. That had never won her any brownie points with her piano teacher, so it was good to finally know that her mother hadn't completely disapproved.

When Greyson tired of playing—finishing with a hauntingly beautiful piece by Debussy, he joined Nash and had a serious talk with Caro's dad, answering a multitude of questions. Basically, the older man put the fear of God into them. He narrowed his eyes finally and said, "I expect you to protect Caro's dignity as well as her tender heart at all times. That's if you know what's good for you." He let that sink in a moment before turning to Nash and asking abruptly, "What do you think your horse's chances are this weekend?" Apparently, the heart-to-heart was over, and they'd been served.

♡♡♡

CARO'S WING IN THE PENTHOUSE WAS TWO FLOORS UP FROM HER parents' suite, so she didn't have any reason to think they would be overheard at night. Her mother had just vaguely pointed them all to their "rooms," letting them know that Caro could show them where to stay. Naturally, they all trooped into her room, and that was that. "I'm sure no one really cares. And besides, Eli has broken them in pretty well," she announced with a smile as she removed Nash's shirt while he was undoing Greyson's pants and Greyson was unbuttoning her blouse. Between the unbuttoning and undoing, there was a lot of hungry kissing going on as well.

"Does this make you feel especially naughty, Caro?" Nash asked. "To be in your childhood bedroom with two men?" He slid his large hand into her panties and told Greyson with a soft moan, "She's wet for us." Looking at Caro, he asked, "What do you want to do? It's lady's choice tonight." His other hand was already wrapped around Greyson's hard, thick shaft as he kissed Caro deeply.

Greyson chuckled and whipped off the rest of his clothes. The others followed suit immediately.

"I'm feeling all mouthy, so let's move over to the bed and make a daisy chain." She scooted over on the large bed and lay on her side. "You do Grey, Nash, I'll do you, and, Grey, you can do me. I am feeling pretty naughty, and that'll get things going nicely." So they made a circle of sorts, each using their lips and tongues in the most exquisite ways. Caro loved watching her men pleasure each other as much as she loved giving and receiving it herself, so she stared as Greyson's hips flexed and squirmed while Nash pumped and deep-throated him. She was very close to orgasm when she panted, "Everyone stop for a moment." The men pulled away with sighs and groans. They too were nearly there. "Now let's shift around and reverse the chain." So now Greyson had Nash, Nash had Caro, and she had Greyson. It took some wiggling around and a lot of laughter, but they figured it out.

They continued in that position for a while, and then Greyson pulled away and gasped in a choked voice, "Shall we all come this way? I'm so close, but I don't feel like I want this to be over so fast. Caro? You're still making the rules, so…?"

"Too late!" Caro shuddered and writhed suddenly as Nash's mouth and fingers brought her over the top. "Ahh, wow. That was a good one, Nash. What were you saying Grey? Oh yeah… something else. You figure it out now. My brain just turned to O-mush." She flopped back onto the bed for a moment, breathing hard.

"She looks pretty ready to me for some double action, don't you think?" Greyson winked at Nash, who was eyeing Caro and Greyson like he was a hungry wolf and they were tasty morsels to be savored.

"Lube?" Nash growled.

With a big smile, Greyson leaped off the bed and went for his bag, quickly producing the bottle they needed. Nash grabbed it and scooted behind Caro where he carefully loosened up her bottom with his fingers and plenty of the slippery stuff. Caro purred like a satisfied cat as he stretched and fondled her, probing with one and then two large fingers. He kissed and nibbled her neck as he increased the pressure with his hand. "Now get on your knees facing away from me and slide down onto my dick. You can control how fast and how deep you want it this way, sweetheart."

Greyson loved watching Caro sink carefully down onto Nash so much, he couldn't help stroking himself. He knew how great it would feel when they were both inside her tight, sweet body. He almost creamed his hand, however, when Caro let out a long-drawn-out moan as she filled her backside with Nash's throbbing dick. He could see that her chest was blooming with a body blush and her nipples stood out like pink diamonds. She closed her eyes, and suddenly Greyson commanded, "Look at me while he's fucking that tight little ass of yours, Caro. I want to see your pleasure."

Her eyes popped open at his brusque order, and she could tell she was getting wetter by the moment. She reached her arms out to Greyson. "Make love to us."

Greyson scooted over on his knees and straddled Nash's legs. He bent down and sucked on Caro's sensitive clit, eliciting another protracted moan from her. He slipped two fingers inside and smiled as he felt the shape of Nash deep within her. Caro shuddered once again with an orgasm, and her eyes closed involuntarily. Greyson reached around and smacked her butt cheek. Her eyes popped open again, and she grinned at him.

"That's right, love. Keep watching." Greyson raised up and carefully fed his weeping cock into her hungry pussy. "Yesss," he groaned as he wrapped his arms around her. "I love you both so much."

Caro couldn't tell if she were coming again or still having one long, amazing orgasm, but the feel of both her men inside her was incredible. Wave after wave of pleasure poured through her as Greyson thrust in and out, rubbing her inside in the most delicious way. The thin membrane that separated their two erections was sensitive, and she felt every inch of both of them. Nash held tightly to her hips as he jutted upward over and over, and Greyson wrapped his arms around her, kissing her as he plowed into her. Faster and faster, deeper and deeper they rutted, until first Nash and then Greyson erupted inside her. It was a glorious outpouring of their arousal and their love. It was also a sticky mess that seeped out of Caro and onto Nash.

"We forgot condoms," Greyson muttered into Caro's neck.

"Eh. S'okay," she mumbled back.

Nash laughed softly. "Y'all are a trip. Anyone else ready for a shower?"

# Twenty-three

The next morning dawned clear and relatively cool. Perfect race weather without a cloud in the sky. Nash's phone drove him from bed, ringing off the hook. Everyone wanted a prerace interview with him. He answered as politely and succinctly as he could manage. Finally, he got a call from his dad.

"When are you going to show up out here, Nash? I have work to do and need someone to keep these vultures out of my hair. I'm so sick of the press and their asinine questions."

"I hear you. Stay cool. I'll be there as soon as I can, Dad. How are Pip and Jorge doing?"

"Pip is as calm as usual. Nothing much gets to that colt unless he thinks you're five minutes late feeding him. That crazy horse loves his food. Jorge, on the other hand, is a bit of a loose cannon."

Nash's antennae went up, and he asked worriedly,

"What's going on with Jorge? Is he nervous? He's not sick, is he?"

"Nah, just the opposite. I'm pretty sure he got laid last night. There were some groupies hanging around here a lot yesterday, and today he's had a sappy grin on his face since he swanned into the barn this morning. Keeps checking his phone when he thinks no one is watching."

Nash, who knew a lot about groupies from his days of rock 'n' roll, chuckled, "Well, good for him. I wasn't aware that jockeys had groupies, but I guess it makes sense."

"Oh sure. Those gals have been around for years. You just weren't paying close enough attention." Then his dad laughed. "And you were never *their* type."

Sighing, Nash said, "I just hope he keeps his head in the game long enough to win the race. Pip isn't going to do it all on his own this time. This is one helluva long race, and it'll take some finesse to do it."

"Don't I know it. I need to get Jorge to focus."

"Have you sat him down and tried to talk to him?"

"I haven't had a chance! Every damn time I turn around, someone sticks a mic in my face and asks me something dumb. I had to hide out in the bathroom just to call you."

"That would explain some of the background noise then." Nash heard something flush just as he said that. "Anyway, I'll get out there and see what I can do to take the pressure off. I know you have a lot to do."

Not wanting to trouble the Whittakers' driver or use any of their cars, Nash scheduled a car to come and get him. Over a late breakfast, he explained to everyone, "I need to go out to Belmont Park and provide some backup for my dad. The press is driving him nuts, and Jorge has his head up his a… I mean in the clouds today. I guess the groupies have found him, and the timing couldn't be worse for his focus."

"Can we help?" Caro asked. "We can go with you."

"Nah, you'd be bored standing around all day unless you want to do a bunch of early gambling. All of you ought to just come whenever you want—depending on how many races you want to see. The gates open at noon, and racing starts at two fifteen, but the Belmont Stakes won't be until between three thirty and four. You can get your seat tickets from will call, and my dad and I'll meet you all in the owner's box before the race."

"Well, I plan to bet on Domino Pip! I might even splurge a hundred dollars." Caro laughed. She was never much of a gambler, and even this amount felt decadent to her. "What about you, Grey?"

"I'll probably do a little better than that, but I've never been a big gambler either. That's always been Nash's thing more than mine."

Nash harrumphed and took a swig of coffee.

"Mom? Dad? Are either of you going to play the ponies, or are you just going to watch?"

Mrs. Whittaker looked serene and put together as she answered. "I love to bet on horse races. It's the one kind of gambling I enjoy because I feel—probably erroneously—that I might have more control over the outcome because I know something about horses. I'm probably kidding myself, but it's more fun than buying a lottery ticket or playing poker. To me anyway."

Her husband smiled fondly at her and chimed in. "I feel rather the same way. A friendly wager now and then is exhilarating, but some forms of gambling just seem like digging a hole, dumping in a pile of money, and then tossing a lighted match on top. At least with horse racing, you have the beauty of the animals, their incredible speed, and all the pageantry and tradition that goes along with a major race. You get some entertainment value for your money." They all joined him in laughing.

## Twenty four

After breakfast, Nash's car arrived, carrying him over the East River to Long Island. Even with traffic, it only took about a half hour. Nash knew that as the races got closer though, the roads would be clogged with people trying to reach the racetrack on time.

When Nash found his father, the older man looked like a nervous wreck. Nash quickly took over answering the myriad questions from the press and must have had his photo taken hundreds of times. He knew his dad needed to deal with getting Jorge sorted out.

Keith Keating found Jorge sitting on a trunk and smiling like a sap over some text on his phone. Jorge quickly pocketed the device upon seeing the expression on his trainer's face. "Hand it over or turn it off, Jorge. And then go talk to some of the other jockeys and get your head in the game.

Now! This is the most important day of your life, so act like it!" Then he stuck out his hand, making a *gimme* motion. "Your agent and I didn't schedule you for any races before the big one so you'd be fresh. *Do not* let us all down!"

With an expression that was one hundred percent more serious than it had been a few seconds ago, Jorge's face reddened. "Sorry, Keith. I'll get it together, I promise. I need to hurry up and go eat something anyway before we get too close to race time." He handed off his phone to his boss and went off to take care of his diet regimen. When he returned an hour later, he seemed like a different man. He smiled cordially and said all the right things to the press before getting ready for his big day.

Security was tight around Domino Pip's stall. No one wanted to see some creep pass a treat to the horse that could be laced with something. The colt was strictly off-limits, and Nash even told the press, "You can take all the shots of him you want—from a distance, *after* he'd been saddled up for the race and is with all the other entries in the paddock." No one was going to annoy the horse now by crowding around him with cameras. Finally, Nash announced, "Interviews are over now. We all need to get to work. We'll talk again after the race." He made a quick trip to place a bet on Domino Pip (trailed annoyingly by some die-hard—and very sticky—journalists) and immediately returned to the stable area.

Finally, after hours of checking and polishing tack and talking strategy with possible outcomes, it was time. Domino Pip's black coat gleamed like obsidian. The colt looked ready.

Jorge took his saddle and assembled with the other jockeys for their weigh-in.

The butterflies in Nash's belly were dancing the salsa in triple speed. "How're you doing, Dad?" he asked unnecessarily.

Keith Keating alternately fidgeted with his collar and cracked his knuckles. He gave Nash a weak smile and then answered, "The good Lord willing, today we'll make history, son. I just wish your mom could see this."

That felt like a stab to the heart, and Nash's voice broke as he said, "Yeah, Dad. Me too. I'm so proud of you though and what you've accomplished with Pip. This is like a dream come true only—without Mom." He gave his dad a sideways hug as they headed to the paddock area. Sometimes even the best things in life were clouded by grief. To comfort himself, Nash counted his blessings — he had his lovers together at last, he had his dad's success to be proud of, and he had this great horse. But his mom... *Better not think about that right now.*

With the jockeys all mounted, the colorful parade to the starting gate began. The crowd sang the words to "New York, New York" exuberantly and joyously off-key along with a Frank Sinatra recording as the horses appeared on the track.

"This is always such a beautiful sight," Nash commented to his dad as the entries were led out. "I'll never get tired of it." The horses themselves were magnificent, and the bright jockey silks added that extra splash of excitement to the tableau. Some of the mounts walked along politely on their own while others fussed and jittered around, requiring a firm grip by the pony rider to keep them in their place. It began as a slow progression. Then they gradually sped up to warm up the racehorses. They never got out of a controlled canter, however. At a mile and a half, this was one heck of a long race, and no one in their right mind would risk fatiguing their horse right before the Belmont Stakes.

Nash and his dad smiled and waved their way to the owners' box amid the sound of cameras clicking and shouts of "good luck!" More than one person brandished a ticket and hollered somewhat good-naturedly, "That horse of yours better win!" Bettors tended to take things personally, Nash knew—not that he had any control over the outcome. He offered friendly waves to those people who cheered for him. Finally, Nash and his father arrived at the private box, where they greeted Greyson, Caro, and her parents. After introducing his dad and trying to look a lot calmer than he felt, he sandwiched himself into the seat between Caro and Greyson. "I need the moral support," he whispered to them. "I've never been so nervous in my life." His dad sat behind him with the Whittakers. They all saw and felt the thousands of cameras pointed at them.

Each of them adjusted their binoculars as the horses made their way around the track to the far side. It was a huge racetrack, and there were no closed-circuit monitors to watch with.

The horses began loading into the starting gate, and Domino Pip took it in stride, slipping into place like a pro. The entry in the number nine position didn't want to go in, however, and the sight of the horse fighting to get free set Nash's nerves even further on edge. The crowd gave a collective gasp as the colt reared up and nearly unseated his jockey, but the handlers finally got him settled. As soon as he was locked into place, the gates flew open, and they were off.

The cheers from the stands were deafening.

Their strategy was to let Domino Pip cruise along until the other ten horses started to tire, and then he'd make his move. He was more of a distance runner than the others—they hoped. As Nash watched, he felt as though he could see each of Pip's long strides in slow motion. So far, so good. The horses all looked comfortably spread out along the far side of the track. This race started out with a long, straight stretch before rounding the curved end of the oval. Domino Pip, who hugged the rail, seemed to Nash to be fighting Jorge to let him run, but Jorge held him back. As they rounded the bend, however, a horse on his outside pulled over in front of Pip, crowding him into the fence. Nash was pretty sure there was some bumping going on, and he swore loudly. His dad hollered, "Foul!"

The crowd groaned as Pip visibly slowed down. "Is he hurt?" cried Caro, grasping Nash's arm.

"I sure hope not. That little shit ought to be disqualified for that lousy move," he stormed.

However, as soon as the bumping rider got far enough ahead of him to maneuver, Jorge pulled Pip's head away from the rail. Pip sailed between two horses and past the horse that had squeezed him. He flew by all the other horses as they thundered down the home stretch. He overtook the lead horse and kept gaining and gaining speed until he crossed the finish line twelve lengths ahead.

No one would ever doubt the black horse with the funny markings ever again. History was made. Triple Crown!

Jorge punched the air in victory as he began his cooldown run with Pip. A sports commentator on horseback tried to catch up with him to get his immediate reaction for the television audience as other news cameras crowded around the owners' box. Nash and his dad hugged everyone in the box and then grasped each other with tears streaming down their handsome faces. Viewers all over the world saw this and wiped their own eyes. The backstory of the spotted-faced, black-and-white colt that no one wanted at the yearling sale became legend.

Eventually, the pandemonium settled a bit, and they all made their way to the winner's circle for the presentation of the August Belmont Memorial Cup trophy and a blanket of white carnations. As the flowers were placed over him, Domino Pip raised his head and let out a loud whinny as if to say, "Yeah, this is me. I did it! I look good in white!" For the record, he'd also looked damn good in red roses and yellow black-eyed Susans. A collage of the three wins went viral instantly.

Domino Pip hadn't beaten Secretariat's 1973 record, but no one held that against him. Suddenly everyone wanted to buy into a piece of the action. The hours after the race were so chaotic with phone calls and messages from all over the world Nash finally made a new message that directed all calls to his agent and turned off his phone.

Domino games quickly began to sell out in toy stores. It became *the* game to play for the first time since the nineteenth century.

Domino Pip hats, T-shirts, and banners appeared everywhere as if out of thin air. He would have his own licensed action figure within a week.

That evening, the plan was to make their appearances at the victory party on the infield of the track. There would be music provided by a leading popular band, dancing, and lots of people who wanted to meet Nash, his dad, and Jorge. They were the men of the hour, for sure.

The senior Whittakers would not be joining them due to a previous engagement, but they made it clear that they were honored to have witnessed the race with Nash and Keith Keating and looked forward to telling their friends about it.

"While this is all very exciting, if it's okay with y'all, I'd prefer to leave on the early side and come back here to celebrate our own way," Nash said with a smile as they got ready to leave the Whittakers' penthouse. They planned to pick up Nash's dad and Jorge from their hotel on the way to the party. "I'll arrange for a driver to take Dad and Jorge back later whenever they want to leave. I'd guess they're both wired but exhausted."

Unfortunately, when they stopped to pick up Keith and Jorge, they had a rude surprise. Keith slid into the back of their limo all smiles, followed by an overly made-up and scantily dressed young blonde who had her hand firmly in Jorge's grasp. Jorge opened his mouth to introduce his date at the same time that Greyson burst out with, "Britney? What are you doing here?" Of all the weird things that could have happened, this one was about three hundred steps below last place in terms of what he'd expected to see.

"Hi, Greysie!" she squeaked. "Hi, Nash. Hi, uh, Carol. Nice to see you all again." She fluttered her eyelashes at Nash.

Jorge's brows knitted, and he looked at Greyson's scowl. "What's going on? How do you know everyone, Britney?"

Jumping right in to explain, Greyson's words stabbed the air. "We were *engaged* up until just a few days ago, but she wanted to get into the best man's pants more than mine. I'm not proud to say that I left her at the altar when she flirted with Nash instead of even looking at me during the ceremony." He didn't feel the need to go into all the other reasons he'd split. This explanation was sufficient.

With an incredulous expression, Jorge's head whipped around to look at Britney in the eye. "Did you plan this on purpose? What kind of game are you playing?"

"Um… nothing," she protested weakly. "My daddy just thought I'd have fun meeting the famous jockey for Domino Pip, so he set it up the other night so's we could meet. That's all." She stroked up and down Jorge's arm and made a purring sound. It wasn't the least bit convincing to anyone. "We drove clear across the country in record time just to see you…"

She started to whisper something in his ear, but Jorge pulled his arm away and narrowed his eyes. "You have some nerve using me like this, Britney. I don't even know what you are trying to accomplish. If you'd wanted to meet Nash, I'd have been happy to introduce you."

"We've already met," Nash said in a flat voice. "The pleasure was all hers."

Caro smothered a tiny gasp while Greyson and Jorge continued to glare at Britney. Nash stared out the window, refusing to return Britney's look. Finally, Jorge asked, "Do you have your phone in your purse?"

Britney blinked at him and snapped, "Course I do."

"Good." He raised his voice and addressed the driver. "Could you please pull over at the next parking lot you come to? We need to unload some excess baggage."

"Jorge, honey! What do you mean? Didn't last night mean anything to you?" Britney whined.

"Don't contact me again, Britney."

"There's a lot of that going on," Greyson muttered, not quite inaudibly.

Britney's lower lip pouted out, and she made a crying noise, although there were no tears—crocodile or otherwise—on her face. "Jorge, baby, you can't just leave me! What if I get mugged? This is New York!"

"Offer your mugger a blowie," Nash snorted. "Maybe he'll pay you." He still wouldn't look at her.

Britney gasped and real tears appeared this time. "My daddy is going to be so mad at me!" she cried. "He'll say I messed up *again* somehow."

Without any fanfare, Jorge waited for the limo to come to a stop, stepped out, and took Britney by the arm. He pulled her out, saying, "I have no idea what your father has to do with this, but I mean it. Don't call me or text me ever again. I will not be used." He got back into the limo and shut the door in her face. "Let's go to the party!" he nearly yelled and slapped out a drum beat on his legs.

"Don't worry, Jorge," Caro interjected. "There will be lots and lots of ladies who're dying to meet you tonight. You're a hot property!" She winked at him and was happy to see relief spread across his face. "And you look very handsome in your suit."

When they got back to the racetrack, the infield had been transformed with a huge stage and a long row of food-and-beverage stations. The music was loud and fun, creating a wonderful party atmosphere, and the dance floor was crowded to bursting with revelers, all gyrating to the music. A screen had been erected above the festivities, and the film of the Belmont Stakes race was projected on it, running on a loop.

As soon as the five of them entered the area, they were swamped with well-wishers, paparazzi, hangers-on, groupies, and generally nice people who were happy for them and wanted to bask in their success for a while. It felt like the Olympics, the Oscars, and Mardi Gras all in one place. Champagne was pressed into their hands from all directions from people wanting to make toasts and congratulate them. Everyone felt as if they were part of history today as they'd seen it happen with their own eyes. They would tell their friends and their families about it for years.

They posed over and over for selfies with their new "friends."

The five of them found it difficult to stick together. Greyson kept a firm grasp on Caro's hand, but Nash and his dad kept getting pulled away into other conversations. Jorge was immediately engulfed into the crowd where he was swamped with folks wanting to know about every step of the race and how it felt to be world famous suddenly. Everyone wanted to hear the story of the already-infamous rail bump and how Jorge had managed to maneuver Domino Pip out of the potentially disastrous jam. The harrowing difficulty of the situation seemed to grow more intense with each telling. Several attentive young ladies passed him their phone numbers as they made eyes at him. *Britney who?* he wondered to himself with a self-satisfied grin.

Unlike Jorge, Nash had a height advantage that allowed him to see over a lot of the crowd and catch glimpses of the rest of his gang. His dad never seemed to stop smiling, and that made Nash's heart swell with happiness. Caro and Greyson weren't swallowed up into quite as many conversations, although people were slowly spreading the word that they had also been part of Chaos back in the day with Nash. This fact raised their cachet tremendously.

Finally, after making nice with as many people as they felt like they could manage, Caro and Greyson hit the dance floor. The music was so loud it made conversation a challenge, so they just held each other and enjoyed the strange solitude the music provided within the massive crowd.

"I'll never get over how good it feels to have you in my arms again," Greyson said in a low voice directed into Caro's ear. She pulled back to gaze into his eyes and then kissed him deeply. With a happy sigh, she laid her head on his shoulder and let the solid warmth of his love seep into her. This whole day had been magical. She would never, ever take these men for granted, no matter what, but to have a day like this was beyond extraordinary.

After what felt like ages, the band announced they were taking a break and would be back on stage in twenty minutes. Caro and Greyson came out of their reverie and looked around for their party. They saw Keith holding court among a colorful crowd, and he was still smiling. Then they located Jorge, who was sitting on the lap of a woman nearly twice his size, accepting a drink from another one. He was apparently done telling his story and had progressed into the fun-and-games stage of the party. "Let's leave him to it," suggested Caro. "He appears to be having the time of his life."

Greyson snorted. "Yep."

But Nash didn't seem to be anywhere they looked.

"Maybe he had to go to the bathroom. Do you want to wait here while I check?"

Caro looked amused and answered, "Not unless you need

to go too. He's a big boy, so I think he can take care of himself in the men's room. We can try his phone…"

"He turned it off, remember?" Greyson said even as he tried to call Nash again. He shook his head almost immediately. "Still off."

They wandered around for another fifteen minutes, and Nash never showed up again. "You don't think he'd have gotten tired and decided to go back to your parents' place, do you?"

"Hmm, no. That doesn't sound like Nash. This is so weird because he's always so easy to spot in a crowd with his long blond hair and being as tall as he is. Let's go ask his dad if he's seen him."

So they shouldered their way through the crowd, winding around people to get to Keith, who was laughing his head off with a couple of men around his age. He appeared to be having the time of his life without a care in the world. When he caught sight of Caro and Greyson, however, and saw their concerned expressions, he sobered immediately and excused himself from his cronies. "What's up with y'all?" he demanded. "Aren't you having any fun?" He tried to smile at his own bad joke, but something about their expressions made him anxious.

"We were, but Caro and I can't find Nash anywhere. When was the last time you spoke to him?"

Keith frowned. "It's been quite a while. But maybe half an hour ago—or more; I'm not sure—I saw him over there." He pointed in the general direction of the main entrance, "Talking to a group of guys. But that was nothing new; he's been talking to people all night. I couldn't see Nash's face while he was talking to them though. It's kind of dark out here to see all that well anyway." He wrinkled his brow and asked, "Have you tried calling him?"

"We did, but there was no answer."

As Caro spoke, Greyson pulled out his phone again, trying the familiar number. Quickly his hopeful expression soured as he said, "Voicemail. He was getting too many calls after the race, so he turned off his phone and forwarded everyone to his agent." He looked at Caro, then Keith. "Now what do we do?"

"Maybe he went backstage with the band! He might be friends with some of them," Caro suggested brightly. "I can go see if they'll let me find out. I'm good with roadies. That's how I met you and Nash in the first place if you'll remember." She gave him a wink and took off without waiting for a reply. Unfortunately, the band was already heading onto the stage by now and getting ready to perform their next set. Nash would have reappeared as well if he'd been back there with them. She got as far as the stage and had a quick conversation with a couple of their guys. She came back to Greyson and Keith looking grim.

"What's wrong?" Greyson asked.

"I talked to those roadies, and one of them said he'd been asked to go find Nash to invite him backstage after the concert was over. He said he noticed Nash leaving with someone out the front gate. So he decided Nash was gone for the night, and he forgot about asking him. He didn't pay any more attention to him after that."

Greyson spun around and took off at a run. He dodged and shoved people left and right as he sped toward the gate, leaving a trail of disgruntled faces in his wake. Once outside the boundary, however, all he found was the limo they'd arrived in pulling up to the gate. Sticking his head inside the vehicle, he nearly shouted at their poor driver, "Did you take Nash somewhere?"

"No. You guys said you wanted to leave around now, so I just got here. I haven't seen anyone but you. What's wrong?" The driver doubled as part of the Whittaker security team and was always alert to anything that sounded like trouble.

"Nash is missing."

"Where is Ms. Whittaker?"

"She's with Nash's dad."

"Please bring her to the car immediately, and I'll alert the security team. Do not leave her unattended." The driver was not about to take any chances with his employer's daughter.

"Shit, you're right. I'll go get all of them. This is so weird. Nash would *never* just leave us."

Greyson tried to get Caro and Keith to come with him to the limo right away, but Caro had a different idea. She dragged Greyson to the stage where she'd talked to the roadies. "We're getting really scared," she told the guy she'd spoken to earlier. "Nash is gone, and this isn't like him. Can you ask the band to make an announcement for me?"

Just then, the deafening music began again, making conversation difficult. The roadie, however, was anxious to be of help and spoke into his headset. "We have a serious situation."

Less than a minute later, the music stopped abruptly, and a voice came over the loudspeaker imploring the crowd, "Nash Keating? Are you here? Please report to the stage immediately." People all over stared at each other in confusion. They all thought they'd just seen him and expected him to make his way forward at any second. But Nash did not show up. When nothing happened, the same voice beseeched the crowd, "If anyone has knowledge of Mr. Keating's whereabouts, please come forward. We have reason to believe that he may have left, and his party needs to know his whereabouts. If anyone saw him leave or who he was with, please step forward and speak to the man with his arm in the air in front of the stage. Thank you for your concern."

A pair of young women shoved their way toward the front and up to the waving roadie. One of them announced, "We were out front taking tickets and checking hand stamps, and we just ended our shift. Mr. Keating was heading toward a limo with some men in suits and may have left with them. I was sorry to see him possibly leaving so early because I wanted to congratulate him and take a photo with him. We didn't see him after our shift ended and we came inside to the party. That's all I know."

Clutching Greyson like a lifeline, Caro looked into his worried expression and said, "I'm scared, Grey."

"Me too," he replied. His face was as white as a sheet.

# Twenty~six

Nash had drinks pressed into his hands over and over. Champagne, whiskey, scotch, beer, whatever. He usually accepted them graciously, took a fake sip, and then surreptitiously deposited them on the nearest table as he moved on to another conversation. Periodically, he checked around to take stock of where his dad and his lovers were. This was not the night to get drunk and disorderly. There were way too many cameras around, and he knew how brutal the press and social media could be if he appeared out of it at all.

When he had a brief lull in his conversations, a group of three large men sidled up to him, and one of them announced in a puffed-up voice, "Mr. Keating, we're part of Senator Branson's staff, and the senator would like to speak to you and congratulate you personally on your historic Triple Crown win." That didn't mean much to Nash, but the guy acted as though he should be flattered. Nash didn't know who the senator was and figured that was because he wasn't from New York. "He is also interested in going into business with you regarding your horse's future… uh… *breeding activities*." The man got a smarmy look on his face as if that should turn Nash on for some reason.

*That figures.* "Where is he?" Nash looked around, thinking, *I couldn't care less about some pompous politician.*

"He's out front in his limo."

"Why can't he come into the party like everyone else?" Nash frowned at the messenger boy. "Doesn't he want to buy a ticket? The fee goes to charity, after all." *Cheapskate.*

"Well, you know… security and all that. And he has had trouble with his leg since his skiing accident last winter. Doesn't like to stand around making small talk. He tried calling you today, but you never called him back."

Nash narrowed his eyes at the man. "Tell him thanks anyway, but I'll pass. I'm not selling shares in the breeding program to anyone." *This sounds weird.*

Giving Nash a steely look, the speaker said, "You'd better talk to him if you know what's good for you and your friends —who are looking pretty cozy over there on the dance floor, I might add. But we could end them quicker than you can blink. There's a sniper with his gun pointed at them right now."

Nash's blood ran cold. The threat was obvious. *From a senator?* He glanced up into the grandstands and realized someone with a rifle could be hiding anywhere. "What did you say his name was?"

"Senator Billson. If you'll just step this way with us." The man took Nash's elbow in a vise grip that he quickly shook off by twisting his arm out of the hold.

"Keep your hands to yourself," Nash growled. *That wasn't even the same name… or was it? Everything is so loud.*

"Then keep walking." Another man closed in on Nash's other side. The third closed in behind him, hemming him in almost completely. The messenger boy kept up an inane stream of jabber, and he and his two buddies smiled stupidly all the way to the exit. As soon as they passed through the gate, two more men crowded around him. They'd been instructed to make it look as much as possible as if Nash wanted to be with them. The scowl on his face should have tipped off someone, but it was dark and the liquor flowed generously. People were too absorbed with their own enjoyment to pay close attention to whether Nash was happy.

When they reached the limo, strategically parked in a poorly lit area, one of the goons rushed ahead to open the back door. The other two grabbed Nash's arms at the same time as one of the newcomers stuck what felt like the barrel of a gun into his back. They shoved him inside the vehicle none too gently, and three got in with him, leaving the others to go get into another car.

*I am so fucking screwed.* Looking around the interior of the limo, Nash saw two men. The one holding a fancy walking stick in his hand was apparently the senator, and the other was… *Oh shit. Chase Hunt.* The limo, to Nash's eye, looked like it probably belonged to a ride-share company. It had none of the personal trappings of a privately owned vehicle, and the whole thing looked a bit worn around the edges. He took all this in within about five seconds. His heart sank as their driver sped away. "Hunt," he said in a flat voice, "and I assume you're Senator…?"

The men in the limo—excluding Chase Hunt, who looked twitchy and a little green except where he had a black eye and a purple bruise on his chin—laughed, sounding nasty rather than amused. The man with the cane explained, "There is no senator, dumbass. But to cut right to the *chase*"—he snickered—"it just so happens that Chase here owes me a considerable amount of money, and you're going to pay it for him because you helped ruin the happiest day of his little girl's life. You and your idiot friends stomped all over her joyous occasion like it was a joke, from what I hear. And now you're going to pay for that. I don't like it when my customers are upset, and I especially don't like it when pretty little brides get their hearts broken." He let that sink in for a moment and added, "And I had to fly all the way out here from LA just to make things right, so you also owe me for my inconvenience." He paused and looked at Nash with his beady eyes. "I think twenty million ought to cover things nicely, don't you?"

"Are you fucking nuts? I don't have that kind of money." Nash realized he was dealing with someone who was either extremely stupid or totally deranged, and it scared him shitless. *I have to stay cool*, he told himself. *Cool down.*

"Maybe not now you don't have it—though that's debatable—but we both know that your funny-looking horse is going to make you a fortune, and furthermore, I hear that lady friend of yours is loaded. Chase here says his daughter thinks you and that Whittaker woman are pretty close. Together, you're like Fort Knox. But I'm a reasonable man. I don't want it all… just my fair share."

Scowling, Nash replied, "So you're kidnapping me and asking me to pay my own ransom? Who does that?"

"I guess you could look at it that way. I prefer to call it a business transaction, but I don't expect to stick around and wait for you to come up with all the cash right now. I want ten million of it now. So we're going to take you to someplace safe and wait for the rest of the money to flow in. Once it does, you're free to go. That is *after* you sign a perfectly legal contract that gives me the first ten million from Domino Pip's future breeding income. The contract has been drawn up by my attorney, and I assure you that it is perfectly legal as well as ironclad. As you can see, I'm not a greedy man. You'll still earn plenty from that horse of yours."

"First of all, we don't even know if Domino Pip is capable of breeding. And second, you may have created a legal-sounding contract, but you can't enforce it by illegal means, you know." *I should shut the fuck up. I probably just made things worse for myself. Shut up, Nash! Just do what you can to protect Caro and Grey… and yourself.*

"It would be fitting for a guy who kisses the groom in the middle of a wedding to have some pansy horse who can't get it up for the ladies, now, wouldn't it? So I take it that sexy Whittaker girl is your beard? I'd love to get my hands on those tits of hers, especially since they're probably wasted on you." Nash's glare could have stripped paint as the guy continued with a nasty snigger, "So what have I done that makes it appear illegal to you?"

"You kidnapped me at gunpoint, asshole!" *And apparently, you're a loan shark, judging from your comment about how much Chase owes you. I don't believe for a minute that you're sad for Britney's ruined wedding.*

As quick as a flash, the fake senator smashed down on Nash's kneecap with the heavy silver handle of his cane, causing Nash to cry out as pain blasted through him. "Manners please! I never saw a gun pointed at you, Mr. Keating. Did you actually see one?" Nash glowered at him, and the jerk went on, "I thought not." He leveled a glare at Nash. "But since you're apparently averse to my reasonable offer, I'm rescinding it. The new offer is fifty million by noon tomorrow. No contract." He looked out the window. "Ah, I see we're here."

They had just pulled up to a warehouse in an unlit and unsavory area.

The goons dragged Nash out of the car, and he discovered that it was difficult to put much weight on his injured leg. He hoped his kneecap was still in one piece after that blow. He gritted his teeth, refusing to give the fake senator the satisfaction of knowing how badly he was injured. He called upon every last ounce of strength he had in his body to walk as normally as possible. One thing was certain—he would not be able to make much of a run for it, even if he were given the chance. The men he assumed were armed closed in around him once more. *I sure as shit hope that sniper has left the track by now and Grey and Caro are safe.*

They marched him into a shabby building, dimly lit only by the moonlight streaking through some filthy high windows, and slammed the door behind them. They were in a cavernous area that looked as if it might have one day been some kind of manufacturing warehouse, but now it was defunct. A few random metal chairs and tables sat in no particular order around the section of the interior where they'd entered. Open wooden beams and saggy old floors gave it a very dilapidated appearance. Piles of rubbish cast shadows in the corners of the space. Nash wasn't surprised that there was no electricity and watched as one of the goons lit what appeared to be a kerosene lantern.

"Hand over your phone," the fake senator demanded.

"Can't." Nash seethed. The cane was raised, this time over Nash's head, and he quickly hollered, "I don't have it!"

Immediately taken aback, his would-be attacker asked, "Who goes out at night with no phone?" He turned to his goons and ordered them, "Frisk him." He took out a gun and pointed it at Nash.

Several hands grabbed at Nash from all sides as he twisted and turned to get away from them. "I said I don't have it on me! Leave me alone, you idiots."

The friskers came away with nothing but Nash's wallet, and their ringleader continued to look perplexed, asking, "Why no phone?"

Glaring, Nash explained as if to someone with a low-level ability to reason clearly, "Because all the people I needed or wanted to talk to were already with me, and I had it turned it off. I was getting too many calls. This was a night to celebrate, not talk business or fend off stupid offers to buy into Domino Pip. He's not for sale, and I don't want or need any partners."

The rat with his wallet rifled through it and spat out, "All this fucker has in here is a driver's license, a few condoms, and about eighty bucks."

"We can always add pickpocketing and ID theft to your list of crimes if you decide to keep it," Nash commented with a snort. "I doubt the condoms would fit—they're not size small." They'd missed the platinum Amex card he kept hidden in a pants pocket separate from his wallet for security purposes.

Shaking with frustration, Senator Fake ordered his flunkies, "Tie him up to a chair."

Nash noticed that Chase Hunt had already flopped himself into one. He sat with his head hanging low as if he had no energy left or was in considerable pain.

"With what?" asked the man Nash was mentally calling Goon One. This guy was looking around the area with a vacant expression as if he thought a rope might miraculously appear. Goon Two seemed a little more on the ball. He undid his belt and whipped it out of his belt loops. Unfortunately for him, his pants instantly dropped, exposing his tighty-whities and pasty, hairy legs. Nash fought not to snicker and had to look away as Goon Two grabbed for his pants. If he weren't so scared, he would have laughed.

*These bozos have to be the worst team of kidnappers in New York. I wonder what would happen if I just walked out the door.* But then, Nash glanced at the very real gun barrel trained on him and decided to stay put until he had a better plan.

"Do something with your pants, Fred!" the ringleader barked. So Goon Two was named Fred. Nash filed that away in case the knowledge could be of use. "Where are the zip ties I told you dipsticks to bring?" He glowered at Goon One and Goon Three while a red-faced Fred hoisted his trousers and put his belt back on properly.

"Oh yeah." Goon Three grinned and fished around in his inside jacket pocket, coming away with a small sack of plastic strips. One look at them had Nash stifling a snort. The ties were only about six inches long and very thin. He'd seen the videos; he knew how to break loose from those things—if they could even manage to tie him up with them. He doubted the ties would even go around his wrists unless they doubled up on them, end-to-end.

Fred grabbed Nash and shoved him into a chair as one of the armed goons pulled out a gun, pointing it at Nash's face. "Put your arms behind you. No funny business."

Nash found he couldn't look at the gun. "I'm not laughing," he remarked, and that earned him a yank on his hair from Goon Three, who stood behind the chair. "Oh, you like my hair? Want to run your fingers through it?" he taunted in a falsetto as he turned around and fluttered his eyelashes. This flustered Goon Three so badly (because he *had* noticed Nash's beautiful locks with some envy), that he didn't notice that Nash had crisscrossed his wrists and made fists with his hands. Trying to strap the band around Nash's large arms proved to be an impossible task until it dawned on him to string two of the ties together.

Finally, Nash heard the unmistakable sound of the tie zipping closed and felt pressure on his wrists. He'd purposefully kept his wrists as far apart as possible, hoping he'd be able to free himself if he got the chance. He became somewhat dismayed when Goon Three then lashed his ankles to the legs of the chair. He also tried to keep his legs planted and not let the ties get too tight. Realizing that his abductors had no immediate means of calling anyone of his contacts on his phone to arrange ransom, he figured he might be there a while and definitely wanted to maintain circulation to his feet. His knee throbbed.

Once Nash seemed to be secured, the fake senator gave him a clop on the head with his cane, saying, "That was for the dick-size allegation." He and his minions moved away from the circle of light to have a confab. Apparently, they erroneously thought the darkness would muffle their voices or something because they didn't try to keep them particularly low.

Goon One asked in a whiny tone, "What are we gonna do now, boss? If we can't call one of his contacts, how are we gonna shake anyone down for the cash? And we can't even bust into his bank account without his phone."

"Yeah, well, I'm trying to work that out. Give me a minute." He looked over at Nash and raised his voice. "What bank do you use?"

With his head now throbbing nearly as badly as his knee, Nash grumbled, "Procter and Gamble." He blinked as the man nodded sagely and then turned away. Nash wondered, not for the first time, how this band of hooligans ever made it in the business of being loan sharks if this was all they could manage. They sure weren't professional kidnappers. *Maybe they usually rough people up for smaller amounts of money?* Nash wondered if inexperienced crooks were more or less dangerous than seasoned criminals—he could see it going either way, but he didn't really want to find out the answer.

Ever so slowly, as the jerks argued among themselves, Nash scooted his chair by increments toward the lantern. He wanted a weapon. Trying to be silent at it, he edged and scooted until he saw Chase Hunt stand up. His heart froze, and he wondered immediately what Chase had in mind. But instead of heading Nash's way, Chase stumbled toward the band of miscreants as he announced, "I know who you can call, and I can get his number right away."

Chase had a hopeful look on his face as if this idea might save his life. He had good reason to feel this way because as soon as the man with the cane saw him approach, he ordered his goons to beat the crap out of him. It was only when Chase kept screaming, "I know how to get you some *seriously big money*," that the goons were ordered to let up on him.

# Twenty~seven

As soon as his security detail called Mr. Whittaker, Caro's parents said good night to their friends and requested (ordered) everyone who was with their daughter to return without delay. So Caro, Greyson, Keith, and Jorge headed back to the Whittakers' penthouse. They were all terrified about what might have happened to Nash.

Greyson insisted on calling the police but was frustrated by their blasé response when they heard that Nash entered a limousine without duress. Explaining to them that the kidnapped party was the owner of the Triple Crown winner only created more exasperation when they answered, "He's probably out celebrating, and he'll be back when he sobers up."

Greyson was so infuriated that he wanted to lash out, but he kept his cool. They said they'd send an officer to the Whittakers' address as soon as someone was available. As he disconnected the call, Greyson muttered, "Yeah, when? Next week?"

Jorge had acted disgruntled when they pried him away from his admirers. He'd been looking forward to a long night of fun and frivolity. But when he realized that Nash's odd disappearance had the feel of kidnapping, he quickly turned serious.

With Quinlan Farrell, the head of his protection team, and a couple of other security employees present, Mr. Whittaker asked everyone, "What do we know so far?"

Greyson spoke up for everyone, saying, "Nash was seen getting into a limo with some men. He apparently didn't fight them, but no one knows how willing he was. The only suspicious character I can think of is Chase Hunt—Britney's father. She and I were engaged, as you know, and recently split up." He added that information for the security team. "Chase was what I'll call 'overly interested' in Nash and seemed to know about the Whittaker family as well. His daughter Britney showed up for the party with Jorge—it seems that she and her family drove all the way from LA just to mess with us. She was pretty upset when we left her on the side of the road. I'm pretty sure I remember her saying that her father would be mad at her for what she called 'messing up again.'"

Jorge interrupted with a groan, "I'm so sorry to have brought Britney into your circle tonight. I had no idea…"

"Oh, Jorge," Caro assured him. "It wasn't your fault. She may have been trying to get close to Nash again, but she's hardly a kidnapper."

"Her father sure could be though," Greyson stated. "He has a gambling problem and, no doubt, debts. There's no telling what kind of people he hangs around with."

The security guys then grilled Greyson for any tidbit of information that might prove helpful. After several minutes of this, however, Jorge's phone rang.

The jockey frowned at his phone and started to ignore the unknown caller, but Quinlan Farrell, the head security guy, barked at him, "Answer that and put it on speaker. Everyone, keep quiet. If it's nothing, fine. If it isn't, then we'll have something more to go on."

Jorge clicked on his speaker button and automatically answered, "*Bueno.*" He'd been answering the phone that way his entire life, even though his English was now impeccable.

The male voice on the other end of the call was silent for a beat and then asked, "Uh... speako Eengleesh?" There was the sound of a nasty laugh.

Jorge snorted. "*Sí,* asshole-o. Whaddya want?"

"Okay, look. Here's the deal. If you and your friends want to see Nash Keating again, we want fifty million dollars by noon tomorrow."

"How am *I* supposed to get that kind of money for you on a jockey's salary?" Jorge exploded into the phone. "Are you crazy? If you have Nash, let me talk to him."

Quinlan smiled at Jorge and nodded his encouragement. If they kept the caller talking, maybe they'd get some real clues as to his whereabouts. As he made a *keep it going* signal with his hand, the man on the phone said, "What is it with you rich people anyway? Always claiming to have no money." He made a disgruntled noise. "So no dice, Shorty. Cough up the cash, or he'll be donating his organs by tomorrow night. All of them. Either way, I get paid."

As Caro nearly fainted from fear, Jorge blanched, and his eyes narrowed. The idea of Nash becoming an unwilling premature organ donor made him sick. And he hated being called Shorty. Jorge took great pride in both his stature as well as his ability to jockey racehorses. "Who is this?" he nearly bellowed.

"Nash's worst nightmare." There was some guffawing in the background, indicating that more people surrounded the speaker.

There was a slapping sound, like two hands smacking together, and then someone muttered, "Heh. Good one, Bull. That makes you sound real badass."

Caro mouthed *Bull?* to Quinlan, and he pointed at her with a nod to indicate that he had heard it too.

Then a familiar voice shouted from the background, "Is everyone else okay?"

There was a lot of garbled yelling all at once, and then a deafening bang. The phone went dead.

Everyone knew Nash's voice. They all wanted to believe that he was alive—for now at least. But that last noise sounded an awful lot like a gunshot…

Caro couldn't take it. She collapsed into Greyson's arms and wept with fear. Greyson tried to be strong for her, but he had to will himself to keep from shaking. The fear he felt had never been more profound. This shit was real.

The security guy immediately contacted his technical team and told them to find out anything they could about a crook named Bull who might have a connection to a habitual problem gambler named Chase Hunt. He addressed the assembled friends and family then and said, "We at least have a name or a nickname to go on, and the next time he calls, we can get a better idea of his location." Taking Jorge's phone, he installed an exclusive app on it. "This will also help," he assured everyone. "When he calls—and he will—we'll be able to track his location. If he wants money, he's not going to let up. I don't think for a minute he'd have shot his hostage. Why he'd shoot someone else, however, is anybody's guess."

♡♡♡

ACROSS TOWN IN THE GRUBBY WAREHOUSE, THE FAKE SENATOR, also known as Bull, had bellowed, "What the fuck are you thinking using my name over the phone, you imbecile!" He pointed his gun at Goon Three, blasted a hole through the man's head, and slammed his phone down. "If anyone else has any great ideas about ratting me out, you're next."

He'd come up with his own nickname when he decided to become a loan shark, thinking that a bull shark sounded tough and menacing, and everyone knew that a bull was virile. He felt it suited him to a tee—when he actually more closely resembled a shar-pei with a face full of premature wrinkles. He was, however, ruthless and mean to the core, with a temper that rivaled a viper. He had a difficult time finding men to work for him because those who know him best feared his wrath and lack of reason.

Nash looked away from the grizzly sight of Goon Three while Chase Hunt puked in the inky gloom surrounding them. If Nash had been pissed off and indignant about being snatched before, now he was also scared. With the cold-blooded murder of Goon Three, the whole scenario suddenly had an alarming new feel to it.

Nash hadn't been clear about who had been on the phone at first, but the "Shorty" reference implied that it was Jorge rather than Greyson. That made sense, since Chase had put in a brief call to Britney before giving them the number. Britney would have known Jorge's number after their time together.

Nash tried to keep hold of the belief that Jorge would know what to do. He was smart and trustworthy, two qualities that might really help in this situation. He was also cool in a crisis, as they had seen when Pip was on the rails during the race; that gave him a real advantage over the kidnappers, who were racing around the warehouse frenetically, clearly in a collective state of panic.

Looking at Fred and waving his gun at Nash, Bull ordered, "Find something to gag that asshole with. Now! And keep your pants on this time, Fred, unless you want him to suck your dick." Bull guffawed at his hilarious statement.

Nash felt nauseated, especially when Fred yanked dead Goon Three's socks off, stuffed one in Nash's mouth, and tied the other one around his head to hold the gag in place. Now he was pissed off, disgusted, *and* petrified. He couldn't help but worry about Caro and Greyson too. *What if they've been snatched off to some other place?* He had no way of knowing the extent of the intended crime, but this Bull creep was far worse than he'd thought at first.

# Twenty-eight

Alternately pacing and clinging to Greyson for moral support and with nothing more constructive to do than fret, Caro finally turned on the television and flipped nervously through channels. She wondered if the news had caught wind of Nash's abduction after the announcement the band had made. Suddenly she called out, "Hey, everyone, come look at this!"

One of the gossip news reporters was showing lousy, poorly lit footage of Nash walking away from the Belmont Park infield with a crowd of men. The reporter's angle for his story was basically, "Look at this jerk. Here we are at this great victory celebration for the Triple Crown winner, and Nash Keating thinks he's too good for his own party. Here he is cutting out early with his buddies. He's probably going off to find some women and get high." Caro went to her computer, and she found that the same crummy videos and accompanying still shots were all over social media. Apparently, there were a lot of people who were jealous enough to slam Nash for the assumed crime of not celebrating properly. Speculation about what he was heading off to do was rampant.

"That reporter is an idiot," Caro muttered disgustedly. "He didn't even realize what he was watching! He could have called the police or gotten the license plate number. Anything! Instead, he just made up stupid lies. Typical." She scrubbed away the hot tears that poured down her cheeks.

The video shots, unfortunately, were not close enough to see much detail, but the security team studied them for clues. Most of the faces were turned away until Nash was about to get into the limo.

Grey spoke up and said with conviction, "That's definitely Nash, but no one else looks at all familiar. When the limo door opened, there might have been someone inside, but it was too hard to see who it was."

As they all sat discussing possibilities, two police officers arrived just in time to hear the second ransom call.

The security team had given Jorge instructions on how to handle things when Bull called back, and Jorge was ready. As soon as he slid his thumb across the screen to accept the call, Jorge flipped the phone into speaker mode. The security guys made sure the conversation was being recorded as everyone crowded around to listen.

"*Bueno?*"

"Hello again, Shorty. Sorry for the rude interruption. I had to get rid of an annoying insect that was bugging me," the caller said with a nasty laugh.

"Is this Señor Bull?" Jorge asked politely. He tried to keep his voice from shaking.

"Maybe. Maybe not."

"All I can give you is five thousand dollars. I don't have any more than that. I got a wife and four kids, and the baby needs heart surgery!" This was a big fat lie of course. Jorge had never been married and had no children.

"Are you shitting me? You need to talk to that Whittaker bitch and get her to cough up the cash. It's probably just chump change to her. And don't try to make me believe you don't know her. My guys saw you arrive with her at the party!"

"Why would she pay you fifty million dollars? We don't even know if you have Nash or if he's okay."

There was silence on the phone so profound, it had to have been muted for a moment, and then there was a gagging noise and some spitting sounds. Someone coughed, and eventually, the caller said, "Okay, I have him on the phone now. Tell them you're alive, Keating."

There was nothing but more hacking and spitting, and then finally, a hoarse voice asked, "Is everyone okay? Who's this?"

"This is Jorge Veracruz. Everyone here is fine. You don't sound like Nash Keating to me though, and I know him well," Jorge argued. "How do I know this is Nash?"

"I'm your boss, Jorge," Nash rasped.

"Everyone knows that." Jorge rolled his eyes. He knew he

was supposed to make this conversation last as long as possible, but this felt ridiculous. "Tell me something only my boss Nash Keating would know."

Apparently, Bull was becoming bored with this conversation and snatched the phone away from Nash's face, growling, "Look, you weasel-faced little pony boy, It's Nash Keating, alright? I want my money, you little shit. All fifty mil. I was going to give you your instructions, but forget that. I'll call you at ten in the morning and tell you where to leave it and where to find Nash. It's up to you to decide whether you want him to be alive when you get to him. We might just return him in pieces." The line went dead again.

Dejectedly, Jorge turned to the security guy and the police officers. They were already plotting the strategy for how to handle getting Nash home safely. "Did I do okay? That Bull guy sounded pretty mad and muy loco."

All three of the men replied with variations of, "You did great, Jorge." He let out a sigh of relief.

♡♡♡

AN HOUR OR SO LATER, THE SECURITY TEAM ANNOUNCED THAT they'd managed to trace the call. Police officers and private security men were deployed at once.

However, when the officers arrived in the predawn hours, it was to find that the fire department was busily trying to put out an inferno that had engulfed the ratty old warehouse.

Caro and Greyson suddenly understood the meaning of

the word terror when they heard that a dead body was discovered in the embers.

Keith's face went stark white, and he had to put his head between his knees. Caro shook like a leaf. Greyson only managed to keep it together by a flimsy thread as he whispered to Caro, "This can't be happening! It can*not* be Nash."

And then a next call came in, and the security team reported, "The person in the fire is apparently male, over six feet tall, and has a bullet hole in his head. *If* the body is that of Mr. Keating, at least we know he didn't burn to death."

Some consolation.

*Twenty Minutes Earlier*

Wanting to distract his captors so he could make his escape, as soon as they wandered off into the gloom once more to plot, Nash again scooted quietly toward the lamp. Realizing, however, that they'd been far too inept to keep eyes on him, he decided to go into sped-up stealth mode. He quickly maneuvered his wrists out of the loose zip ties and took off his shoes. That gave him the ability to slide the ties off his ankles. Not bothering to take the time to put his shoes back on, he reached toward the lamp and looked at how far he was from the door. He knew it would only take a second for one of them to see him in the full light of the lamp, so instead of continuing to illuminate himself, he grabbed and hurled the lamp toward his captors. It exploded on the nasty wooden floor and immediately set fire to the refuse that was lying around. While his captors stood, paralyzed by surprise, wondering what had happened, Nash limped as quickly as possible out the door. He knew he just had seconds before they would be after him, and he also knew they were armed.

Nash's leg throbbed with pain as he awkwardly tried to run away from both the fire and the gunmen. The area was deserted, and he had no phone, so coming up with a plan on the fly was proving difficult. He tried to stay in the shadows as much as possible, but then he heard shouts as Bull and his goons fought each other to get through the door first. They seemed more concerned with their own safety than with catching up to him for now, but he knew that wouldn't last.

"You were supposed to watch him, Fred!" he heard Bull shout, and Nash wondered if Fred would soon meet the same grizzly fate as Goon Three. "Where is that fucker?!"

Fred had no answer, it seemed, but there was no gunshot.

Seeing that his escape route was a mostly long, open stretch of parking area that provided nothing in the way of cover, Nash did the best he could by wedging himself behind a smelly dumpster next to a concrete block wall. From there, he tried to see which way they were going. Unfortunately, what he heard was, "Let's split up and each look for him." Apparently, they weren't all that stupid after all. That must have been why Fred still breathed. Bull recognized his need for Fred's eyes and ears.

The building was really burning now, and it unfortunately also robbed Nash of the cover of night. The flames were bright and causing quite the nighttime glow. Any minute now, Nash expected to hear sirens. If he did, it would be a welcome sound. Sadly, no one seemed inclined to report the fire. Certainly not Bull or his guys.

With his heart pounding so hard he could see his own pulse beating in his eyes, Nash heard approaching footsteps. It sounded like one man. He crouched down as low as his hiding place allowed and held his breath—both to stay quiet and to avoid breathing in the acrid smoke mixed with the stench from the dumpster. This wasn't an area that had regular trash service, that was certain.

Finally, there it was. As the flames rose higher and higher into the dark sky, the blessed sound of approaching sirens made his heart swell.

But just as he began to feel some minor mental relief, he was aware of the unmistakable sound of a gun cocking, and the lunatic voice of Bull saying, "There you are. You might just be more trouble than you're worth, Keating." Turning his head to the side, Nash found himself face-to-face with the barrel of a Glock.

At the sounds of sirens approaching, all the goons immediately gave up their hunt for Nash and raced toward the limo and backup car. Leaving the limo alone, they all piled into the car and roughly shoved Chase Hunt out of the back seat when he tried to get in with them. As they burned rubber getting away, Chase picked himself up off his ass in the parking area, swearing a blue streak. With no other means of escape, Chase looked at the limo and thought to himself, "Why not?"

He quickly hotwired the limo and gunned it to get out of there.

Just as Nash was contemplating his possible last living thoughts, a firetruck barreled into the area. Its headlights were pointed toward the fire, missing his dumpster hiding place and, unfortunately, Bull as well. They also missed the limo that was closing in on Bull and his hostage.

In a split-second decision, Chase decided to stop and get Bull into the limo, even though his first thought was to steal the car and get as far away from Bull as possible. France, possibly… or Tahiti. *But maybe if I help him now, he'll reward me later,* he thought naïvely. He lowered the window and shouted, "Get in the car!"

Glaring, Bull waved the gun in Nash's face and said, "Hop in, and no funny business."

Stiffly, Nash squeezed himself out of his crappy hiding place and got into the car. As soon as Bull pulled his second leg into the car —before he even had a chance to close the door—Chase smashed his foot on the accelerator. Bull lost his balance and nearly fell out. As he gripped the open car door, Bull felt the gun being wrenched from his other hand. Heaving himself into a sitting position with the door finally closed, he looked at Nash, who had the Glock now pointed at Bull's head.

Nash snarled, "Pull over right now, Chase. If you don't, you and Bull here will both have holes in your heads to match your buddy's back there in the warehouse."

"Believe him, Chase. Thanks to you, he has the gun," Bull croaked shakily.

Bull was far less scary with no weapon, Nash decided. Still cranky though. Nash was also relieved to see that Bull's cane had been lost somewhere in the commotion. It certainly felt different to be the one in charge of the situation. Nash wondered briefly what it said about him that he was happy about pointing a lethal weapon at someone. *It's all about survival, I guess.*

Cringing at the idea of having the gun pointed at the back of his head, Chase pulled over. Nash climbed out of the vehicle, dragging Bull by the arm. He aimed the gun at Chase's face until he was also clear of the vehicle.

Brandishing the Glock at them, Nash ordered the men, "Move away from the limo." As both Chase and Bull stepped out of the way, Nash got into the driver's seat and sped off. Remembering Caro's statement about escaping like Bonnie and Clyde brought a relieved smile to his face. It was such a good feeling to be away from those creeps at the warehouse, but he still worried about everyone else. The only thing he could think to do was to go to the Whittakers' place. If they were safe, that's where he thought he'd have the best chance of finding them. *I'm such a dope for not having a phone with me though.*

As he finally reached some traffic and approached Manhattan, Nash slowed to a more leisurely pace. He certainly did not want to be pulled over for speeding with a loaded firearm next to him—*and* driving with no license. His sense of direction kicked in and he had a decent notion of how to get to the Whittakers' penthouse, so he pointed the limo in that direction. Shaking with adrenaline, he looked around the interior of the vehicle, wondering if it had any kind of Bluetooth phone service—*not that I've memorized anyone's number.* Then it occurred to him to wonder if he was also driving a car the goons had stolen. *Lord, I hope not.*

Dawn was just starting to break as the buildings began to look familiar. He'd made it. He'd found the penthouse. Parking the limo illegally in an alley, he shoved the Glock under the seat, locked the doors, and took off for the lobby of the high-rise. He'd left the car running because he had no idea how to turn it off after Chase had hotwired it. The doorman greeted Nash with only a mildly startled look at his disheveled appearance when he gave the man his name. As soon as the doorman got his approval, he directed Nash to go on up.

By the time the elevator reached the penthouse, everyone had crowded around the doors to see Nash for themselves. Nash gave them all an enormous, though weary, smile as he took in their thankful tears and grins. "You're all safe. Thank God," he breathed out in a relieved whisper.

Caro threw herself at him, sobbing, and Greyson wrapped his long arms around them both, burying his face on Nash's neck. Keith shoved his way forward and swung his arm around Nash and Greyson's shoulders. Jorge grinned from ear to ear, and the Whittakers smiled, looking relieved. There were also a bunch of people Nash didn't know—who turned out to be the security team. After the immediate shock of seeing Nash more or less in one piece wore off, suddenly, everyone wanted to talk at once. They had a million questions.

Nash looked at everyone with love and asked, "Do you all mind if I get out of these filthy clothes and take a quick shower? I'll answer everyone as soon as I don't smell like rotten garbage."

And sure enough, they all became aware at the same time that he reeked. His previously beautiful suit was streaked with filth, and he had rips in his jacket and pants. He was also strangely shoeless. Everyone peppered Nash with more questions until Caro's mother spoke up. "Let's let the poor man clean up, and then we'll all find out what he's been through."

Nash was relieved that the elevator could take him up to Caro's floor. His leg throbbed horribly, and he didn't think he could navigate two flights of stairs. Caro and Greyson accompanied him up to the room, holding on to him as he walked. Had he been on his own, they might have noticed his limp, but they were crowding him too much. They both changed their tops while he showered, shoving the smoky dumpster smell into the laundry hamper.

♡♡♡

FIFTEEN MINUTES LATER, NASH REAPPEARED DOWNSTAIRS IN clean jeans and a comfortable shirt. His hair was still damp, but he seemed somewhat refreshed despite the dark circles beneath his eyes. While he'd been cleaning up, Mrs. Whittaker had an impromptu breakfast buffet set out in the dining room. There was enough food for at least twenty people, and their cook stood by to make omelets on request. Best of all, there was a lot of fresh coffee.

Not only were the security guys back in attendance, but they were also joined by the original police officers who'd been present for Bull's second call. Nash immediately told the officers, "I left a limousine in the alley around the corner. It has a loaded Glock in it that was used to kill a guy. I don't know his name, but he worked for a loan shark called Bull. The gun has my prints on it because I took the weapon from its owner after he'd used it. It's under the front seat of the car. I don't know whether the vehicle is stolen or belongs to Bull, but Bull and Chase Hunt are on foot somewhere in the vicinity of the warehouse fire I escaped from—unless they got someone to pick them up. Given the kind of losers Bull has working for him, I kind of doubt they came back to retrieve him though."

Naturally, this statement spurred a multitude of questions, and Nash patiently answered each one.

It took a couple of hours for the police to get the full picture of what happened, and when they were all done, Nash asked the Whittakers, "Do you have a doctor you could recommend? I need someone to take a look at my knee."

I t turned out that Nash's kneecap was not shattered by Bull's blow with his cane, so lots of ice and a few painkillers did the job of fixing him up.

Chase Hunt and Bull were apprehended, just as Nash predicted, not far from the warehouse fire. They were discovered having a brawl in the middle of the street. Chase was accusing Bull of being incompetent, and Bull was cursing at Chase for being stupid. They were truly made for one another.

Chase sang like a canary and got some favorable treatment after he explained in meticulous detail everything he knew about Bull's loan shark operation and the murder of Goon Three. It was discovered, however, that Chase had a long history of fraud and scamming people with his wife and daughter. His wife had already escaped to parts unknown by the time this came to light.

Britney tried to continue dancing, but she eventually got too lazy and out of shape when no one would hire her. She had developed a reputation for constantly being late to rehearsals, and no one wanted to put up with that. She eventually took a job in a movie theater cleaning up spilled drinks and popcorn. At least she saw a lot of movies that way. But when people asked, she told them she had a job in the film industry. In time, she found someone who was enamored with her fake boobs enough to marry her, and they stayed married for two whole years.

Bull was charged with kidnapping—helped by the video that had circulated in the press. He also faced murder charges, along with several other nasty crimes—enough to put him in the penitentiary for life.

There was momentary discussion about charging Nash with setting the warehouse fire but given his life-or-death circumstances and the fact that the building owner didn't give a shit, that never happened. There was no intent of arson —just escape. It had saved the owner the cost of demolition, and he didn't even plan to file an insurance claim.

# Thirty-two

Once they said their goodbyes to the Whittakers, promised to visit soon, and extended an open invitation to Best Life Farm, Caro, Greyson, and Nash happily returned to Kentucky. Nash threw himself into figuring out the ins and outs of managing Domino Pip's career.

"What do you think about continuing to race him, Dad? Are you for or against the idea? He's still young and fit, but I don't want anything to happen to him before we stand him to stud. If all goes well, we could be looking at over twenty years of good breeding time—depending on the success or failure of his progeny."

"On the other hand, son, we could be missing out on some great wins if he still races, but I understand what you're saying. If he'd been gelded like some of those jerks who didn't want him recommended, then I'd say let's race him for sure, but there is always the risk of injury or worse. So I think it's time to focus on the breeding program too." He laughed and continued, "I know we're going to be inundated with buy-in requests. We'll need to stand firm in our resolve to keep it in the family."

"I agree," Nash said with a grin. So that part of Domino Pip's future was settled at least.

"I have another question for you, Dad. This isn't related to Pip; it's about Elvis. Grey said you knew all about him sending the horse to me, and yet you let me stew about how Elvis showed up for months. Why?"

"Son, look. I made a promise to Greyson, and a promise is a promise. I didn't know until he told me the other day that a letter had been lost. I figured he'd had his reasons for the secrecy, and I didn't understand that it was all just a mix-up. Maybe if I had said something, it would have straightened things out between you sooner, and I apologize to you for that—but not for keeping quiet the way I promised to do."

Nash nodded pensively. "I don't know… maybe it all happened the way it did for a reason. We needed Caro too, and I wouldn't have known how to contact her. Maybe Greyson could have, but… no sense worrying about it. We're all together now, and we're happy."

"And that's what's important," Keith agreed.

They also decided to up the security around the farm, but that posed a new conundrum because Caro had proposed another interesting idea. One that she personally wanted to spearhead.

Shortly after they'd arrived home, Caro invited her brother Eli, his husband Tanner, and wife Zoë to Best Life

Farm for a big family cookout, with swimming and pony rides for anyone who was interested. Greyson also decided it would be a wonderful opportunity to have his family drive down from Indiana, and he'd be able to introduce everyone. The guest list grew and grew as friends, nannies, and mannies were all added to the mix, but the result was a truly incredible day. Tanner and Zoë especially enjoyed having a social event that the press was not allowed to attend.

Besides everyone's delight in getting together, two days prior to the party, Dreamboat Annie had decided to give birth to her foal—a tiny palomino filly whom they immediately named Blondie. As Greyson explained with a laugh, "Her name was preordained."

The vet had proclaimed the new arrival fit as a fiddle, much to everyone's relief.

Dreamboat Annie displayed her amazingly sweet nature by allowing the children in—chaperoned—one at a time to admire little Blondie. The kids brought the new mama chunks of carrot and stroked her neck, and the gentle little mare not only allowed it, but she also seemed to be proud of her achievement. She was a loving mama who kept a watchful eye on her foal. The children were spellbound and looked on with big fascinated eyes.

Caro took all this in and began to formulate an idea.

♡♡♡

"I HAVE A PLAN THAT I'VE BEEN RESEARCHING, AND I WANT TO run by you both and Keith," Caro announced one morning as they were all getting dressed.

"Sure. We can talk to him over breakfast. You've probably noticed how much time he's been spending here for dinners and breakfasts. I don't even think he goes home anymore." Nash wiggled his eyebrows and continued, "He seems rather enamored with the lovely Angela."

Laughing, Caro agreed. "Yes, I've noticed that she's bought some new clothes and recently added pretty high-lights to her hair. She has a much more, shall we say, satisfied demeanor too."

"Well, I'm all for it. She's nice, and if she makes my dad happy, she makes me happy."

Greyson chuckled. "Those crazy kids."

"Angela is only around forty-five. She lost her husband when he was deployed to Afghanistan, and they never had kids, so this is wonderful for her."

They all trooped into the dining room, where Keith was reading and sipping coffee. He looked up with a relaxed grin on his handsome face. "Morning!"

Just then Angela swooped into the room with a Belgian waffle on one plate, and an omelet on the other that she set down. Looking a little surprised, she exclaimed, "Oh! I didn't know y'all were up yet. I'll just go make some more waffles, or... um, here, someone, take this." She attempted to pass the beautiful omelet to one of them.

"Nonsense, Angela," Caro soothed her. "Enjoy your

breakfast with Keith, and then you can get us something. We can enjoy our coffee and juice first. We're in no hurry."

Angela blushed, but she sat down.

Nash broke the ensuing silence by saying with a grin, "Welcome to the family, Angela."

Her jaw dropped at the same time Keith spluttered. But he quickly recovered himself, and announced, "She's a treasure," as he beamed at everyone. Angela's blush deepened, and she ducked her head. Keith leaned over and kissed her cheek.

"We're delighted for you," Caro assured them. Then she looked at Keith and ordered with mock authority, "Just don't go stealing the best cook in Kentucky. We'd all starve if it were left up to me, and I don't know how well these two manage in the kitchen."

"Oh, go on." Angela giggled. Then she sheepishly asked, "Do you have any objection, Caro, if I move out and into Keith's house with him? We'd have a lot more room over there, and I would still be close enough for all the cooking here."

"Just don't go taking my dogs with you." Nash laughed. "The traitors."

"Whatever makes you happy works for us," Caro agreed with a smile. "Anyway, your love life is your business, and we respect that. I have something else to discuss, however." She looked to make sure she had everyone's attention. "I've been researching equine therapy programs recently. I think it's time the Mötley Crüe had more of a job to do than keeping their pasture mowed." Everyone smiled at the image of those horses happily grazing on the beautiful Kentucky bluegrass. "What do you all think about starting a program for autistic kids?" Her excitement was apparent as her thoughts poured out. "The kids learn skills and gain responsibility, and they are often soothed by the nature and sheer size of the horses. We could match each of them up to their very own, or we could rotate them around—I'm not sure, but we have so many great horses out there who'd love the attention as much as the kids would love to give it. Maybe it could be a weekly thing."

"Are you suggesting we teach them to ride?" Nash asked. "We'd certainly have to look into insurance issues for something like that."

"Eventually, if they want to ride, yes. And we can certainly afford insurance. If not, they can groom the horses and just have a friend. I'm sure each of the kids will have different needs and challenges. I'd love to look into it more closely, but I need to have everyone on board with this."

Keith looked at his son and smiled. "I think she's onto something special, Nash, what do you think?"

"I think we need to look seriously at liability issues. The therapy program will have to be a separate corporate entity in case anyone was ever, perish the thought, injured by a horse. It's pretty obvious we're going to be making a shit ton of money with Pip, and we don't want any lawsuits, frivolous or otherwise, from greedy parents."

Greyson grimaced and muttered, "I've sure had enough of greedy parents." Then his expression brightened up, and he added, "Maybe some of the kids would also like music lessons."

"I love that idea, Grey! Music and horses are two of the greatest pleasures I can think of, and it would be wonderful to share them with kids who have special needs." Caro didn't want her plans to worry everyone, so she continued, "I can speak to a lawyer about forming a corporation, and I'll get some advice about insurance. There are several programs like this around the country, so I'll talk to them about what works and what doesn't. I just think this would be a match made in heaven, and it would give the horses a purpose. Some of them need jobs to be happy."

So over the next weeks, Caro's time was spent commuting now and then to Frankfort when Zoë needed her help with the literacy foundation and researching equine therapy programs. In truth, Zoë's foundation didn't require a lot of effort from Caro at this point, so it all worked out great. Knowing that Caro needed to lead her own life, Zoë also made sure not to monopolize her. She was the best of friends in that way.

# Thirty-three

A couple of weeks after Domino Pip's famous Triple Crown win and the story breaking about Nash's subsequent abduction—clearing up any notion that he felt he was "too cool for his own party"—Nash received an interesting phone call. While it seemed as if he'd heard everything so far from legitimate reporters, nosy tabloids, a few hungry authors, and lots of folks who claimed to be related to him and wanted to cash in on his notoriety (and fortune), this offer sounded like fun, and Nash couldn't wait to share the news with his dad, Caro, and Greyson.

Over dinner that night, he announced, "I got a call today from a couple of movie producers. They're the independent production house called Twenty-First Century Wolves that recently won the Oscar for Best Movie, so I know they're legit. They want to make a movie about Domino Pip and the subsequent drama that followed. They'd first send someone to interview all of us to write the screenplay, and then we'd have to endure having a movie crew here for a while, but it might be fun. What do y'all think?"

Greyson's eyes lit up, and he answered, "I love the idea, but only under one condition."

"What's that?"

"That you, Caro, and I have complete control over the music. We compose the theme, title music, background clips, all of it. Well, maybe not sound effects because that's another thing, but wouldn't this be great if we could make an entire soundtrack for a movie? I've always wanted to."

"I think that's a brilliant idea," Caro added. "We're not Chaos anymore though, so how about a new name for our trio?"

Nash got a wide grin and answered, "Passion."

"Yes!" Greyson and Caro agreed.

That afternoon Nash left for a while to do a mysterious errand. That night he revealed to Caro and Greyson what he'd done. He'd found a talented tattoo artist who fixed his broken heart. Now the tattoo showed two sides of the heart bisected by a flowing ribbon that was inscribed with their names in a flowing script.

"You told me you'd fix it, and you did," he told his lovers. "And now my broken heart is healed. I wanted to celebrate how much love I have for both y'all." He kissed them one after the other. "And it's still a reminder to me to do the right thing."

♡♡♡

IT DIDN'T HAPPEN OVERNIGHT, BUT EVENTUALLY, BEST LIFE FARM added a small building that included a music room, a business office, and playrooms for various ages. They hired a dedicated staff of people who were well educated in how to work with autistic kids, and the program became enormously successful. The Mötley Crüe never looked so good with all their lovely grooming and attention, and Greyson was in his element giving piano lessons to a few of the kids. The kids thrived and bloomed, and their parents were eternally grateful for a program that they both enjoyed for free and their children adored. It wasn't without the occasional drama, but it made a big difference in the lives of families who had special kids.

After the initial movie about Domino Pip's miraculous story and Nash's misadventures was completed and won rave reviews, the Twenty-First Century Wolves decided to also make a documentary about the Best Life Farm Equine Therapy Program. It garnered them a second Academy Award. The guys who ran the studio became Hollywood royalty.

Nash, Caro, and Greyson's ensemble Passion also grew successfully. They found a new calling in composing, performing, and producing, and this gave them an incredible sense of accomplishment. Their only problem was that there was always something keeping them busy, and there weren't enough hours in the day.

Without fail, however, they religiously took out time at least three days a week to ride their horses—often more when they could. It was their favorite way to relax, and Greyson became quite the horseman under Nash and Caro's tutelage. He never wanted to learn to jump, however, preferring to stay earthbound with Gene Simmons. It worked for them.

# Thirty-four

A year after they'd all moved in together, Greyson and Nash were adjusting their ties and pinning their boutonnieres to their lapels. "It sure is a lot more fun and feels way better to be getting ready for *this* wedding, doesn't it?" Greyson asked.

"You said it. And I couldn't be happier. Ready to head out there?" Nash clapped Greyson on the back. "Don't forget your lines."

"Don't worry. I've rehearsed them over and over, and I can always read them."

They'd hired a local carpenter to build a picturesque gazebo on the property just for the purpose of this wedding, and it was now liberally festooned with seasonal flowers. Their friends and families had already gathered in front of it in rows of white chairs where everyone looked splendid and happy. It was a sparkling, early-fall day, so the colors were just beginning to show on the trees, making the whole farm look like a painting.

Greyson and Nash took their places next to Nash's dad, and they turned to look down the center aisle where Caro, looking delicious as always, walked in time to the music toward them. She winked at her men and stood to the side.

The music grew louder as it changed to Mendelssohn's wedding march, and everyone stood. Angela, dressed beautifully in a tea-length ivory gown, made her procession toward Keith on the arm of her older brother. Her smile seemed to light up the world.

When the couple stood before him, the newly ordained officiant Greyson welcomed everyone to the wedding. Nash was his dad's best man, and he stood looking proud at his father's side. His thoughts drifted as they often did, to his mother, and he mused to himself, *She would have approved of this, and she'd have loved it.* He felt a calm sense of peace looking at the adoration in his father's eyes.

♡♡♡

LATER THAT NIGHT, NASH BROACHED A TOPIC THEY'D TOUCHED on a few times, never making any headway with it. The guests had departed hours earlier, and the three of them were relaxing in the living room, having a rare night of quiet—save for Greyson's soft piano playing. There was a lovely blaze going in the fireplace, and the dogs were all sacked out in front of it. This was a homey, domestic scene that Nash loved but he'd never expected. His heart felt full to bursting with contentment.

"How do y'all feel about our commitment?" he suddenly asked.

Greyson stopped playing the piano, and Caro looked up from her book. They regarded him with mild surprise. Caro was the first to speak up, and she asked, "Are you referring to us being committed to each other? If so, I think our actions already prove that we're in this forever, Nash."

"Yes, that's true, and it is what I'm referring to, but do you need any kind of formal promise, document, whatever to make us official?" He wondered if he had a case of wedding fever.

Greyson snorted. "Are you proposing, Nash? If so, that sounds a little weak. You can do better than that."

"Do I need to propose to y'all? I'm just checking your pulses, so to speak. That's all. And what about having kids? We all enjoy them. Do we want some of our own?"

Caro took a deep breath. "Quite honestly, I used to think I wanted to have a couple of them, but over the years, I've sort of lost that feeling. Maybe it's because of my wonderful nieces and nephews and the kids we see here all the time, but I don't have any burning desire for any of my own, actually. I hope that doesn't make me sound terrible. And if it's a deal-breaker for either of you guys, I'm certainly still open to discussing it."

"Our part in making a baby is way easier than yours, Caro," Greyson observed. "If it's not something you want to do, then we shouldn't pressure you." He looked at Nash. "How do you feel about it?"

"Kind of like Caro. I think we're doing great the way we are, and I've never seen myself as a father, actually. I just want to make sure I'm not expecting either of you to miss out on something you'll regret. But I also have no idea how you tell a kid he or she has three parents. That just seems awkward to me."

"I think we should just continue the way we are," Greyson said with a nod. "We're happy, busy with things we love to do, we have extended family we cherish, and I personally don't need anything more either. I don't need a piece of paper to prove how much I love both of you. And we've already written our wills, made each other power-of-attorney for health issues, and given access to medical records. I'm not sure what else we need or how a three-way marriage would work anyway. There isn't any way to make one legal… yet."

Caro added, "Tanner and Zoë made a verbal promise privately to Eli after they were married. It was basically so he'd feel as important and included as possible after being so devastated by thinking he'd lost Tanner. Eli told me about it, and it was beautiful. But we've always come together as equal parts of the three, so it's a different story for us."

"Do we need to make vows?" Nash pushed.

"Only if one of us needs them. But I think we're already a done deal," she said. "Do you need vows, Nash? You're the one bringing it up."

"I don't need them. Just checking." He grinned. "So how

about we all show each other how much we love one another? Shall we head to bed?"

"I'm up for that," Greyson said with a soft laugh.

"Let's go," Caro agreed.

Nash let the dogs out one last time and then met Caro and Greyson in the bedroom a few minutes later. He found them already proclaiming their love to one another in the most carnal way. "Sorry, buddy, we couldn't wait," Greyson said with a groan as Caro deep-throated him. Nash stood spellbound for a moment, enjoying the sight of the man and woman he loved so dearly. Greyson stood next to the bed, grasping the headboard for support while Caro knelt in front of him. Their sculpted bodies seemed to gleam in the moonlight that poured in from the windows.

"You're both so beautiful," Nash whispered. He approached them and stroked their heads. "And so precious to me. When I lived here by myself, I used to dream of the two of you, but it was never as good as the reality."

Caro tried to smile around Greyson's dick but found that her mouth was too full. She gave a little nod instead and made an affirmative noise in her throat, causing Greyson to groan again.

Through his groan, Greyson murmured, "Very true. I used to do the same thing. We're so lucky we managed to find our way back together."

"We can thank Elvis and Pip for that." Nash chuckled. "God, life is good."

Caro pulled off of Greyson and complained, "You're

wearing too many clothes, Nash. Let me suck you too. Please."

Nash's clothes disappeared in a rush. He sidled up next to Greyson and placed a hand on his face. Drawing him forward, Nash kissed him deeply. Their tongues united and clashed, in and out, almost dueling.

Caro popped off of Greyson for a moment and engulfed Nash, satisfied by his immediate groan of approval. She clasped both of them in her hands and used her mouth back and forth between them, over and over, stroking and licking. She sucked and kissed them until they both gasped at her to stop before they came in her face.

"I need to be inside you, Caro," Nash demanded.

"Me too," Greyson agreed in a strained voice.

"Shall we try the thing?" Caro asked. "This seems like as good a time as any, and I'm up for a little adventure."

Knowing exactly what she meant because they'd discussed this possibility a few times, Greyson directed her, "Lie back on the bed first so we can loosen you up. I think at least two orgasms are recommended, don't you agree, Nash?"

"I like the sound of that," she purred. Caro made herself comfortable while Nash went in search of the bottle of lube— finally finding it in the bathroom—and Greyson set his efforts toward giving Caro the best head she'd ever experienced. He sucked and licked, prodded and probed, and basically made a banquet of her.

Within minutes, Caro was a squirming mess on the bed, shouting his name over and over. Nash stood by and chuckled at their combined enthusiasm. He grinned as Caro writhed in ecstasy, knowing firsthand just how talented Greyson was with his mouth and fingers. Idly he wondered if it had to do with all that piano playing. *But then guitar playing also limbers up my fingers, so…* He chuckled to himself. *And I'm not too shabby on the piano either…*

Greyson sat back and made room for Nash to join the fun, so Nash climbed onto the bed. He too went after Caro like she was the most delicious thing he could imagine and managed to carry her into two more orgasms almost immediately.

Caro sat panting and enjoying the view as each man lubed up the other's dick, giving each other greedy looks. Nash lay beside Caro and smiled expectantly. He lifted her on top of him, facing upward, and carefully slipped his erection inside her pulsating pussy from behind. She had another mini-gasm just from that.

"You ready, Caro?" Greyson asked. He had a concerned look on his face. "If this hurts, say so please. It's no good if you're not enjoying it too."

"I'm so ready," she promised.

Greyson slipped a finger into her vagina alongside Nash's shaft. Nash groaned with Caro this time. "That feels amazing," he growled. "Use another one as soon as Caro relaxes a little."

"I'm ready, Grey. Go ahead."

Greyson added another finger. It was a very, very tight fit, even with all the lube. He stroked in and out, relishing the feel of Nash's hardness against his hand while being enveloped by Caro's hot, wet vise grip. Ever so gradually, he felt less resistance from her muscles until, finally, he bent over and sucked her clit into his mouth.

Caro nearly blew apart with all the contrasting sensations going on. Greyson's hot mouth, his pulsating tongue, Nash's steel-hardness inside her while Greyson's fingers slipped in and out. She felt everything with heightened senses, bursting with love for her men. "I'm ready, Grey. Do it now."

Greyson pulled back and added a little more lube to his erection. Then he ever so carefully fed the head of his dick into Caro, next to Nash. Caro fought to remain relaxed, but the reality of having both men fuck her simultaneously was mind-blowing. This felt nothing like their previous DP sessions, where one was in front, and one was behind. She'd watched the videos online and knew this could be done, but she had no idea how emotional it would make her.

"We're all making love together as one," she whispered. "This is incredible. Can you go deeper, Grey?"

"Am I hurting you?" he asked.

"Not really. It's strange and beautiful all at once. I never imagined this. Please, Grey, more."

Greyson shoved himself inside her and heard her immediately cry out.

"Is it too much?"

"It's perfect. We're perfect. The perfect three."

Nash finally spoke up. "I've never loved both of you more than I do at this very moment. We've been through hell and back in so many ways, but now we have perfection." He and Greyson began to thrust in and out, stroking each other simultaneously as they stretched and massaged Caro from the inside. By the time they all collapsed in a huge, throbbing tangle of arms and legs, they'd fulfilled their wildest dreams of satisfaction.

"I don't know how others do it," Greyson said softly, "But this is our way."

<br>

The End

<br>

Have you read *The Rule of 3*?<br>
Don't miss out on the rest of the fun.

_Acknowledgments_

Congratulations to Denise Kaszuba for winning the naming contest I created for this book. She came up with the name Chaos for the rock band, saying it was inspired by the chaos generated by her beloved grandson. I love that, and it's a terrific name for a band! Well done, Denise, and I hope you enjoy the story.

This book was a challenge for me in several ways. It began after I'd started writing a different one, only to discover that this story was calling to me in a louder voice. I've wanted to write Caro's book ever since I completed _The Rule of 3_ two years ago, but things got in the way one after the other. I'm happy I finally got Caro back with her men. I'm just sorry that the process was interrupted by so many issues and trips out of state, making the book take longer than it should have.

I grew up with horses, and they were such a huge part of my life; they were also a very emotional topic for me to tackle. I wasn't sure I could do it until I decided that I could assign personalities to the different horses in this book that reminded me of some of mine. That made it fun! For instance, I had an American Saddlebred mare who had the same terrible habit of blowing up every time I mounted her as

Lady G does with Caro in this book. Anyone standing nearby scattered to get out of the way. She would always squeal loudly and throw a tantrum before she could settle down. My trainer, who *never* favored a gentle approach to anything, seemed to find it both hilarious and character building for me, so he didn't try to fix it. I quickly learned how to stay on after the first embarrassing splat onto my butt. And I had a Quarter Horse who had Gene Simmons' (the pinto—not his namesake) personality to a tee. He was fat, had fantastic smooth gaits, was beautifully trained, and was the sweetest horse ever. The proud cut story was from another one of my horses who, unfortunately, was one of the jerks about it. He used to break things all the time to get to the mares, and those ladies thought he was hot stuff. I didn't have him for very long because we didn't fit well. But he went to a father and son who appreciated him, and he respected them (unlike how he reacted to me). Win-win. There were many other equally funny or interesting stories, so maybe they'll show up in other books.

A considerable tribute goes to the 2022 Kentucky Derby winner Rich Strike and his jockey Sonny Leon. That race was so exciting and unusual that I had to incorporate as much of it as possible into the book. Rich Strike looks nothing like my Domino Pip, but the particulars of what happened on the track are the same, as is the fact of his last-minute entry due to a scratched horse. Sometimes fact is stranger than fiction, and I could not resist using it.

A difficulty I faced while writing was that we had the brilliant (?) idea of adding a new Gordon Setter puppy to our family, and this little girl is the cutest little monster on wheels (paws?). She challenges me every day by waking me up way before sunrise and then tries to chew the computer or jump on my head if I spend too much time writing and not paying her adequate attention. I know we'll look back on puppyhood and laugh someday, but I hope it's sooner rather than later. Our other dog has learned to hide outdoors when things get to be too much for her. Usually, they're besties, but we all have our limits. Some days, I must admit, I had to throw in the towel and realize that I would not be able to write. Eventually, however, I learned to make good use of those god-awful early morning hours when the dogs would fall asleep after breakfast (the bums!), things would quiet down, and I could write undisturbed.

(Added later) Things with the puppy are improving. Hallelujah! I'm beginning to feel human again by getting a full night's sleep—more or less.

Complaining aside, I have some people to thank who are amazing. My author friends, especially Ava and Sutton, have bolstered me up and advised me in innumerable ways, and I will be forever grateful. The writing community is a wonderful one.

Huge thanks to my composer for writing the beautiful music to go with my song lyrics. He has a busy life with many projects *and* a full-time job, plus they have a baby to raise. He cheerfully accepted my challenge to write the music, and I am extremely grateful for that. His musical talent is incredible. He prefers anonymity on this project, so I will honor that.

My husband always chimes in with ideas and opinions, and while we don't always agree, his input is invaluable. He makes the best sounding board ever. His encouragement is something I cherish.

My beta reader Susan has had a tough time recently with her own serious challenges, and still she's made time to weigh in on the manuscripts I send her. I do it in pieces, but it's different each time she gets something. I tend to write and revise a lot. So thank you, Susan, for putting up with me and being a terrific friend. It was a great day when I answered her email and we struck up a friendship. Her opinions are valued like gold.

As always, my wonderful editor Amy Maranville proved invaluable, not just in sprucing up the sometimes-garbled messes I hand her but also in supporting my idea to include the section about equine therapy for autistic kids. I have limited personal experience with the disorder and was very happy to have her advice. Also, working with Amy is fun!

Thank you to Linda at Victory Editing, who was brought in to do the proofreading job at the last minute when a scheduling issue prompted the change. It pays to be flexible in this job.

Dar Albert of Wicked Smart Design stepped up again, redesigned my cover for *The Rule of 3*, and designed the companion cover for *The Passion of 3* when I decided to make them a duet. I love the new look and how well they go together. She is so talented and… well… wicked smart!

Most of all, thank you, dear readers, for continuing to purchase and borrow my crazy stories. You're what this is all about, and without your acceptance and support, I might as well just send emails to myself to satisfy my compulsion to write.

Please leave a review when you finish a book. Each book represents weeks, months, and sometimes years of dedicated effort, and it's both costly and emotionally challenging to put something so personal out there for others to read. Authors depend on reviews and those stars that are so simple to leave once you've finished reading.

If you'd like to stay in touch, please sign up for my newsletter. https://landing.mailerlite.com/webforms/landing/m6f3i7 I generally mail one out once a month.

Also, I love to hear from readers. info@ariellatalix.com

For more information, please visit my website www.AriellaTalix.com

Happy Reading!
Ariella Talix

# Books by Ariella Talix

Every book is a standalone story with no cliffhanger.

Each series is more fun when read in order, however. Often characters show up again because I can't help myself.


### **Contemporary Romance**

The Drummonds:

Porter the Importer

Make Believe

The Artist


Lovers in Louisville (Spin-off from The Drummonds):

Save Her

Saving Him

Savor This


### **Contemporary MMF Romance**

The Perfect Number (Spin-off from Savor This):

The Rule of 3

The Passion of 3


Living the Fantasy:

Just Curious

Compelling Urges

-

Standalone:

Group Hug

-

<u>Honeybee Hollow Series:</u>

Jack of Hearts MMF novella—a spin-off from Group Hug

<u>Buddy System Small-town, MMF, Military romance</u>

<u>Everybody Knows Small-town MF Romance</u>


## <u>Historical MMF Romance</u>

Hearts of Gold:

The Golden Rush

Fiddle and Fire

Casting Vows


## <u>Anthologies</u>

Double Down on Love (*Jack of Hearts*) with the Kentuckiana
Romance Writers

The Drummonds

Lovers in Louisville

The Perfect Number

Living the Fantasy